Sick Girl Screams

Sick Girl Screams

by SJ Townend

Brigids Gate
PRESS

Sick Girl Screams

Edited by S.D. Vassallo

Proofread and formatted by Stephanie Ellis
Cover illustration and design by Daniella Batsheva

First Edition: October 2024

ISBN (paperback): 978-1-957537-97-9
ISBN (ebook): 978-1-957537-96-2
Library of Congress Control Number: 2024947517

BRIGIDS GATE PRESS
Overland Park, Kansas
www.brigidsgatepress.com

Printed in the United States of America

Dedicated to Dorothy Davies who bought my first ever story, shared my love for Ray Bradbury, and gave me the confidence to write, and to my mother and father, RIP.

Content Warnings

Step Inside: suggested child abuse, suggested violence, child neglect

No Place Like Home: eating disorders, suggested child abuse, miscarriage, death, gore, blood

We Still Don't Use the Garage: death, alcoholism, homelessness

Circle: suicide, mental health (bipolar, mania), blood, grief

A Piece Missing: suggested child murder, gore, death, mental health (postnatal depression), grief, existentialism

Neon Fly: gore, murder, death, blood

It Started with Placental Encapsulation: gore, blood, suggested domestic abuse, misogyny, death, violence, grief

The Dangers of Ill-Prepared Shellfish: domestic violence, gore, suggested rape, body horror, death, gaslighting, blood, forced marriage

Juliet, Juliet: drug abuse, addiction, gore, death, blood, maggots, mental health (depression), grief

The Beauty Parlour: body mutilation, murder, gore, assault

Sick Girl: self-harm, gore, drug abuse, addiction, mental health (hypochondria), blood

The Cool Kids: gore, murder, bullying, blood, self-mutilation

Cosmic Spin Class on Deck 112: loss of a child, gore, mental health (depression), grief, existentialism

Labourers Wanted: domestic violence, gore, mutilation, assault, suggested rape, misogyny, body horror, gaslighting, blood, eyes

All the Parts of a Mermaid that I Can Recall: body horror, mutilation, misogyny, domestic violence, blood, gore

Every Cloud: blood, self-harm, mental health (depression), miscarriage, existentialism, body horror, death

I Pull My Blanket Up Beneath My Chin: suggested child abuse, gore, religion

One Lie for One Soul: religion, blasphemy, murder, gore, blood, miscarriage, death

Black Metal in a White Room: body horror, blood, gore, mutilation, eyes, tooth/mouth horror, surgical horror

In His Memory: dementia, grief, suggested violence against an animal, murder, body horror, death, existentialism

Hag Stone: eyes, blood, gore, body horror, loss, death

Christingle Service: mental health (depression), drug abuse, suggested child abuse, loss of a child, miscarriage, religion, blasphemy, death, suggested suicide

How to Read a Woman: misogyny, eyes, body horror, death, suggested sexual assault, predatory behaviour (stalking), death

Contents

Introduction

By Robert Shearman

I don't know what the J stands for. The J in the middle of her name: SJ Townend. I know the S. The S is easy, and I think that Sarah is perfectly fine, as good a name as any. But the J remains a mystery. I suppose I could just ask her. But I haven't quite dared to, for reasons I shall try to explain.

It's easy to make the mistake that you get to know the writer through their stories. That you have a clear image of the person bashing away at the keyboard—what they believe in, their fears, their hopes, their passions even—that they're laying themselves bare just for the reader to gawp at. But writers are expert at distortion. We're good with words, after all, and we know their power—as much as to mislead as to inform. I sometimes think those of us who write weird fiction do it to hide ourselves from the world—our true selves, at least. All good writing is a form of self-revelation, no matter how hard we might try to conceal it, we chip away at little bits of what we are to pepper an otherwise invented narrative and make it come alive. But the weirder the tale gets, the more we might hope we're burying all the really fragile stuff beneath layers of tricksy metaphor and absurdist flourish. Here I sit, safe in my writer cave, and outside I'm dazzling them with lots of sparkling madness to distract them—they'll never find the entrance to the cave now!

What struck me so forcefully when I first began reading Sarah's stories is that she is far more courageous than that. And, yes, her tales *do* dazzle and the madness *does* sparkle, they are truly bizarre: in them you'll find a woman who can control the weather by bleeding, another who vomits up physical memories of her childhood. In an apocalyptic landscape people surgically alter their bodies to look like all the animals we've made extinct through climate change, and show them off as they party on towards oblivion. There are times Sarah's imagination leaps so high it can make you feel queasy with the vertigo.

But there's a hard, granite truth to these flights of fancy. Sarah has no interest in living inside a cave. She wants to present herself to the reader in as unflinching a manner as possible. *Sick Girl Screams* is not just a collection of short stories, it's an experience—intense and personal, and often uncomfortably intimate. These may be stories of haunted houses and alien invasions and nightmare worlds in which you'll fade from existence if you stop being entertaining enough. They are also tales of domestic abuse, and manic depression, and self-harm, and drug addiction, and the painful effect of just refusing to be submerged by all the shit that life can fling at you.

These are stories of resilience. Of women resisting the temptation to be defined by the horrors of what has been done to them, and what they have done to themselves. And not all of Sarah's heroines make it through intact, and none of them is unscathed—but they come to recognise that they have to fight. Many of the tales in this book are frightening and brutal, and the imagery may even disgust, but each one also feels weirdly optimistic, that even if the fight is lost, that at least the courage was found so that it was fought at all. So, no, Sarah doesn't choose to live in a cave, because her characters have done with that. And the confrontational anger of her stories draws blood.

Sick Girl Screams, then, reads to me as a personal journey. And if the path that journey takes is sometimes winding and sometimes seems to be leading you in wild, different directions, that surely is the point. This is a crazy road map through a startling new writer's very psyche, exposed for all to see, with none of the ugly bits airbrushed away: of routes considered and not necessarily taken, and with detours that may lead you somewhere dark or somewhere redemptive. And along the way, she never fails to impress with her absolute stark sincerity.

We talk short stories sometimes, Sarah and I, and we swap ideas back and forth like it's a party game. (At the moment we're particularly keen on gargoyles. We both clearly have a lot of gargoyle trauma we need to work through.) I always know wherever I push an idea, she'll push it along further. No matter how much I might bend reality, she knows how to give it an extra twist—and somehow find a way of making it truthful and honest. For me, I'll confess it: writing weird fiction has often just been an extension of telling jokes. For Sarah, it's something much more complex. Oh, her stories are funny, all right, in the most macabre of ways. But never mind how caustic her sense of humour, the stories are never framed as comedies as such—they're never designed to let the reader off the hook as simply as that. Some of the tales in *Sick Girl Screams* built up to a punchline, and then blindsided me with something so cruelly detached they made me actually wince. Sarah's jokes are grounded by the idea we live in a world as ridiculous, as contradictory, and sometimes as callous as this, and that we don't call it out and rail against it more forcefully. There'd be something a little indecent at merely laughing at her tales, like getting the giggles at an especially grisly funeral. With these stories she *dares* you to react, and to care, and to feel. One day she said to me, quite suddenly, when we were ping-ponging back our gargoyle tales: "These stories really happened to me, you know." From anyone else that might have seemed ludicrous. But I knew exactly what she was saying. Because these tales are impossible—mad!—and at the same time they have the force of lived history.

And to take a leaf from her writing, and speak frankly: I owe Sarah a debt of thanks. She wrote to me maybe a year ago to say she'd read a story of mine that had chimed for her. At the time I wasn't in a very good place. I think I had just lost my faith in writing somewhat, and certainly in writing short stories. I had turned out so many of my own, and I couldn't see the heart in them any longer. To be polite—probably nothing more—I asked if I could read a story of hers in return—and at the time it upset me. I couldn't deal with it, it was full of that sense of purpose I felt I'd lost. I sulked for a bit. I didn't know what to say. It took me a few months to write back … and to beg for some more of her stories. And the more SJ Townend I read, the more I realised I wanted to write for myself again. Sarah *loves* short stories. She is so excited by the form, by reading them and being inspired by them and inventing new ones of her own. There's a wonderful generosity to Sarah's fiction—and part of that comes from the sense that that these stories are not merely voyages of discovery for *us*, but voyages of self-discovery for *her*. Many of them are written in the present tense, so you get to experience them in extreme close-up, in the moment they're being created, with every heartbeat. And the immediacy of it feels like a privilege, that you're witnessing a writer work out who they are in real time.

This is an extraordinary debut collection. It's new and it's urgent and sometimes it'll make you laugh and oftentimes it'll make you hurt. And it does that thrilling thing that all really good fiction should do. It convinces you that the writer is making herself present to you, and she's unapologetic about it in all her complexity. I don't know what the J stands for. I don't need to know. She's given me enough. She gets to keep some secrets for herself.

Step Inside

Have you ever been so lost in a book the protagonist wears your shoes, and you, theirs, and you take their journey together? Have you ever been so distracted you bite your nails down to stumps as you delve six feet deep into that thriller? So trapped, your coffee grows cold, untouched? Engaged so completely that your lonely heart cries like a wolf under a strong moon as you tear through the last few pages of a romance? Ever been so captivated you swear you catch sight of fantastical creatures with pointed ears and knife-sharp tiger teeth leaping from the page and dancing in between blades of grass as you read on the bench at the park?

Have you ever fallen so deeply into a book?

So absorbed, you know even before you've finished it, you will scour the library, the local bookstore, the internet, and purchase and gather every single story, novella, essay, and poetry collection the author has ever written. You want to hang onto the author's every word like a coat on a hook, like a child's tightly curled fingers around the string of their brand-new red balloon. You want to savour the author's use of language, drink down their expression of self, inhale their poignant paragraph structure and distinct turn of phrase for just a little longer after the novel in your hand is done.

You're so very lost in the universe the book creates, its zoetrope of colour soaring upward from the black-on-white prose.

You rush the preparation of food for your children and partner, attempting to pass off a microwaved ready-meal as home-cooked—no-one even notices—just so you can sit down and read for a little while longer. In this way, you can spend less time standing at the kitchen counter, peeling, chopping, frying, and stirring. Oh, to indulge for a further minute, an hour. To run your eyes over the author's words for just a moment longer, to delve a smidgen deeper into that storyline, to be whisked away for one minute more—You *need* to know what happens next.

Today, you end up so engrossed in a story, so very tied up in the characters and the storyline and the ambience, the throws of it all, that when your four-year-old daughter—whom you bore from your very own womb—asks if she can use the toilets at the park, you nod without even a brief look up from the novel in your hands …

And so, off she skips.

Have you ever been so ensnared in a plot and that *quirky protagonist* and *unreliable narrator* and that story arc you have never explored before, that you let your daughter enter the lightless block of cubicles behind the bushes, just out of sight, completely alone, to empty her bladder?

From the bench where you are sat, engrossed, you don't look up to protect her on her journey. All it would take is a quick glance, but the author's words whip you up, up, and away from the greyness of the October skies which loom overhead. The story takes you to an entirely different place, an escape of sorts.

And in this moment, you don't think twice as your child skips off solo. The fruit of your loins heads towards the unstaffed park facilities, the toilets with the flooded floors and empty soap dispensers, the smashed strip light and ever-dripping tap.

Well, my dear, that is when you will find me: the antagonist in the grim tale of your mundane storybook life. Or should I say, that is when I will find your child.

I am here.

In the beetle-black end cubicle I lurk, with claws which silence with one rip, and dead eyes which flush away dreams and souls. Here is where your child will find me as I wait for them.

And I have been waiting for all of time … to end their time.

My dear, will you put your book down after five minutes? Ten? After your daughter's red balloon—which has long since floated up into the raincloud-laden skies—has become swallowed whole?

How long until you notice she is gone, has not returned?

Oh, what I have done?

And what will you do?

No Place Like Home

Return.

Louisa hears the call again as she takes a left down St. Christopher Lane, but the voice has no obvious source.

Lately, she has been practicing mindfulness. She tries to live in hope, and has been doing the work to stay 'in recovery,' but no matter how many items her present-self counts, sees, feels, and smells to try and quash the darkness within her, she can't shift the feeling of existential dread.

Inside her something rouses.

She finds herself driving towards the Jacobean cottage she had grown up in—as she has done the last few nights after her nine-to-five—taking the non-essential detour on her commute home. Halfway down the A-road, miles from either her place of work or her apartment in the city, she eases her foot from the accelerator on approaching the familiar string of trees, the boarded-up local shop she used to purchase comics from as a child.

She mulls, *why am I here again?* as her wheels slow. Her mind is a flurry, a snowstorm on this bright spring day. She cannot recall what her motive had been for taking this route, yet here she is, driving through the small village in which she had been raised. It is as if her childhood home is whispering out to her: *come visit.*

The white cottage comes into view. From her car, she sees its dark crown of thatch-work ahead, poking up above the broad wych elm she had climbed, aged seven or eight, in an attempt to escape from the garden. Sitting in her faux-leather seat, she clutches her knee and recalls how it had smarted when she had fallen from the tree, how her leg had bled for hours afterwards. Her mother had sent her to her room with wet tissue and refused to allow her back down for dinner.

Like a black hole, she thinks, as the fence around the front of the cottage grows larger and the stretch of road between her and the gate shortens. She practices her therapist's teachings. *Five things I can see. Four things I can smell. Three things I can hear.* But her focus on the present is broken.

Step inside.

The gravitas of the call has been growing stronger all week. As a young girl, the front door of the house, with its apex porch canopy, had often reminded her somewhat of a moustached mouth. But she knows the cottage has no true mouth, it is a building after all. *Just a building*, she tells herself; a cottage can make no noise.

There it is, she thinks as she sees it, the cottage, which is half-swallowed by the shadow of the looming tree. Her car idles up on the pavement outside the drive. The house sits, unspeaking, in a silence broken only by the whoosh of passing vehicles.

She feels cold, still, unable to pull away as she puts her car into park; the cottage, a steel pin, her body, a butterfly. White stone walls. Red wooden shutters. A trail of wisteria, not yet in bud, bound to a weathered lattice trellis, the stubborn roots of the plant penetrating the wall like invasive thoughts. Creeping green-grey fronds, all skeletal fingers, stretch over the arch above the front door.

Her stomach aches, just like it would before Measurement Day. She has to get out to take a look at the old building she had in the past called home. Has to.

The garden had once been wild, when Louisa's parents had purchased the house some thirty-odd years back. Louisa, a toddler the day they moved in, had thought the original garden was beautiful—something from a fairy tale.

Growing up in the house, she had come to realise fairy tales are often quite unnerving: all wolves and goblins and cursed spinning wheels, tragedy and transcendence. Her mother, when she had had the time, would read her stories from books, with princesses and dragons on the cover, tales of women lucky enough to be rescued, blessed enough to win husbands. The Ugly Sisters never got to marry, her mother would say, because they had bad genes, were too old, haggard, did not take care of themselves.

Feeling the chill of her parked spot in the shade, Louisa unbuckles her seat belt and cloaks her cardigan around her petite frame. She closes her eyes and tries to picture the original garden in summertime, with its array of chipped, faded gnomes, carved forest creatures, overgrown beds of St. John's Wort, and white clouds of *Gypsophilia*. The wild rosebushes had shouted colour with their blooms of reds and pinks. *A witch's paradise*, her younger self had thought.

During the spring of her first year at the cottage, Louisa's mother had ripped up all the flowers bar the trailing Wisteria which had become practically woven into the stone of the wall, making it 'too costly' to remove, and her father had paid for the lawn to be sealed over with tarmac and gravel.

Perhaps her parents had been right to create sterile order from the chaos of nature. Gardening, after all, her mother would say, is grubby. Hard work for little gain. At least they'd allowed Louisa to keep and tend to one small terracotta flowerpot. She recalls watering the fuchsia plant in its orange container. How she'd loved to pop open early the pink and purple buds, although her mother had always made her sweep up the petals.

Her parents no longer live at the cottage. After Louisa's mother had died nearly a decade ago, Louisa's father had sold up, himself unwell, and had moved into a hospice. Shortly after this, he'd moved on to the crematorium, riding the funeral-black coat-tails of his wife. He'd left the profit from the house sale to a military charity. Not a penny had passed to Louisa.

Louisa feels silly describing herself as an 'orphan' at thirty-five to her colleagues in the office, but she finds it stops them in their tracks when they start to ask probing questions. *Where are you spending Christmas? Easter? Will you be visiting family?* She is not one for small talk, prefers her own company, which is lucky, with no family left and no sweet love waiting for her at her tiny apartment.

Today, sitting outside of the cottage, she focuses on her breath-work, takes account of the whiff of diesel, the soft blue-and-cobweb shade of the sky, the way the fabric of her woollen skirt feels underneath her fingertips. She is in no rush to get home and has no urgency to be anywhere, except for here, at the cottage. Years have passed since she last set foot inside.

Once her anxiety passes, she opens her door and gets out from the car. *I'll just take a quick peek, see what they did with the garden, pretend to be a passerby taking an interest in the Wisteria, or lost and in need of direction*, she thinks, always one for forward planning and being in control. However, with mounting bills, a dodgy boiler her landlord is stalling to fix, and a stream of new colleagues always asking questions of her, so many questions of recent, she has felt very much out of control.

A sickness turns in her stomach as she stands outside the closed gates. An intruder in the story of her own life is how she feels. On tiptoes, she peers over the top of the fence. The fuchsia bush is no longer there—this, she had suspected would be the case—but where the pot had once sat are plentiful new planters of colourful flowers. She feels she should smile at this sight but the muscles in her face won't agree.

From the downstairs window, a curtain twitch distracts her. Louisa is unsure if the dark shape at the window is a person or the back of a chair or a heavy coat hung on a peg, until the shape disappears and reappears, merry-faced, and opening the front door.

Before Louisa has time to move, her eyes meet with the eyes of the lady at the door. Louisa instructs her feet to march onwards—to make herself simply a passerby passing by—but they do not respond, and before she has a chance to escape, the lady is in the drive, is opening the gate, is inviting her in.

"You must be Louisa." The lady has a dusty blue apron on. Her voice is cheery, as if she spends her days baking brownies and singing to children. Her eyes are a little too bright.

Louisa cannot deny this, she is indeed Louisa, and finds herself quietly replying affirmatively so. "Yes, do I know you?" she asks, although she knows she has never met this lady before.

"I suppose you wouldn't. I recognise you from the photograph album. We bought the house from your father about ten years ago, before he ... He left a few things behind ..." The lady's sentences trail off as she picks at a lump of something like pastry on the cuff of her blouse.

"Oh, I see," Louisa says, tongue-tied. The small port wine birthmark above Louisa's left eye must be a solid identity giveaway. She pulls out a long wisp of hair from her bun.

"Would you like to take the album?"

Louisa blushes. "I suppose so." There is only one album she can recall: an annotated, chronological display of Louisa's life, the extended baby book her mother had pored over at pivotal times each year. Louisa does not want the album. At all. But, she decides, the leather-bound documentation of her childhood is safer, perhaps, in her own hands.

"Your parents must have been ever so proud of you, to keep such ... records."

Louisa shifts from foot to foot, drawing a blank, unsure how best to respond. Proud? She has never felt more ashamed.

Come inside.

The two words carry on the spring breeze, becoming distorted by the up-whoosh of a passing Fiesta, and Louisa is not sure if the words come from her head, the lady, or the house.

Step in.

Irrespective of their origin, despite the clement weather, the soft invitation sends shivers down Louisa's spine. No, she thinks, that was not the lady's voice. Her lips didn't move. Must've been the house. The house, the house wants me to go in.

"Please, come in for a cuppa." This time, Louisa is certain it is the lady inviting her in and not the house. "See what we've done to the place."

Louisa stares at the lady's mouth as it shapes out each word, and before she has a chance to make her excuses and leave, the lady takes Louisa's hand and Louisa finds herself following the lady—who Louisa learns is called Anna—into the cottage.

Like the last sweet in the box, the chocolate-wrapped Turkish delight that no-one really likes, Louisa puts up no resistance, despite her apprehension. An urgency to go inside is a pull which she cannot fight.

They stop in the hallway where the lady slips off her garden shoes.

It's cold inside, Anna apologises for this. "Such thick stone walls. Brilliant for insulation in the winter, but the house takes forever to warm up when the heating's off." Anna slides on well-worn sheepskin slippers. "But of course, you'll know that. You grew up here, didn't you? I expect you've such fond childhood memories."

Goosebumps like pinpricks spread up Louisa's arms as she slips off her shoes and places them by Anna's. It is an odd thing, she thinks, to expose your feet to a stranger. She hopes Anna doesn't notice how her toenails are unpainted or spot the bunions on the side of each big toe, the result of years of forcing her teenage self into shoes a little too small.

Louisa feels fifteen again. Ugly, as if entirely naked, and at school, in a dream. She has always felt this way in this house. The entrance hall is familiar yet not; the same, yet so very different. Despite the layout being identical as it had always been, the decor is modern, and each available space is filled with trinkets and fresh-cut flowers. The aroma of baked goods just pulled from the oven fills the air.

As Louisa follows Anna through to the kitchen, the grandfather clock in the hall chimes six times. Louisa jumps, feeling ice in her heart as if someone has walked over her grave. "I'm sure you remember Little Ben." Anna smiles. "So symbolic of another era."

Something about the interior of the property is unsettling, misaligned, like when one sees one's reflection in a mirror responding out of sync, sneering with a slight delay. Each counterfeit room is a treacherous dimension away from the ones in her true childhood home.

Louisa finds herself unable to speak in anything but monosyllabic responses. "Yes," she eventually replies.

"You might recognise a few things of your dad's here and there. We cleared most of it away, but my husband wanted to keep some of the furnishings."

Mum and Dad. The words pinball in Louisa's brain. She had never used such informal terms for her parents. Her father had insisted he call her by his army rank—Major Jones—and her mother had always been Mother.

Louisa nods at the right moments as Anna guides her round downstairs. Anna does not ask questions. Louisa is glad of the one-way conversation. Always better than questions.

In the front room, on the mantelpiece, people Louisa will never know smile from ornate, mismatched frames. Colourful cushions which clash with the striped sofa suite are covered in pet hair. *Mother would never have tolerated such a higgle-piggle display, such mess,* Louisa thinks as she weaves in Anna's slipstream, into the kitchen.

"Take a seat."

Louisa perches. Anna serves tea and cake and tells Louisa how they have redecorated the master bedroom, retiled the bathroom. In truth, much of the interior looks completely different through Louisa's eyes, apart from the few items which belonged to her parents dotted around.

Louisa pushes Victoria sponge around her plate with the fork in a repeating figure-of-eight pattern until it crumbles into small morsels. No more than a few mouthfuls pass between her lips. Once her tea is drunk, she thanks Anna for her hospitality. "I must be getting on now." Getting on for what exactly, she is not sure, but she has spent long enough in the property. The very bones of her feel hollow.

Don't leave. The words come, not from Anna.

Louisa fastens the top button of her cardigan and wedges her hands in prayer position between her thighs.

"Please," Anna says, "let me get you the album and show you upstairs."

Again, Louisa is unable to excuse herself and follows, gliding from room to room, nodding and forcing smiles.

The watercolour of the property her father had commissioned a local artist to paint still hangs on the landing, a thick slug of dust atop its frame. Out of Anna's field of view, Louisa cannot help but correct the jaunty angle of the painting, aligning it with the white coving above.

"This must've been your room. We haven't got around to decorating in here yet, only got as far as taking down the posters." Anna opens the door at the end of the landing to the room with green wallpaper speckled with tiny white flowers which is scratched and torn in places next to the bed.

Louisa recalls her teen hunger pangs, recalls chewing on balls of crumpled daisies in an attempt to quell a gnarling stomach. Pale rectangles adorn the otherwise bare walls, ghost marks of Kate Moss centrefolds and all the other heroine-chic supermodels. Thinspiration.

"Ah yes," Louisa says.

The narrow wooden bed her father had built, because it was cheaper than buying a new one, is still there. How uncomfortable it had been, how her feet used to press up against the end wall. She'd had to sleep on her side, in the foetal position, after puberty had brought on an unwanted growth spurt. Her father, though aware of this, had never offered to purchase something larger, despite Louisa's requests and sleepless nights.

Anna encourages her to enter the room. Louisa does so and becomes horribly lost between four walls she knows like the back of her hands. She stands in place, unsure which way to turn, then retreats from the room, her eyes wet.

"We kept the bed," Anna says. She follows Louisa out before brushing in front of her along the narrow strip of landing to take the lead. Louisa notices the exaggerated smile fall from Anna's face for perhaps the first time as Anna passes. "In case we were blessed with the sound of pattering feet." The floorboards of the old cottage creak as they make their way back downstairs.

In the dining room, Anna presents Louisa with the album from a shelf above a makeshift desk. It had sat there gathering dust, the album, next to the complete works of Dickens—a collection of eighteen antique books her mother had cherished. Louisa had never once seen either of her parents read anything, let alone classical literature, but her mother had commented once on how she liked the linear pattern the books made in the centre of the shelf, admired the symmetry of the spines aligned. She would dust around it bi-weekly, had said having such proud works of quality made her feel like she lived in a show home.

"Enjoy," Anna says and smiles as if she is trying to make her mind up about something.

"Yes." Louisa hurries on her shoes. "I've really got to go now." Anna opens the front door and Louisa steps out of the house.

"Goodbye. Do drop by any time." Anna waves from the porch.

Don't leave. Whispers. Louisa strides across the driveway without looking back, utters a courteous thank you under her breath to Anna, while clutching the album under her arm.

I am leaving, she thinks. *You can't stop me.*

Louisa makes it back to her car—*five things I can see, four things I can smell*—and sits and focuses on slowing her breathing and then opens the photograph album. A brief leaf through the first few pages reminds her it is not something she wants to revisit.

Louisa, at the start of each academic year, standing in her bedroom with her hair scraped back in pigtails, her school uniform too tight, her mother complaining about having to fork out for new kilts and shirts, and *would you please stop growing*. Next to each of these annual keepsakes, another photo. Louisa, not in uniform, posing in greyed underwear. A discarded tape measure coiled by her feet. Measurement Day. Each photo is detailed underneath with the date, her age, and weight, like some sort of Bridget Jones's diary entry, or prison mug-shot catalogue.

She presses the heels of her hands into her eyes, holds back tears, then throws the album onto the passenger seat where it falls open somewhere near the end pages. She cusses under her breath, clunks her belt, and pulls away.

How cruel her mother had been to track her weight like that. In the photo which screams up at her from the passenger seat, Louisa is sixteen years old, five stone three pounds, hollow-cheeked, hips jutting like a broken umbrella. *I looked terrible,* Louisa thinks as the image catches her eye. *Three things I can hear—*

You looked great. The whisper. She pulls up a mile down the road and ditches the album in a roadside bin.

As soon as she gets home, Louisa comes out of recovery, binges on everything she can from her cupboards. Cookies, crisps, raw jelly cubes, long-life juice. Nearly a decade clean, the trip to her old family home has unstitched years of hard work. She downs a pint of warm water, knowing this will make it hurt less, will help to flush everything out, then kneels in front of her toilet.

Two fingers slide down her throat. Sugar-rich calories come back up. Once she finishes bringing up biscuits and pastries and apple juice, up comes the grandfather clock.

Louisa rubs her bloodshot eyes. The acidic juices on her fingertips which burn her sclera are washed away by the tears which come with her sickness.

She had not expected to vomit up the clock, yet there it is. She wipes her face on her sleeve, runs cool water over her hands, splashes her mouth and dries it again, then slumps against the bathroom radiator.

The clock is heavy and almost as tall as her. There is not really room for it in her small fifth-floor apartment and the sight of it only reminds her of unhappy times. Too weak, after her purge, to shift the wood and metal beast with its pendulum tie, she decides to drag it only so far, and leaves it in the shower-come-bath. She draws across the white nylon shower curtain to hide her production, the plastic rings at the top of the fabric *pap pap papping* along the steel pole, then slinks to bed.

That night, she wakes every hour as the clock strikes, but it does not yield its normal dong—it whispers instead, *come home*.

Each time the clock's voice wakes her, she panics, thinks she is back in the cottage, but on turning on the light, she sees the rich teal paint of her apartment bedroom walls, her poster of David Bowie, and on her bedside table, the pile of *Hello* magazines Karen at work passes to her, and manages to soothe herself back to sleep.

Of course, the bingeing and purging continue full force. The next day, after work, she brings up the first of the Dickens collection. After wiping the vomit from her face, she lifts up *The Pickwick Papers*, opens the first page, but instead of finding antiquated prose, each page says the same thing: *Come inside, come home*.

It is enough to make a girl sick, and sick she is again. A block of cheese. Two thirds of a loaf of sourdough. Countless snack-size bars of chocolate. Once she has feasted, she emits the rest of the Dickens collection. The membranes on the inside of her mouth bleed onto the pages as each is birthed. *These books at least,* she thinks, *are light enough to carry out of the bathroom.* She lugs them out in armfuls, pushes across the tea lights and oil burner from the single shelf in her kitchen-come-diner, and arranges the books there.

At the weekend, the watercolour of the cottage comes up, frame and all. *Come back,* the creeping Wisteria whispers through the glass, from the canvas trapped beneath. She hides the painting in her larder and, to silence its call, wraps it in a beach towel.

Each night, she sleeps with cotton wool stuffed in her ears, but still the hushed calls of items from the home address of her youth seem to beg. These parts, these relics of her childhood, she can't bring herself to throw out. Over the next few months, she purges and purges and produces many more objects.

Her small apartment grows cramped. It's as if the walls press in, but it is not the walls, it is the building presence of myriad nostalgic ghosts which decorate like funeral flowers the city-coffin in which Louisa currently dwells.

Weight falls from her near-skeletal frame. Yet Louisa still feels too big, like she is taking up too much space, and her sickness gives her back some control.

Christmas time. Louisa scatters a few strips of threadbare tinsel around her apartment, but there's little space left for a tree. *And what purpose is a tree for one?* she thinks. Christmas, at least, is a chance to rest. And by rest she means time to eat and vomit in peace.

In her father's rocking chair, which now holds centre-space in the kitchen-come-diner, she sits. The bones of her buttocks press firm, ache, on the leather pad. She feels the hardness of the seat, despite the thick clothing she wears to keep out the bite of cold, to cover the dense lanugo down which has made a hair-coat of her arms and legs, and stares at the hamper she received on Friday at work in the Secret Santa. The red ribbon holding the balloon of cellophane packaging closed unties easily.

This purge is fruitful. She works through shortbread, marzipan-stuffed dates, other cinnamon-sweet delicacies, then takes herself to the bathroom. Here, pressed between a set of mahogany nesting tables, her mother's prized blue-and-white china, and her father's tool kit, she kneels by her porcelain altar and makes herself throw up. This time she brings forth her childhood bed, slicked in bright blood. It pins her to the wall until she struggles and tips it forwards, bringing it to rest against the window. Each of its wooden slats beckon her home. Her thin frame shaking, she plugs her ears with cotton wool, then sidles her way out of the bathroom.

The soreness in her throat is overwhelming, yet, as she steps on the scales she keeps by her bed, she is still too heavy. Too much. Her stomach burns. Back to the kitchen she goes for one more binge. There is always more that can be purged. Standing there, shivering, her thin bare feet numb to the cold laminate floor, she finishes off the Christmas cake.

Louisa's heart races, the taste of royal icing overridden by the bile and acids which already warm her tongue. Her clothes hang from her angular body like a child wearing its mother's wedding dress. She thinks of her own parents—the cottage, and tape measures—and runs back into the bathroom.

Now, it comes, on a wave of terrible pain. Sheathed in red-streaked mucus, it slides up in one big heave: an eight-month-old foetus. A foetus. In truth, a near fully formed baby; the baby who never made it. Her baby. Through her mouth, she gives birth to death.

A 'late-term miscarriage' the midwife had called it. Louisa and Matthew had preferred 'Honey.' Honey had been Louisa's reason for ending her purging all those years ago. Matthew had told her time and time again, to be pregnant and ill would not bode well for the baby. And then he had told her goodbye, just a few weeks after Honey's delivery. Said he could not cope with the grief. With Louisa's grief. Louisa's grief, he had said, had taken up too much space. It had eaten into the transient happiness they had once shared together.

He had not come to visit, not once, when Louisa had returned home to her parents to recover from the loss. Matthew did not even visit when Louisa's mother had insisted Louisa should try to move on and had forced her to scatter her baby's ashes.

Louisa had sat on the bottom step of the stairs in the hallway of the cottage, her belly still loose from pregnancy, and had stared, wan faced, for weeks in between broken, medicated sleep, at the grandfather clock. She'd listened to it pass time like the wind, her heart skipping a beat each time it had let out its hourly chime. Forever waiting for Matthew.

In some sort of postnatal psychosis, Louisa, under her mother's forceful hand, had eventually tipped out the contents of the pink urn onto her fuchsia bush outside the cottage. So much ash from such a little thing. The fuchsia became an intrepid explorer, all bone-grey skeleton, lost to the avalanche. It'd taken weeks for the white powder which had been Honey to disperse.

First, Honey had blustered up into the elm's branches. Then, she had been carried away on the wings of a strong autumn gale.

Louisa had remained at the cottage until each last speck of her baby had been blown away, then she had returned to the city. Louisa had known she would not be able to stay in recovery, and could never recover from her loss, if she had stayed with her parents. She hadn't returned to the place her baby's ashes had been dropped for years, not until something had started calling her back.

Honey, in lifeless form, floats in the toilet bowl of Louisa's apartment. The foetus does not whine, does not move, does not beat, yet from its perfectly formed, rosebud mouth, with no movement of lips or opening of eyes, Louisa thinks she hears her baby cry: *Come home.*

Her heart throbbing in her neck, Louisa wants to rescue her lost little one from the toilet bowl. Fish her out. To hold Honey again, even without breath inside of such tiny lungs, this is what Louisa has an urgency to do.

Louisa loses control of her breathing. *You're just hyperventilating, there's nothing wrong,* those would have been her mother's words.

Three things I can hear, two things I can taste—she does not get the chance to think about the one thing she could touch.

In rising, a second wave of pain comes which causes Louisa to buckle. She slips on blood and vomit—to purge is not tidy—Mother would not have approved—and Louisa is thin, like the ghost of the voice she hears calling her home. She falls too fast, does not think to reach out and grab the sink to steady herself as she goes. Her head slams on the tiled floor.

Unconscious, she vomits again. Slippery organ meat the size of a dinner plate contuses her raw throat on its way up. This chokes her. As she delivers the afterbirth she blacks out.

And then she is in her car again, driving towards her old family home, the Jacobean cottage. Louisa feels empty, light, as if her body is nothing but dust on a blank canvas, ash in the wind. Her hand moves like an automaton's sliding her gears down into first.

This time, she does not park on the road outside. Instead, she pulls up in the gravelled drive. She un-clicks her seat belt and opens the car door.

Come inside, come home.

Louisa steps out and drops her car keys onto the stone chippings. Crunch. Her hands are unable to hold anything other than her chest as sadness engorges her more so than any food ever has.

Following the trail of blood which meanders across the tarmac, across the path, down the steps, her feet are unable to navigate anywhere else than along the route which takes her to the front door of the cottage.

Her mother opens the door. Louisa slides off her shoes. The grandfather clock in the hallway dongs, but on its dial, Louisa sees no numbers, no moving hands, just the face of a man she perhaps once loved. Young blue eyes flicker, distort there, where the two and ten should be, as if trapped in the clock like an image from a dream washed deep within her brain.

She follows her mother, who follows the line of smeared blood through to the hallway, then up the stairs. The door to her parents' bedroom they pass is wide open. Louisa sees her father there, pipe in hand, rocking in his leather-pad chair. He nods and grunts as they pass. Her mother pushes open the door to Louisa's bedroom. Posters of supermodels are tacked above the bed. From their paper prisons, the wiry models snarl and growl at Louisa as she steps in the room.

There, on top of the quilt, Honey sleeps, her birdlike chest rising and falling, each throaty breath rasping with the wetness of blood and amnion.

"You should rest," Louisa's mother says, pinching between sharp fingernails the parchment-thin skin of Louisa's waist, her other hand holding a numberless snaking tape measure, "tomorrow, we will take your readings."

We Still Don't Use the Garage

First published in Secret Attic, 2020

This morning, I flipped the calendar page over and revealed the month I've been waiting for, then I cracked open a celebratory beer. The big red cross is in sight now, but we still don't use the garage.

Nearly ten years we've been here: Keith, his dog Rusty, John and I. Rusty's a funny old beast: born with one eye blue, the other green. They're like glazed marbles now. He must be on his last legs. When he goes, we'll probably have a little service in the back garden, like. A few sausage rolls, John can play some Clapton numbers on the guitar. We'll make a day out of it. Do the best we can by the old mutt. No idea why Keith called him Rusty though; he's clearly brindle. Should've called him Bowie, but like the rest of us he's more grey wire than hair now.

Keith, bless him, felted the dining room table back in ninety-six so we could play *Texas Hold'em* for coppers or matchsticks. None of us knew the rules at first, but we muddled through and now it's become a regular event. None of them can read me for custard. Proper poker face, I tell thee. John took all the pennies down Asda last week though, cashed them up in that big slot machine. Took a percentage, mind, but we had enough in the penny pot for a take-home rotisserie chicken dinner. Everything costs something ninety-nine, doesn't it?

Four pack of beer, four ninety-nine.

New set of socks, eight ninety-nine.

Best of Deep Purple on compact disc, ten ninety-nine.

Must think we're fools, those shopkeepers. We can tell those prices are just a penny shy of the next rung. We're not a penny short of a pound, a sandwich short of a picnic. Except for houses though, they tend to be rounded up to the nearest five or ten 'k,' don't they? I keep my matchsticks hidden in a Tupperware box I found in the cupboard next to the sink now—they're worth more than coin on games night.

He's a good egg is Keith, terrible cook though—could screw up a Pot Noodle given half a chance. We met outside of Currys Electricals back in the winter of two thousand and two: Keith, John and I. Rusty was a pup. I had a terrible case of frostbite, fingertips blackened so bad I couldn't roll me own. Keith shared his blanket in exchange for some rolling papers, and he made me cigarettes all winter from them. Good egg, that lad. Sad backstory, but good egg. We stayed in touch like, on the town centre front-line, best friends now.

We've a four-ring hob in our 'galley kitchen,' a power shower upstairs, and a large television with five channels in the front room. Makes a change to have the sound up and I can't say I miss watching all the shows at once through the glass of Currys Electricals. Nothing to see out the front window though. Too quiet—there's no footfall at all. Good job we're not relying on that for our beer money anymore. Has its advantages, though, living on a quiet street.

I took the master bedroom. The boys were more than happy to share the spare. I say *boys*, but we're all in our fifties now.

I think.

Jack, he's the oldest, pretty much keeps himself to himself. I've had more words out of the dog than out of 'e. More sense too. Neat spirits can do that to a soul, though, can't they, over the years? Chips away at your noggin, corrodes the ol' cerebellum, so I've heard. I stick to me Special Brew or a nice box-wine if I'm feeling fruity. The fridge has got more to say. I'd forgotten how lush a chilled beer on the patio was in the heat of the summer, mind. Hums like a rascal, though, that refrigerator. Buzzing constantly, letting us know it's still there. Thought about unplugging it and putting it out in the garden for a bit, but we didn't want the neighbours complaining about anything. Didn't want the neighbours full stop, if I'm honest. Instead of moving on down the street, though, I just move into another room if the fridge-buzz gets on me nerves. Can't complain, hey?

Time distorts things, I think. All manner of sins can be forgotten about with the passing of the seasons. It's funny how things turn out when you look back over twenty-odd years, don't you think? And they have been odd, for me at least. I'm the first to admit I made a mess of my youth. The bottle, red wine that is, never brought me said promises of *unoaked, full-bodied essence of the Rhone valley*. It brought me a divorce and took my job. Struck off the building site for being five times the legal limit. I spent my forties in the stairwell of the NCP. Save the wine for special occasions now, stick to beer for the daytime. If it's under eight percent it's not really alcohol, is it? Still chain the old coffin nails like it's going out of fashion, mind.

We have our happy routines: Job Centre on a Monday, Wetherspoon's on a Thursday, kebabs on a Friday at the start of the month, then beans with a flipped egg to garnish when the giro runs dry. We've got a plate each and one spare in case one breaks. We don't have friends over for food. Not until we've cleared out the garage, anyway, made a little more space. The boys keep the kitchen clean, and I do the lounge. The bathroom is no man's land: it's functional but you wouldn't want to be trapped in there for longer than needs be.

In and out.

Swift.

Good job I'm a bit handy with a power tool—there was plenty to be getting on with at first, but I've fixed the place up a treat. All the equipment was here so I haven't needed to purchase a thing. Bolt cutters, electric drill, mallet. I've put an extra bolt on the front door, and we've panelled up the back.

When I first arrived, his bed was off the ground. I wasn't used to that, felt regal yet unsafe, like I was being carried in a sedan chair through the night. Most strange. Pine slats, medium-to-firm mattress, and he had those Egyptian cotton sheets—the ones that hold the heat in. They were in need of a wash, though, even by my standards. Took it apart and the slats are in the garage now. Mattress rests on the floor as do I.

As soon as I was in, I did what I needed to do, then I tossed my old sweater and jeans on the floor and used his shower gel. God, that first shower. The water felt like liquid gold compared to the three-point sponging I'd been giving myself in the public toilets downtown. The leisure centre staff had just stopped letting me in to use the washroom facilities, too, so I really appreciated his generosity. Ha. Plus, I'd rather have stunk like a bin full of smoked kippers than stayed in that Westland Hostel. Full of wasters going nowhere fast that place.

Washed away years of street life under the power-jet head, I did, that first night. It went cold at the end, though, which woke me up a treat. Penance for my sins I suppose. I've figured out the combi-boiler since and now sometimes I spend over an hour in the bath, bubbles up to me chin, making up for lost time. Slept like a log after. Always do now.

He was a man of habit, I'll give him that, a creature of repetition and order. He even folded his under-crackers. Who does that? Someone with too much spare time or too little beer in the fridge, that's who. Have to admit, though, I've taken to a clean pair each day now we've figured out the washing machine. What a treat.

Once I'd got out of the shower that first night home, and dried myself off, I bundled my old clothes into a ball and stuffed them in the bin. The bin matched the toilet brush. Très chic. Next, I slipped into something fancy: *cashmere* the label said. From Marks and Spencer's. I laughed I did. I had to sit down it made me laugh so hard. I'd only ever been in that shop once and I got carried out in handcuffs. I had a good old rummage in his wardrobe; my bottom half needed covering too. I remember thinking, given all that freedom of a job—an office worker of some sort I think, penpusher probably—bricks and mortar, money, why would anyone choose five *identical* pairs of slacks?

Six-foot on the nose I reckon, thirty-four-inch waist. On the right side of thirteen stone. He'd been a tall lad at school, and I'd been knee high to a high knee. Times changed though. Some of us mature later than others, after all, and some of us live for longer too.

Snap. Perfect match.

He was a good size for a grown man. Felt it too. Nearly did my back in when I moved in.

He drank good coffee, mind, and his freezer was full of those *ready meals* you put in the microwave.

Twist that dial. Prick that lid.

Five minutes and thirty seconds.

Ping and it's good to go.

Domestic bliss. I've never eaten so much in one sitting. Had to undo me top button. His top button. My top button.

Couple of weeks later, once I'd worked my way through his comestibles, I had to nip out and get more supplies. Didn't have a choice. Man needs feeding, doesn't he? Maxed out his contactless on beers, obviously. Didn't want to overspend on his card, you know, take the mick, like. Not immediately anyway. Slow and steady. Luckily, I'd found a twenty in his wallet that first day, so I came back fully loaded—brought the boys back too. They've been here ever since. I like the company, mind, but they can be scruffy old b'stards at times.

His life looked dull as ditchwater. I've tried to read his books, but *The Railway Stations of Devon and Cornwall* and *The Complete Works of Thomas Hardy* don't really tickle my fancy. I'm more of a *Mirror* man, or the occasional lad's mag. You know, gadgets and stuff. Splash the odd drop of his *Old Spice* on the old boat race after a shave, though, especially if it's my night to go down the pub. Not brought a lady back yet mind, but you never know when it could happen, getting lucky that is. I hear being a homeowner is quite the lady lure. You've got to always be prepared and take a few risks every now and again.

When it arrives, I always open the post. It's my gaff so I do the admin. It's just a quick check usually to make sure the direct debits are still being collected. Sometimes, there'll be a one-off bill I can settle online anonymously, but I'm getting those less and less. I can't believe how much the council tax is round these parts though—it's more than I earned in a month when I was a brickie. Mind you that was nearly thirty years back. Keith found a stash of notes in the bottom of the wardrobe—must've been about three grand or so. Old Roy must have been saving up for the apocalypse or something. Should've used a bank, silly old boy. Since having a roof over my head, getting an account was easy as pie. Got me one of my own cards, too, now mind. One with a *PIN code*.

We always make sure one of us is in. There's honour among thieves, see. John doesn't go out much anyway which is handy, because Keith and myself love a brew or three down the Ring O' Bells of a Thursday, side of darts, pool. One of us is always locked in. Just in case anyone snooping catches wind.

I keep looking at the red cross on the calendar and I'm wondering which of them legal beagles I'm going to let handle this case. They're all a bunch of wankers, Keith says. He's probably right. Got to get me one though—can't do this alone, it's a two-man job. Got a few cards from my last trip downtown, I have. Put on his smartest suit I did, fits me a treat. Looks like royalty in it, I do.

We're both size nine and a half which is lucky. He gifted me some lovely leather penny loafers which are perfect for driving. It's my yard, so the boys and I've agreed—I get the Aston Martin DB5 and I'm keeping the keys to the garage. No questions asked. When I do nip out for a spin, I take his black leather driving gloves and waxed jacket from the hall and a handkerchief to hold over my nose. Just to get it out of the garage, mind. Worse than a public toilet it is. Much worse.

No photos anywhere when I first arrived, except a sepia one in the hallway. Looks old as time, must be his parents or grandparents. Not a popular gene pool from what I can gather. Poor old chap can't have had any family. That, our measurements and our schooling are the only similarities we've got, I guess. Oh, and we're the only two allowed in the garage. No-one's come after him anyway and he's still paying all the bills.

He was a mean man and he died with little, yet he still had more than I. I saw him often, Sneddon, with his snide glares, passing me as I sat cap-in-hand outside of County Stores, through hot or cold, rain, wind, and snow, down North Street. Never gave me the time of day let alone a quid. We'd sat side by side at school, Roy Sneddon and I. Surnames and the alphabet meant we sat side by side in the register, so we were put side by side in the class for a good five years at least. Five years of Sneddon's sneaking eyes running up and down my answers every day. Bloody cheat. Can't stand liars. It was enough to drive a man crazy, I tell thee.

Following him home had been a doddle. He seemed oblivious to my presence. In fact, he seemed unaware of anything but the pain in his chest which he clutched like a wild rabbit as he climbed the first step that led up to his abode. Key in nook, I saw his humped frame launch through the door, and he fell into the hallway. I stood and watched. I stood, watched and laughed silently as I knew my moment had come. He could only have been a few months older than me, yet time had not treated him as kindly.

I guess you could say I'm house-proud now. Fed up of hoovering those bloody dog hairs off the sofa, though, that's for sure. Will have to have a word with old Keith about that later. Maybe I'll knock up a kennel in the garden for the old beast? Rusty, not Keith. I'm not an animal. Not sure it'll last long enough though. Maybe I should just start digging instead? Under the cover of night, of course. Wouldn't want the neighbours catching wind, thinking anything suspicious was going on, as I'm running out of space in the garage.

Do I feel guilt I expect you're wondering? Not at all. Death comes to us all, some a little sooner than nature intended. *Carpe diem.* That was our old school motto. If I hadn't seized this opportunity, it'd just have rolled into the hands of the state. And they've got more than enough, haven't they?

Nearly ten years ago, from behind the hydrangea, I crept, carrying my worldly possessions on my back and in my pockets. Not another soul was watching as death swept his away. A rind of moon clung onto the midnight sky that night, smiling at me, giving me the signal, the go-ahead, the okay. I lunged over his sprawled carcass which lay blocking my new front door, avoiding eye contact just like he had done every time he walked on by downtown. I was unsure if he'd taken his last breath, so inside, I waited. The moon slid behind a blanket of cloud. I stood and I waited, then I dragged him through.

I look at the red cross on the calendar again, one more time for confirmation. Seventeen days and the law says this'll all be mine. The bricks and mortar, the house, the garage.

Squatters' rights.

His house, his clothes, his bed, his car. Mine now.

I took the cane for him on more than one occasion. He should never have copied my school work. Thing is, I was never a grass you see. There's a big red cross on the calendar this month and we still don't use the garage.

Circle

I wake at midnight with a gasp of pain. Father said I was born with pain inside me, it will always be a part of who I am. I wonder, is it the same pain I saw in his dead eyes before I closed them for the final time? And if it is, did his hurt pour into me, or mine into him?

The thing with dagger-blade teeth which imprison an even sharper tongue has been with me ever since I found Father. Lop-ears roll down its sides and drag along the floor. It creeps, it pours, it dresses in shadows. Its hearing is impeccable. I cry in silence each evening when it's near because if a single, grey tear splashes on my beige pillowcase, it'll pounce and pin me down and slap me into and through dreadful slumber. From dawn the following day, I'll be seven shades tired, and it'll loosely follow me, haunting my heart, forcing me to see life through its black blood-stained lens. I'll spend the morning trying to shake it off. I'll douse it with cheap whisky to block out its cruel whispers, and then fall into an abyss of daymare-filled, restless sleep.

Only I can see it, but we all sense its presence. My husband says he knows it's here by my aura, the way I don't wear my hair, and the fact I refuse to leave the house. Through these dark days, he'll take over childcare, the chores. *Mummy's having a moment.* And through these periods, he'll sleep in the box room.

"No Sam, not tonight," my husband will say to our boy while searching for diplomatic phrasing, my actions having made a lighthouse of me. "Mummy needs the bed to herself. If you wake and can't resettle, come hop in with me."

I gasp for air again and clutch my sore chest. Bed-sheets sodden with dank sweat swim stale beneath me, but at least my bed is my own again, and now, minutes past midnight, I once more feel alive.

It's gone.

Before I woke, in the last moments of my nightmare, I swear I heard it jump down from my chest and scurry off.

My ribcage, now freed to breathe deeply, feels bruised. The veil of darkness and tiredness, the sadness that dripped from me, that flooded our family for days, weeks, a month, has lifted. My lungs ache because I can inhale again without resistance.

I've done little but sleep and cry since I found and buried Father. But this isn't grief, not wholly—Father and I weren't close. At all. His death may've triggered this down phase, who knows, but this cyclic curse has movements no scientist or prophet can predict.

Now, my head feels clear. I rub sleep from my eyes. The body odour stench I've allowed to manifest suddenly disgusts me. It's the middle of the night, witching hour, and I'm fully awake. I stretch out the pain which I can now rename 'relief.'

12.13 a.m. I shed my clothing and climb in the shower. Here, I sing to myself—loudly enough to entertain a small money spider (now the only thing watching me), quietly enough not to wake my family. Once dry, I cross the landing and take in the night-time beauty of my two favourite sleeping souls. The pair are curled up together, a mesh of dark curls, freckles and Snoopy duvet. Glorious.

In my kitchen, I pour tea and load up my online shopping basket with doorstep-delivered art supplies: white spirit, badger-hair brushes, acrylics and oils. I don't know how long this uptime stint will last—no-one knows—but now, in this moment, lightning is bolting through my vessels where blood ran blue-cold before, and with it flows an overpowering urge: buy, sing, create, dance, move.

12.30 a.m. Time to paint.

Productivity comes in bursts and fits and I've not lifted a brush for weeks. I sink my tea and note I've several hours 'til sunrise, so, eager as wildfire, I head out to our garage-come-art studio. The swinging lamp stutters on and with it comes the radio. I yank off the rags which I'd tossed over my paintings, and stand—hands on hips—and stare.

With biased eyes, it's nigh impossible to see the good and bad within each piece. The black and the white. But I do see the quality in what I do. I see why people say I've talent, why my work sells, yet I still struggle to like any of my paintings. And that is why they remain here, strung up in the garage. A wall of faces. Forty-three portraits to be precise.

At first, I painted family—living and long gone—from photos and memory and once I'd drawn every blood connection, I drew the few friends I've clung onto over the years. Then, I started to paint, quite obsessively, everyone I came into contact with. Myra who runs the village shop. Our postman. The checkout girl who doesn't do small talk and whom I always make a beeline for if she's free. Random parents at the school gate whom I interact with for just long enough to capture the essence and symmetry of their faces. Everyone I ever meet.

I've a style it's fair to say. Every face is true to form, vivid. Each is a diverse celebration of the individual; however, each portrait shares one common flaw. I never stop blaming myself for it. And yet it seems to be the reason galleries book me, the feature critics always praise: the eye contact. Or rather, the lack of it. Each face carries eyes which do anything but follow you round the room.

I mount a canvas on my easel, squirt out primer on my palette, and mull, but I've no idea whom to paint—I haven't left the house in six days, so I decide once more to try to capture *it* on canvas: the thing that haunts me. But when it's not with me—and I feel it's far, far away right now—when it's not burning its snout against mine and its claws of smoke and hate aren't anchored to my breast—I've no idea what it looks like. So now, in the middle of the night, with more surplus energy than anyone else could ever care for, I draw a blank.

I put my brush down. I've a journey to make in the morning. I figure I'll find a new project then. I twist up the volume dial, close my eyes, and dance, and when I get bored, I play with hoarded garage junk: clothing, books, box-fresh devices to spiralize vegetables, endless tat I've ordered in a frenzy of mind. Rarely bin anything, even packaging, and when I'm not being sat upon and I'm jaunting on a high, if I'm not painting, or singing, or dancing, or online shopping, I'm organising. When the hellish cloud that looms is not around, I always find something that needs to be done.

Must've dozed off around five. My husband wakes me with decaf coffee and a smile.

"Get much done, love?" he asks. I feel incandescent in his love. Never reprimands, never judges, no matter how far along either end of the see-saw I'm lost. The only aspect of me we've ever argued about is medication: makes me sleepy, gain a few pounds. He's quite insistent about it. But prescriptions make a piano of only white keys of me; I become unable to play the sad songs, and sometimes, we need the sad songs, for balance.

"No painting, no," I say and take the mug and return the smile. "But I packed down all the delivery boxes. And date-ordered all the *National Geographics*." I point to a mountainous stack of cardboard and a large crate.

"Lovely. I'm sure that'll be helpful, you know, next time we need to rapidly find an article about"—his eyes flit to the box—"*'Why Jamaican Reggae and Finnish Saunas have UNESCO status'*." I punch him playfully in the belly.

"We've three hundred and thirty-one editions," I say and slurp the bitter liquid.

He reaches out his hand, places it on top of mine; it's digging into my breastbone. He holds it still, tight, quietens my busy hand. I've been scratching at my birthmark unaware. I fiddle with my port wine stain when manic.

"You okay to have Sam today? I need to go in," he says. It's the school holidays. A pang of guilt. He's taken the last few days off work to care for our son whilst I've been having 'downtime.'

"Yes. Busy day ahead, actually. Bit of an adventure on the cards," I say and march him back into the house. "I'm going to pick up the tin. Sam can play driver's mate."

"If you're sure."

And I've never been surer.

My father dealt with most of his belongings himself before he got ill. But after he died, a hospice nurse called me. He'd given her a tin to hold onto, to pass onto me. I've not felt up to the drive until today but right now, I'm jonesing to discover—what did he feel was so important for me to have?

I let Sam sit in the front next to me. Says he feels safer here, the front has airbags. (I drive like I talk when I'm out and about: fast. Always. There's never enough time to fit everything in.) I look at all seven years of my son and feel a volcanic eruption of pride and dopamine exploding in my heart. His smile often moves me to tears. Happy tears. Not the tears that come when I can't leave my bedroom and my chest is gripped in a night-vice.

We chat for the duration of the trip, or I chat, Sam nods and smiles. As we pull up in the hospice car park, Sam says he doesn't want to get out, and I understand. The building shouts of death and decay, with its old infrastructure all Rivers Styx and Acheron, so I rush in and out and bring back the tin and ponder, shall I, coalmine canary, peek first, alone?

My father was a dark soul, but I'm convinced he wouldn't leave me anything unsuitable for young eyes. The one time he met Sam, he showered him with warmth. My son received more birthday cards and gifts from Father than I ever did. I say, "Let's open it together," and Sam's face lights up. His happiness is the wind beneath my wings and today I'm soaring high.

We drive to a cafe, and I treat us both to hot chocolates. Sam touches me on the arm, all wide-eyed, a frame of panic to his face. "You're bleeding, Mum," he says. I reach for a napkin and dab at my chest. Without realising, I've taken off the top layer of my fist-sized birthmark swirl.

Shaped and shaded like a two-tone yin-yang: half of it is crimson, the other side, pale pink. Hermann Rorschach might see two entwined lovers, curled speech marks, or two tadpoles looped together, each with an eye the colour of the other. I see a yin-yang symbol, the melding of two opposites. I was bullied for it at school, but I've come to accept it's just another part of who I am.

"So I am. I'm such a naughty picker." The bleeding eases and leaves small, pinprick balls of red cresting my skin. I reassure: *Mummy is fine.* Sam calms and I let myself become distracted by the waiting staff, the lady behind the counter, patrons. My mind's eye is rampant. It documents and stores every face. I will paint them all later, once Sam's gone to bed.

"Let's open the tin, shall we?" I say. I let him lift off the metal lid. Inside is a slip of paper and an old sepia photograph: a clearing in a wood. Sam, expecting cash, is disappointed. I pull a twenty from my purse and tell him to go and choose a piece of cake, *keep the change.* Sam approaches the counter and grins at the spread of fondant fancies.

I turn over the sheet of paper and try to make sense of it. A single word, 'sorry,' is scrawled in the centre. Around it are seven names which I read over, again and again. One name is Father's, another, Mother's. She died when I was small. The other five names, however, I've no clue. And what is most peculiar? They're all written in a circle, spread around the sheet like numbers on a clock.

Before we leave the cafe, I need to make a call.

Sam is sticky-fingered and content, so I sneak outside and dial the only lady I can think of who may be able to help.

I pace through all seventeen rings until she answers the phone.

"Yes."

"Hi. Martha." I don't need to say anything else. She knows it's me.

Ice follows. We spoke briefly at Father's funeral, made polite exchanges, praised the floral arrangements, but prior to that? We've not spoken in years.

Not a word. I know she's still at the end of the line, I can hear the crackle of my grandmother's elderly lungs.

"It's about Father."

"Gathered so."

"Can I come over?"

"Not today. Frightfully busy."

She's ninety-six, the oldest person I've ever painted. Her face hangs top left in my garage gallery. Her oil-paint, grey-fish-eyes—like those in all my other paintings—stare anywhere but at your own.

"Of course," I say. "Of course." I tell her, quick-fire, about the tin and its contents and just ask outright if she can help before she can hang up. "Any ideas? What does it mean?"

Silence. I can see an outline of Sam through the frosted cafe window. He's getting restless, the sugar's kicking in. I dab at my raw chest and continue to rattle back and forth along the pavement outside the cafe.

"Can't help you, dear." I sense a change in her tone. Less Victorian matriarch, more lost sheep. She's pulled back from the phone mouthpiece.

"Really? Nothing?" I say, patience thinning.

"I expect it's just his way of apologising."

"For what? Is this to do with Mum?"

"Not directly, dear. More to do with you." A long pause ensues. "You, and the way you are. I suggest you read nothing more into it." And with that, she hangs up.

And there's nothing I need more in my life right now than to read more into it.

I place the items back into this Pandora's box from Father, go back in to shimmy Sam out, and speed back to the car.

We drive to a park so Sam can play, and I can investigate further. Double-time, I stroll around the perimeter with my eyes set firm on my phone screen. My folks were local people, so I probe locally: village pub, corner shop, bowling green. I cyber-stalk and click and call multiple names and numbers in search of the five contacts on the circle-shaped list, all the while I draft and redraft possible explanations.

Father's dead.

Mother's dead.

Three of the other members of the circle also turn out to be dead. This comes as no great surprise—my parents were old when they had me.

Number six is alive. Bingo.

I contact his relatives to learn he has dementia—doesn't remember who my parents are when I ask after them.

I've one name left, Margaret Millard. Alive. And now, after sweet-talking the penultimate connection, I also have her address.

Since the stroke of midnight, my mind has been switched to 'on.' Neural messages are surging fast, making a computer processor of my brain. I lean against a tree and close my eyes to rest but all I see is cerebral-fire. I see, feel, breathe, the warm, frenetic buzz of flickering Christmas tree lights mid-July. I can accomplish more in a day when I'm out of the deep end of the lagoon of my sickness than I could in a lifetime of treading water. Or so it feels. There's nothing I can't do right now—except rest.

Margaret lets us in. Her eyes radiate a kindness. She brings us fruit loaf and tea and directs Sam to a box of toys she keeps for her own grandchildren.

I show Margaret the photo.

"That's the clearing half-way up Three-Mile-Hill, before you reach the farm. Haven't been up there for years."

She flags up the walking stick propped by the front door then shrugs at her own knees.

Her words flow tardily, or, I'm processing them too quickly.

"Why would he leave me a photo of it? And why's your name part of this circle?" I say and push the slip towards her.

She stalls, offers more tea, travels to the kitchen and back to gather a tub of sugar and a teaspoon. "Do you really want to know, dear?"

I've both feet in now, in this damn circle. Whatever truth she's keeping from me, I won't be leaving until I hear it.

"Of course," I say.

She looks over at Sam. His attention is with the toys. Lost in a fantasy of yellowed, plastic farm animals.

"It was a séance."

"A what?"

"More of an offering, really. Séances were usually held indoors." Margaret, eyes narrow, head tilted back, appears to be studying the images her memories are creating.

"And these were the people involved?" I ask.

"Yes."

"In the woods?"

"Your mother, lovely woman. Struggling to conceive."

I push the biscuit around the edge of my saucer and feel the furrow in my brow deepen.

"A small sacrifice was made. Didn't go so well first time. We had to go back up."

"I'm sorry, what? A sacrifice—?"

"It was dark, of course—these things are always done at night—and as we were stood spread out in our circle, none of us could catch it. Mr. Bream managed to nick it, I think. I could see its fear though. Beetle-black, beady eyes. I remember seeing the glint of its blood on its white fur by the light of the paraffin lamps we'd placed at the five points of the star. But none of us could move fast enough to catch it."

"Catch what?" My voice comes out loud.

Sam looks up. "Mummy?"

"It's alright, love. Won't be long."

"Mummy, your neck."

"Oh dear, your neck's bleeding." Margaret passes me a tissue. I dab at the edge of the tip of the yin I've been subconsciously shredding.

"Catch what?" I say again, softer.

"The rabbit. To evoke new life in your mother, to help ease you into this spiritual plane, Mr. Bream needed to sacrifice something. One-in, one-out, if you like."

"Someone killed a rabbit?"

"It failed first time. Poor little bugger. All white fur, it didn't stand a chance, stood out like a sore thumb. It was bleeding pretty badly as it skittered off into the darkness. Such a lively one. Spirited. We all wanted to carry on, but he said we needed to make the full sacrifice in the centre of the circle. Something needed to die in the centre."

"Fuck." I feel tension creep into my shoulders. The tissue is sodden with red. Margaret proffers a clean one. "You went back?"

"Yes." She pauses, shifts in her seat. "Sure you want me to continue? You're white as a sheet, duck."

Mother had been desperate to conceive, Father said she was over the moon when she found out she was pregnant. The only time I saw pure love in his eyes was when he spoke of her. I fell pregnant easily with Sam, but I can understand the urge to become a parent. But this? This is ludicrous. Otherworldly. No wonder Father didn't tell me this. Mother died shortly after giving birth to me, and Father, despite raising me solo, grew emotionally distant. His heart hardened.

"Yes. Please. I need to know." I'm welling up. In the well-lit room, a dark shadow pours out from behind Margaret's chair, onto her rug. "Please."

"We returned with a fresh rabbit the following week. A black one. Runtish, sick-looking thing. All bones, no meat. It was the last in the shop, we had no choice. We went ahead anyway, despite the manual specifying 'white.' The candle of time was burning fast for your mother. She was pushing forty."

"What happened to that rabbit?"

"Slashed from neck to tail under a strong moon. Gave up more than enough blood to cover your mother's stomach. Your father drank a half-pint, then vomited into the emptiness of the forest behind him."

"Jesus—"

"He wasn't involved, dear. Not in our church."

"—Christ."

"You came along nine months later—one bonny baby for the price of two, scrappy kits. She was overjoyed. Such a shame she passed so soon after."

I feel sick. I collect my scrambled thoughts, thank her for the tea, grab Sam, and leave.

Should I drive to the forest, find the spot where this ritual occurred? I just can't.

Sam asks over and over: "Why are you crying, Mummy?"

But I can't and won't burden him with the filth I've just heard. Every time I look in the rearview mirror to overtake, switch lanes as I shuttle home at breakneck speed, I see the creeping shadow.

It's back. Ribbons of darkness spool from the back seat of my car into the driver's footwell. Tendrils of sadness and doom roll under my chair and weave up and around me. Cruel whispers only I can hear begin again: *You're worthless, nothing.* I feel it in my lap, weighing me down. It plucks at my heart strings with talons of melancholy. Only I can hear the coercive swansong it plays. It's back, and I need to get home and in my room.

I'm a mess when I pull up. My husband eases me out of my clothes, into my pyjamas, and tucks me up in bed.

An hour passes. In the darkness, I hear it panting, twitching, waiting to hurl itself onto me. I'm exhausted but I don't want it to drag me back down its slope. I know it's stronger in the dark, so I reach for and switch on the bedside light and watch it recoil into the corner, with its long, black ears of velveteen fog and a face I can never remember when I'm up and well enough to paint. But now, I see it with clarity. It makes a shaking child of my heart. White, empty eyes glower at me, vacant yet filled with the magnitude and permanence of death. It whisper-shouts: *Séance Girl. Child of Séance.*

I drag myself out of bed. Have to push on through this depth of despair and woe. I hiss at it. In a skirmish, it vanishes beneath the bed. By the dim light of the bedside table, I dress, then check on my husband and child. Fast asleep. On the landing, I cry in silence. It's better Sam doesn't see me like this, safer.

Safer without you.

Safer without me? My son's safer without me?

I stumble down the stairs and head out to the garage.

It's close. Draining me. I must paint it away. I can see it; I can picture it. If I trap it on canvas, it may no longer have power. I'm not thinking straight.

I swirl black and white on a palette and fling and dash until the stretched canvas in front of me is splattered. It's awash with everything but colour: emotion, contrast, bipolarity.

Useless. Terrible.

This piece does not feel like it's helping. I abandon it, pick up a fresh canvas. The last thing I feel like doing as I writhe around at the bottom of this pit is painting, but paint I must.

I churn out image after image of everyone I've seen today. They are poor pieces. My radiant muse isn't present, just this beast of darkness. The people in the nursing home, the waitress, Margaret, Mother and Father in their prime, the others from the circle. Up and up go more and more bad portraits, and of course, none of them are looking at me. I've never managed to master eyes.

I'm being torn in two directions. Siamese twin babies, Yin and Yang, connected at the hip, are each trying to crawl free.

No-one should exist with two spirits in one skin.

Almost every ounce of oxygen is sucked from my blood as it presses up against me. I recline on the cold, concrete floor and let it take its place on my tired chest.

Liberate me.

On my ribcage, this thing, dark as funeral pyre smoke, white devil eyes, stares directly into my soul, my two, trapped souls.

Séance child. Should not be here.

And I realise, it is right. This is why I lead this life of pain. Why I swing pendulous, an unstable chandelier, from one peak to the next, stopping only to sit in the trough of the nether whilst my brain fails.

Should not be here.

Was never meant to be.

With every last mote of energy I've left, I stand and drag across the chest-high stack of empty cardboard boxes from the corner I'd so neatly stacked whilst tweaking last night. I re-stack them up as tall as I can in the centre of the garage, box upon box upon box.

The twenty-metre extension cable which brings power out from the house is easy to yank free. I wind it halfway in. Thick, blue, plastic-coated cable coils up and around the yellow levered bobbin in my hands. I climb atop the boxes and throw the three-pin plug over an exposed garage rafter. It dangles back down. I fasten it in place and tie the plugged end around my neck, a noose, a circle.

Do it, Séance Child.

The thing of shadows is here, around me. It grabs and forces my head up to face the sea of portraits which cover the walls. And I am lost in an ocean of ruinous burgundy and black waves. For the first time, and maybe the last, I see them watching me. Falcon-eyed. All of them. They stare directly at me.

The eyes of every portrait are now mastering me. Every pair of pupils is thick, hard, and strong: burning into me, challenging me without words. The pupils of myriad familiar faces chant in the silent voice of the white-eyed, black-bodied devil hare: *No-one should exist, two spirits in one skin. Do it, séance girl.*

I close my eyes. A spinning zoetrope, two teardrop shapes in shades of dark and light red—both bloody—are entwined as if in battle for my soul. Loony tunes. That's all, folks.

I tighten the cord, jump up, swing my legs forward, and kick back on the stack of cardboard below. The thing that too often helps to drag me down watches on. But tonight, it does not attempt to help me down as plastic rope burns my neck.

A machine beeps. Again, and again. Does this mean I'm alive? Or trapped in some kind of audio torture chamber? Hell? It's not hell. I open my eyes. My boys are here. Both with red, wet eyes.

"Mummy's awake," says Sam. I try to lift my hand to take hold of his, to touch him. It takes effort, a world of effort, but my arm still works. I send a message to my toes, my calves, my legs. They move. I'm back in my body. I've no idea where I've been. I remember my portraits staring at me, judging, then I recall a sensation which sends a shudder down my body. Pain kicks in. I don't want to let go of Sam's hand, but I have to lift it to feel where the soreness is. My neck's on fire, shoulders too. My head is pounding.

"Don't, love. Please, leave it. Don't move the dressings." My husband takes my other hand. Sam drapes himself over me and starts to cry fresh tears.

"Where are we?" I ask.

My husband cut me down. I am without recollection of this. He heard something crash in the night, and concerned, came out to check on me.

"I found you just in time. What the hell were you doing?" He breaks down. They're both sobbing. I want to cry but I can't. I'm in physical agony, but otherwise, I feel borderline happy, at peace, I'm okay.

I try to recount my last moments in the garage, try to recapture the vision that made me behave the way I did, but I can't. All I can recall are the portraits and a feeling of bleakness and how something had wanted me to swing from the rafters.

I feel disgusted with myself. That my partner saw me like that, dangling, limp. And my son, my young, impressionable child, watched me get trollied out unconscious to an ambulance. The shame of it. I throw up in a cardboard dish.

I hear my child crying, and this is remedy enough. Nearly dying has taught me how much I want to live.

I spend several weeks in this room. People check my temperature and blood pressure relentlessly, yet I sleep better than I have in years. I don't know if it's the new medication the medics are insisting I must take, or the fact that I appear to have reached rock bottom and the only other direction I can move on is upwards. But I feel … well.

I dress to leave. Sam and my husband are with me. Sam's drawing pictures, wants to be an artist like me. My husband tells me Sam has developed a penchant for the darker shades, for charcoal, grey and rust pastels. "What are you drawing?" I ask.

He looks up but doesn't look me in the eye.

"Look at me, Sam. Let me see your beautiful face."

I look at my partner who asks me not to push it.

Sam muffles something: *forests, trees, the woods at night, and all the creatures that don't sleep within it,* and then, still not making eye contact, he speaks again, louder, "Mummy, it's gone. Your yin-yang mark. Gone."

He carries on with his grim sketch. I notice each owl, squirrel, and badger, wears a tight leash around their neck.

I raise a hand to my breastbone. Now my bandages are gone, all I can feel is the burn scar around my neck. I walk into the bathroom to check in the mirror. My boy is right. I turn and look at my husband who shrugs and carries on packing my bag. Like my foggy memories of that night in the garage, memories I know I won't miss, it's gone. My birthmark demons have washed away like prints in the sand. All I see are a décolletage of smooth pale skin bar a constellation of freckles, and a ring of bruising further up my neck.

Weeks pass and things feel different. I feel different. I can sleep, nothing weighs me down, makes an infernal armchair of my chest. I paint. Every character I've met over the past few weeks appears on the wall of my gallery garage, but I don't paint out there. Sam won't allow it. Our box room has become a miniature indoor studio. I've mastered eyes. I hope this doesn't devalue my work, because I feel happier with each piece.

My husband hasn't once claimed victory over the collection of medicine bottles and pill packets that now sit in our medicine cabinet. I observe my son and the artistic talent he seems to have inherited—morbid as it might often be—and my heart swells. My mind speaks clarion for the first time in forever. It declares from every ounce, every cell of my body, that I'll never try to leave again. I could never inflict such pain on the pair of them.

But although he never leaves my side, sleeps in between us every night in bed, follows me like a friendly ghost, my son still won't, can't look me in the eye. My husband says Sam's afraid to look at me. Says he sees something different in my eyes. Where everyone else sees my pupils and my amber irises, Sam sees swirls of black and white.

It's a warm Tuesday evening. I hear a knock at the door. I've been internet shopping again, whilst riding this perpetual, sleepless, upswing that is now my nearly merry life. It's a parcel addressed to Sam, something I've ordered for him.

I bring it through, sit next to him on the carpeted floor of the lounge, and push the large gift towards him. He thanks me and I feel a pang of sadness that he's opening it without a single look my way. I grab his chin, cup it in my hand, and draw his face up to look at mine. "Look at me. I'm here. I'm never leaving you; I promise," I say and his eyes are looking straight into mine for the first time since that night and his eyes are full of fear and hurt and a power, a force, that is stronger than anything the darkness has ever threatened me with. It's the overwhelming strength of a terrified love that a young child has for a parent they've witnessed dance the closest dance with death.

"But how do I know? I keep having nightmares. About you, your body. Every night. Then I feel this pushing feeling on my chest."

I bring my finger up to his lips and shush him. I don't want to hear what he's about to say. I hug him in close and comfort him as his tears flow. I struggle to hold back mine. Minutes pass which fill an eternity. I encourage him to open the gift. He rips into the brown tape package and unfolds the flaps. An almost-smile pulls at the corners of his lips.

"Canvases. For me? Proper canvases?"

"Yes. So you can paint, express yourself. Want to go up now, do something together?"

He smiles but his eyes sink and again flit away from the direction of my loving stare. "I would Mummy, but I'm tired. Really, really tired."

Its half past three in the afternoon.

He places the canvas back down. A shadow creeps out from underneath, from within the folded cardboard packaging. It swells and grows and sits to the side of my boy. My heart thrums and not because of my balancing medication. I fear I've seen this shape before. It looks at me with white hole eyes and then shifts its glare directly to my son.

"Need to go to bed, Mummy. Tired," he says and rises to his feet. As he leaves the room and climbs up the stairs, I watch helplessly, frozen with dread, as this horrific creature of darkness follows him up.

I'm unable to cry or scream. Medication has me muted like a de-strung harp, but inside, I'm shattering with fear. And I now know for certain I've passed on more than my artistic skills to my son.

A Piece Missing

First published in Dark Matter Magazine, 2022

All six screaming monitors gathered like nestling owlets in the pocket of her apron fall silent as soon as she crosses the threshold. The distress of the baby had been hideous to hear, but the silence which follows—as the monitors return to a lowly crackle of static interference—feels asphyxiating. Back inside, she can no longer hear the baby. Her baby. Had it been her baby she had heard?

Up the stairs her feet carry her, as they have a thousand times before, along the hallway towards the furthest room which is also the smallest. The door, like her front door, like all doors in her home which has become her house, a house, is stoppered open, wedged fully ajar, and the wind which pushes in through the agape window makes ghosts of baby's breath from the delicate white net curtains.

She draws her arms tight around herself and rubs the sides of her bare arms with red-raw, muddy palms. The cot-bed—bar one of the paired monitors which sits crackling gently with the static of lost promises on the centre of the small mattress—like the rest of the hollow room, lies empty. She doesn't notice how filthy her hands are though. Her mind is on other things, in other places. She can't see the dirt, or perhaps, she chooses not to.

Despite her chill, she can't pull down the window. *What if what I have lost wants to return?* she thinks.

Not here, she thinks. *Whatever it is I am looking for, it is not here. Perhaps the next room?*

She moves through all of the rooms, checks in all of the cupboards, searches and pries under stale bedding, under each dusty cushion. Nada. The breeze continues to move in and out of the building like air through lungs and gives a dusting of goosebumps to her skin. She finds nothing. Nothing. Zilch.

The staircase groans as she makes her way down it to search the ground floor. It is as if the house feels her despair. *Why am I so sad, is this not what I wanted?* she thinks as she continues on her search and makes her way through to the last room she has not yet checked: the kitchen. She sees within a moment what she's searching for is not there. In her heart, she knows she'll not find it there or maybe anywhere, especially not in the kitchen where cutlery and unsafe things are kept. What she does find there, though, is a mountain of dirty dishes. All of her dishes have been used; they clutter the tabletop. The washing up seems endless in her home. Her house. A house.

She slides her finger over the smooth curve of a greasy plate and, on noticing the brown crescent of dirt under each of her fingernails, she lifts the plate up and decides now would be a good a time as any to wash it. *My hands will benefit from the chore,* she thinks. On touching the plate, she forgets what she's been searching for, forgets why she's in the kitchen, has a feeling like the feeling one gets when one moves from one room to another in search of something, forgetting what it is they're searching for the moment they enter a different room.

She fills up the sink with warm, soapy suds. Dipping her sullied hands into it, pushing them deep below the surface until they can't be seen any more will provide some release, she hopes, and the porcelain does need to be cleaned.

No time like the present, she sighs, although she is not sure what time it is because the wall-mounted clock has been stuck for a long time. Its second hand clicks on beat like a metronome but never advances past twelve. It has been five-to-three for days now. Perhaps a month. *A new battery,* she thinks. *Or maybe it's beyond repair. Sometimes, things do break beyond repair.* She says this aloud and hears herself saying it, but it does not sound like her voice. Was it a recording of her voice? *Was that a recording of my voice?* she thinks and says the words aloud again to be sure. But she can't be sure of anything.

I might, she thinks, *be stuck here at the sink forever if the clock cannot be fixed.* The pile of plates to her side looms, seems to lengthen like shadows at dusk. She makes a start on it and many ticks pass by as she soaks and scrubs and rinses the mound of dirty porcelain, but it never seems to deplete.

She rubs her tired eyes with a dry patch of a part of her arm just between the elbow and her wrist, a part of her which she cannot recall the name of, and on opening her eyes, she finds she is no longer at the helm of her own kitchen, taking pride in its appearance, its order, but is standing at a sink she does not recognise, washing dishes she has no memory of using.

The big hand is still stuck between two and three, the little hand on the eleven. The pattern on the splash back tiles seems familiar. *This must be home,* she thinks, the constants in the house giving her some reassurance.

In the translucent version of herself she catches in the sheen of the glass in the window above the kitchen sink, she thinks she sees a streak of bloodied dirt on her left cheek, or maybe on her right—she has never been very good at understanding reflections—so she soaks and wrings a clean cloth which she lifts from a tub which she always keeps between the lines of the edge of the back of the sink and the glass window.

The windowsill, she thinks as she tries to recall how the mark may have been made, *is made of the most beautiful tapestry of glazed tiles.* She dabs at the mark on her cheek and dabs again and rubs until it fades and then returns her focus to the dishes.

The largest plate is precariously balanced on the side of the mound of washing up. She carefully pulls it free and places it into the water and finds a rhythm with the tick-tick passing of stationary time. Despite her efforts—the clean pile to her left does seem to grow slightly—the dirty pile to her right swells in magnitude. At least, she notices, her hands are becoming cleaner, free of grime. But her baby monitors still just crackle quietly, yielding no clues.

She lifts an oval serving dish which perhaps a roast turkey had been presented on, carved up into smaller morsels on, dispatched as brown slices onto a myriad of smaller dining plates. All from a meal perhaps reminiscent of happier times, yet it is a meal she does not remember cooking or eating. She submerges the oval dish into the sink. As she pushes off grease and minuscule fibres of meat and buffs the centre of the dish, she cries out and drops the dish down into the water again.

Fuck! she says, and gingerly lifts the plate back out and brings it closer to her tired eyes for examination.

There, within the markings of the fat settled and stained from an old burnt bird's carcass, she sees an imprint of a familiar face. Drawing a deep breath, she feels a rush of something not altogether awful nor altogether pleasant quicksilver through her veins. *It's him,* she thinks. *Husband.* She traces over the sticky, brown lines which swerve and bend and twist and straighten and portray the face of her husband. But it is not any face of her husband. Not his sleeping face, his face full of laughter or sadness, his cross face he makes when he reprimands her for leaving the front door wide open when neither of them are inside; it is a face only she, she hopes, might recognise: his face at orgasm.

This is the last time she remembers seeing his face, this face; it is the last clear memory she has of her husband. They haven't made love in over a year. She tries to remember if she has seen him since then, since he came last, inside of her; she squeezes the base of her palm against her forehead in thought. He still lives in the house; this she knows because she's seen large leather shoes by the front door. Also, she can see his shed door right now, opened out towards the raised beds of the large garden as she looks through her own faint glass reflection, out towards the acre of land on which the house sits. *His shed, this is where he often is,* she recalls, *pottering, doing something with French beans.* And if he is not here, living with her, then *the shed door would not be open,* she thinks. *A keen gardener,* she recalls. *My husband is quite green-fingered. But when did I last study his face?*

In the image of him on the cream plate in her hands, she sees his eyes are closed. His head is tipped back yet his chin is dropped towards his chest and his mouth is wide open. Like the door to the house, door to the shed, windows in each and every room, always waiting for something to return.

She rubs her eyes, and, in the pop of a bubble, the image is gone. Such a strange sight to behold, had she imagined it? She moves on to the next dirty plate. *What a strange day,* she thinks. *What an odd vision.*

She works her way through a few more plates, trance like, finding the repetition of the chore meditative. She looks down at another plate and this time, does not feel as surprised to see an image. This time, it is less clear, but it is there: coiled spine, disproportionately large eyes, small nubs. She sees it clearly and when she scrubs harder, the image appears stronger. It is an embryo; no, it is more advanced—a foetus.

She places the plate down in the suds, pulls it up again. This time, the foetus is swollen. It appears larger, more refined, as if a trimester has passed: clear limbs, a defined nose, an umbilical cord, where before she'd seen just smears of sauce and gravy. She dips and lifts the plate, moves her sponge over the image, each stroke in time with the click of the stuck clock. The image mutates. It twists and spins around, and there, on the foetus on the plate, is the face of a child. A baby. Her baby?

Its eyes too, like her husband's had been, are screwed closed. The baby's cheeks are high apples, and its mouth is pranged wide open. Strangers would say they saw her husband's face, in the face of the baby. She has a clear memory—perhaps the only crisp memory she'll have this day—of the baby: the shade of red its cheeks would turn, accompanied by the noise it would make when nothing she could do would settle it. Could it, could this, be her baby, this face on a foetus on a dirty dinner plate?

Her heart is confused. It tries to beat in time with the stuck clock hand, but finds itself syncopated, faster, lost. Her own heart and the clock are the only sounds she can hear, because the baby monitors stashed tight in her apron pocket are screaming out with nothing but silence.

She dips the plate, fearful the baby's face may vanish, yet also keen to end this delusion. She pulls it up and out of the suds again. The face is gone—a new image appears. She turns the plate like the steering wheel of a car angling a sharp series of crooks in the road until she finds its position. Until she can see what it this time the plate wants to show her.

It is a tree, this time. Not a face, a willow tree. Drooping branches hang heavily to the right, its trunk bows slightly to the left. *I know this tree*, she thinks. She recognises this tree because it is the tree at the far end of the garden.

She drops the plate into the sink. A foam spray bursts up, the edges of which tickle white the work counter. Clasping the monitors tightly down in the deep pocket of her apron so they do not escape or smash, she runs back out of the house, down her front path, and around the back. She keeps on running past the shed, its door still ajar.

"Love, what's up?" she hears a tall, gaunt, shadow say as she hops and steps and bounds over tumps of grass and scattered terracotta pots and spades and bundles of bamboo cane and sacks of fertiliser. It is a shadow which has thrown itself into the garden. She looks up. She knows this shape, this shape, which is speaking, asking her if she is okay, calling her love, but she cannot see who, precisely, it is.

"I can't stop," she replies. Where its face should be, she sees the face she saw on the plate. Not the sex face—but the face of a screaming child. A crying baby: balled cheeks, red cheeks, tonsils, with watering eyes which won't stop watering.

She hears again: "Love, what's up?" but she sees the baby, open maw, face of eternal scream, superimposed where the face of the gaunt shadow which has given itself to the garden should be.

She ignores the tall shape with the gardening fork in its hand and picks up pace. She must get to the tree. It is as if the plate has spoken to her, offered guidance in all the ways the expensive baby monitors she'd ordered six-fold, one for each room, had failed.

The tree.

The willow tree which bows to the side. Maybe by the tree she'll find what she thinks she's been searching for, been keeping the windows open for. What she has lost. She drops to her knees on reaching the tree and places her hands on the mound of earth piled up high underneath it. *Feels cold to the touch*, she thinks. *But there's nothing here. Just dirt, a tree.*

It is a tree which has been here for longer than she has, much longer—and she feels like she has been here already for an immeasurable length of time. A tear rolls down her cheek, weaves a wonky path. It meanders towards her chin, itself unsure if it is being shed in relief or in sadness. The tear rolls off and shoots like an arrow on target straight down, as if drawn towards the mound of soil. In this moment, she has the urge to draw her own face closer to the heap. It is as if it is calling to her, this pile of earth which is stacked up under the willow tree.

Her lips are now kiss-close to the tip of the heap. *Should I?* she thinks, but she is doing what she is thinking of doing before she has had a chance to reason. Her tongue probes into the mound, presses against and into the mud, and her hands scoop up more, in preparation for her mouth.

The hunger overriding her is insatiable. She tries to curb it with what is in front of her by filling her mouth with several scoopfuls of mud. She chews on small clumps of soil and handfuls of grass-topped turf. She masticates until something hard hits her molars: something familiar. Something which is not food, not nutritious, not what she thinks she is looking for cracks hard against grinding teeth. She plays with it with her tongue, cleans it, and then with thumb and finger, pulls it out: a small, flat, piece of porcelain.

She admires the smooth, found treasure in her muddied palm. This is not like any of the porcelain she has ever served food on in her home, her house, a house; it is like no dish or plate she has ever washed or stacked. This piece is white with bold, blue, shining lines; navy, hatched pictures. On this small piece, which is no larger than a large coin, she sees the edge of a blue willow tree.

The embossed blue branches she strokes with her fingertip, she admires, are not unlike—in shape and angle—the ones which shelter her from the autumnal sun now. She sits on folded knees and continues to search for more broken pieces of chinoiserie-patterned pottery in the dirt. With her tongue, she cleans each new piece she retrieves from the pile, greets each like a long-lost friend with her lips, and then arranges them to her side, on a patch of flattened grass.

Without the constant tick of the kitchen clock, she loses all awareness of time. She loses herself almost but not quite completely in what she's doing, even though she isn't entirely sure why she's doing what she's doing. Her hands dig and scoop further. She pulls out piece after piece and cleans each free from organic matter and humus and grub larvae and other things which dwell in the dirt with the tip of her tongue and the wetness of her saliva.

To her side, the shape of an old plate forms, and on it, she sees the story appear. This time, it is not a mirage, not her imagination, not anything she is unsure of, because this time, she knows this story to be real.

As a child, her own mother would spout the tale of the blue willow plate. Of this, she can be sure. Childhood memories alone are set in the stone of her mind. *To be the child,* she thinks, *and not the mother, makes for happier times.*

In the collection of smashed, worn fragments she gathers and assembles from the pile of mud, she sees the two lovers. She recalls her mother telling her the story of the blue willow plate while serving her sliced apple on a version of this broken treasure which she continues to dig to unearth. One of the pair on the plate, the woman, is promised to another, a man whom she does not love, so the original lovers elope, but they are caught. Due to their forbidden love, they're banished to a faraway island. But the Gods take pity on them and transform the lovers into a pair of swallows who fly free.

A similar plate telling the same tale now lies in pieces on the grass, and is nearly complete, all apart from one chunk. One small piece which she knows is where the image of the two swallows who face each other in a permanent state of amorous conjunction is absent. The sight of the incomplete plate deeply disturbs her, so she digs. She digs deeper and deeper, and searches for this last piece, but she knows, deep within herself, in a place within herself into which she can't dig any deeper, she will never find it. The plate will remain fragmented, like her thoughts—if they are even her thoughts and not just the superimposed thoughts of the person writing this story as if it were about this woman when it may be about the author herself.

Her hands scoop down as she spits soil, small pebbles, and crushed snail shells from her mouth. She scoops until she strikes something hard and large with her fingertips. Clearing the layers of sifted dirt, she pulls up not one but two items, each of a similar size, to the surface. Her tears come hard and fast now and each time she wipes her cheeks, more mud and dirt and a little blood from a selection of small cuts and scrapes on her hands now have become smeared onto her face. She lays the two objects, body-like objects, side by side, and stares neither at them nor at anything else. She knows she has seen this before, this pair, but not in a dirty plate, nor in the blue willow story, nor in a dream. Or perhaps in a dream, if this, this real-life experience, is not in fact a dream.

On the left lies a clumsily stuffed skin-suit, once a baby. She probes the human sack with muddied tips and feels both sharp and smooth edges inside it. She remembers *yes, I emptied it of its pain, filled it with fragments of broken china.* To the right, almost identical, the mirror image—although she has never been very good at understanding reflection—is an old, porcelain doll caked in the mud in which it was buried. She turns the doll over, so it lies on its face. Her finger traces over where it's been broken and taped back up. *This one I filled with something crimson and wet, a material altogether softer. It holds the pain of the other within it,* she remembers. *Afterwards, they both slept so well.*

It is then she becomes more disturbed and jumps up suddenly because all six baby monitors start to scream at once. The burst of cries shocks her backwards.

She steadies herself and grabs the two lifeless bodies and places them back, deep down in a hole, the hole, their hole. Mud and grit and blue-white china pieces rooster-tail through the air as she rushes to fill the void back in. The constant wailing feels like a fork on a plate, and it only grows louder. She kicks back the top layer and runs back up the garden. Her baby is back. She hears it scream. Somewhere, everywhere in the house, something is screaming. Her baby must've found its way back in. Somehow. She can hear her baby on the monitors nestled in her apron pocket. Her baby. A baby. Had she had a baby?

With each step forward, her hold on the truth slips. As she gains proximity to her home, the house, a house, she sees the tall shape leaning against the open-doored shed. It talks to her, susurrates something, but all she hears is the persistent, piercing scream of a child.

She looks to the tall shape's face. *Perhaps I can try to read its lips,* she thinks, *it is speaking to me, trying to say something important, a clue.* But where nose, eyes, lips, and adult skin should sit, she sees instead the face of a porcelain doll with willow buds bursting out through every one of its orifices. White-green, cotton-soft buds push through china nostrils, poke out like caged prisoners' hands through ear holes and rosebud lips. It's not who she thought it would be, the tall shape standing by the shed. But who did she think it was? Her memory draws a blank. There are no hints or images or shadows in the space of her mind. She runs faster back towards the house, cheetahs through the wide-open front door.

All six screaming monitors gathered like nestling owlets in the pocket of her apron fall silent as soon as she crosses the threshold. The distress of the baby had been hideous to hear, but the silence which follows—as the monitors return to a lowly crackle of static interference—feels asphyxiating. Back inside, she can no longer hear the baby. Her baby. Had it been her baby she had heard?

Up the stairs her feet carry her, as they have a thousand times before, along the hallway towards the furthest room which is also the smallest. The door, like her front door, like all doors in her home which has become her house, a house, is stoppered open, wedged fully ajar, and the wind which pushes in through the agape window makes ghosts of baby's breath from the delicate white net curtains.

Neon Fly

First published by Ghost Orchid Press, 2021

A swarm of fluorescent-green flies hover above Mother's head as she's taken for cremation by the army. Buckled over in pain, her guts are being digested from the inside out. I can smell the rot from her—putrescine, cadaverine, death's call—through the transparent wall which separates us. A web of foamy green plaque which carries chunks of congealed blood creeps from the decay that has perforated her bowels. A time ago, I would've shielded my daughter's eyes, but she has seen it all before. We're all damaged goods now, even those of us who are clean.

Mother looks up, one eye now gone, her face nearly unrecognisable, and mouths the only words left to be said: "I love you. Look after Eden." I blow a kiss at Mother, pull a little harder on Eden's hand, and walk with great pace in the other direction.

I'm not going to cry—I genuinely feel no urge to anymore. Relief. I feel relief instead. My poor mother will be put out of her misery in just a few moments. The cull has been going on for so long now, no-one cries any more—global desensitisation. The nation's tears are spent.

We stomp past the organic fruit snack stall. Eden eyes up the fresh pineapple fingers, the slices of rich red watermelon, and the deep orange carrot batons. "We'll eat on the ship," I tell her and beckon her onwards.

Over the years, the majority of the world's population has led a lifestyle of poor-quality food choices, and so, like the ocean and the soils on planet

Earth, their bodies have become infested with nano-plastics. Microscopic pieces of polyethylene, PVC, and Styrofoam have accumulated in the intestines of anyone with a less than perfect organic feeding regime.

There was a trend, a hundred years or so back, for people to pool all of their plastics inside of a large, emptied plastic bottle. 'Eco-bricks.' Walls and garden dens were built with them, but these mummified pseudo-environmental projects became fast submerged beneath soils and created reservoirs rich in accumulated poisons which drained into nearby arable land. This magnified the scale of Earth's plastic problem. A fine noxious snow of crude oil excrement soon dusted over everything and bio-accumulated within our soil. Within our water. Our food. Most of our people.

Bacteria modified by scientists to break these plastics down proved successful to a degree in the oceans, but these same genetically-modified, plastic-feeders are also drawn to the motes of plastic which saturate ninety-nine percent of the population's innards. Once inside the body, these bastard microbes consume the plastic they find there. And also the flesh. They gnaw their way out.

Nicknamed 'Piranha' bacteria, the infection is untreatable. Once infected, a painful death follows, as does a tell-tale ring of neon greenfly which feed upon the microbes. Another mutant food chain. The neon fly headdress the infected like an emerald halo crown.

Oceans, lakes, rivers, all now glow green. All waterways are caked in thick sludge and stink of rot and decay as all life within perishes. Flies—neon lights in the night—swarm everywhere. They hover over the freshly deceased and the not so freshly deceased, feed on the Piranha bacteria, lay eggs, and spread their repulsive maggots. A stench worse than a butcher's trashcan hangs thick in death-pockets. And the survivors? Well, we wear scarves over our face if we have to brave the outdoors.

"I love you," I shout back from the other side of the Perspex screen which stretches sky-high and keeps us forever separate from the contaminated.

"This way, madam." A guard hurries us into the tunnel which leads toward the interplanetary screening zone. I know we'll pass, myself and Eden. I've known since school what we put into our mouth is what we become. I turned down plateful after plateful of food as a child. I knew my mother cut corners. She dished up processed meats, offal, cheaply farmed nutrient-depleted vegetables. I turned it all down. The thought of the disasters she'd serve each evening still turn my stomach now. She'd send me unfed to my room, furious I'd refused the meals she'd toiled over so hard. She'd scrape the contents of my plate onto her own. I wish I could've stopped her. I knew it was all bad.

I left home as soon as I could, fell pregnant shortly after, and had Eden. Her father was taken by the neon fly. He lied about what he ate. I grieved for our brief relationship, then found solace elsewhere, with the People of the Organic Food Order. I raised Eden with them, in the commune. Those were some of the best days of my life.

We still visited Mother and stayed at her house, but we never ate her food. Our cooperative of like-minded thinkers, farmers, and eco-warriors worked our large patch of land organically. We ate sparsely, but we ate well. No shreds of plastic poisoned our bodies; we gave nothing to the bacteria and the neon fly which follow to feast upon.

When we received the letter from the World Government inviting us onto Rocket 23, I was hopeful for a better future for myself and my daughter, hopeful perhaps some of the other barefoot children Eden had grown up with, had pulled snails and slugs from the organic lettuces and radishes with, would be on board too.

Who knows where we'll end up once we land. We don't even know how many people are being sent.

Before the neon fly came, the World Government's plans for shipping out the rich, the elite, the leaders and their families from our polluted planet had been kept secret. But the truth had eventually spilled. The government had been terra-forming Mars for decades.

Many of those who'd been on the elite list had already perished from the green plaque. Or, like Mother, had been found to be infected and had been pushed alive into funeral pyres which pumped dirty, green-black smoke into Earth's increasingly fucked atmosphere.

And so, with the decimation of the elite, the invitation to escape to Mars opened up to civilians.

If civilians, like myself and Eden, can prove we aren't contaminated, are clean of plastic, bacteria and neon fly, then, we too can qualify as Earth Seeds for a place in one of the twenty-three rockets being launched this week.

"Mummy, I'm hungry." Eden squeezes my hand. She didn't even shed a tear when her grandmother was led away for combustion. I'm so glad we are leaving this planet. "Can I get something out of the bag?"

"Not now, Eden." I'm pulling my entire belongings along behind me in a wheeled flight case. One wheel squeaks loudly on each revolution. It was annoying at first. Now, it's the least of my concerns and it's drowned out by the noise of all the other anxious voices which babble around us. Eden pulls hers along behind us too. "There's food onboard. Good, clean food. That much, we've been promised. We just need to get through the checks."

I pick up the pace. The remnants of the World Government say there are enough spaces for all the uncontaminated, but I don't believe a word, and our seats are in the last rocket. I want to make sure we get on that damn spaceship.

We barge past the other Earth Seed hopefuls. The first checkpoint is directly ahead. There, we'll be examined medically for any signs of the green plaque. At the second check point, our IQ will be tested. Academic limits have been placed on those wishing to seed the red planet. We are to be re-homed up there in living quarters with our equivalents. I've forewarned Eden of this, told her to dumb things down, but I can tell she's fearful of lying.

"Mum, please, I'm starving," she says. The whine in her voice grates.

"Not now, Edes."

She's petrified of the whole process ahead of us. How do I know this? Well, wouldn't you be? Plus, when she's nervous, she gets hungry.

At the physical interrogation, I struggle to remember when I last took painkillers. The lady assessing me flicks a look over to a more senior member of the investigation squad. I panic—I can't not get on this ship. We can't. To stay would be to perish, for certain. I make something up, pluck a date from thin air, which seems to placate her, and she taps the information into her electronic device. How will they check anyway? Could they check? My heart revs, a wave of sickness shoots up my gullet. To be found lying is instant dismissal from the project. She waves us through to the next investigation panel.

We smash through the physical and head towards the second checkpoint, but the crowd thickens as we approach it. I lose Eden for ten minutes. Feels like hours. I break into a sweat as I push through the throngs of other desperate civilians, in search of my six-year-old. Where is Eden? She's always by my side, we even share a bed. For her not to be with me feels like a limb is missing. I search hard. I ask every person who will make eye contact with me where she is until I find her slouched down against a wall, her eyes wet with tears.

"Thank God, Eden. I thought I'd lost you," I say. I grab and hug my child and check her over in the way a loving mother does, and then wipe her curls from her eyes. With her cheek pressed against my bosom, my heart rate drops a little. She's all I have left in this world, and the next. She smells so sweet, her hair is so soft. But she pulls away, looks to her feet.

"What's wrong?" I ask.

"Nothing, Mummy. I thought … I thought I'd lost you. I was so hungry and scared—"

"Hold my hand," I say. "We just need to clear the second gate and then we're through to interplanetary passport control." Her awkward body language, the odd, defensive twist of her torso sings to me like an out of tune piano. Every part of her is there, arms, legs, black and white keys, but all is not how it should be.

"I don't feel well, Mummy," she says as she grapples with her waist.

"Really? Do you think you can hold it together until we get on board?" There is desperation in my voice which I'm sure she senses. I have never felt so panicked. Eden nods, squeezes my hand in response, follows me as I stride along. I want to ask her more questions, check my baby is okay, but the large signs mounted every hundred metres along the channel we are herded down informs me we don't have time for small talk. I will not miss this rocket. We cannot miss this opportunity.

I reach for and rub my passport. It is there, as it is always, underneath the skin of my upper arm. It contains a lifetime's worth of history and evidence and documentation which will allow us to embark on our new lives, up there, on that small red dot. It's nearly invisible to us—not because it's daytime, but because clouds of green-grey pollution have made a hazy, almost impenetrable mess of Earth's sky. Am I making the right decision? I remind myself of the list I drafted which I left behind in the house I no longer own. I know the contents of my list by heart. It consists of two columns, 'reasons to stay' and 'reasons to go.' The 'reasons to stay' column contains only one bullet point: 'Mother may recover', but by now, Mother will be nothing more than hot white ash and dust.

BANG. BANG.

We freeze, Eden and I. I crane my head back to locate the source of the sound and spot an armed guard, a rifle still in his hand. I grab my daughter's head and force her with me down and onto the floor behind a row of fixed seating. We huddle in silence, entwined with each other and the handles of our luggage cases.

"It's the army," I whisper in her ear. I stroke her hair out from her eyes once more. She shakes. They don't normally use guns to assassinate the contaminated—too messy.

"Security breach attempt," the guard shouts to the silenced hall. "We've shot the runner. Man down. Civilians, as you were."

We slowly stand, Eden all a quiver. She takes her hand away from where it had been pressed into her stomach and points out the dead man a hundred feet away. He lies in a marbling pool of green and red which ekes out across the floor like an inflating balloon, an expanding universe, a spreading plague. Like most disgusting things, our eyes are immediately drawn to it and repulsed by it—nature's warning.

"How did he make it through the first check?" she asks.

"No idea," I reply. "Guess there's always the risk someone might try and break through. Someone contaminated but desperate enough to see Mars before they die."

"But they would bring the flies with them," Eden says. Her words tumble out fast yet reedy. "It could infect our new home." Panic thrums in my daughter's widening eyes. The whites of her eyes are haunting.

"It's not contagious though, darling. Not if people stay well, eat well, treat Mars with respect. Hopefully the flies and the Piranha bacteria will become a distant memory; a nightmare we can all forget about. With time."

"Like Earth. Like how we can forget about Earth?"

"Yes. Like Earth."

We make it through the final gates, through the air lock, and onto Rocket 23. I smile with just my mouth at Eden. She tilts her head, reads me, so I look away. I swear, my young daughter is so perceptive she can almost read my mind when she looks into my eyes. "We've made it," I say. I try to sound as positive as I can, but I know she detects trepidation in my words. I'm not even sure I believe myself anymore.

An official directs one hundred or so of us through to a seated area onboard the rocket where we belt up for take-off. The air is conditioned, the decor clinical and economical. Eden nabs a window seat—a small oval eye, one of perhaps two hundred in total from which we can both see out from, and I shove our bags in the overhead compartment.

"Wave goodbye to Earth," I say as we rise up, into, and through the clouds, as we break the ionosphere and pierce into space, as we leave the pull of our wasted planet's gravity behind. Goodbye home, goodbye roots, goodbye first love. Goodbye Mother. Goodbye Mother Earth.

"Farewell, Earth," Eden says, with a wave of her tiny fingers. I reach over to see it off too. Good riddance.

The concrete launch pad becomes a curve of grey. The curve of grey becomes an arc of sludge-green. The sludge-green becomes a distant, ruined dot, encapsulated by a fuzzy neon green halo. The once-blue oceans found in photographs of Earth taken from space are no longer present. It is truly now just a green planet.

We sit quietly.

A light flashes above our heads. It informs us we're free to unbuckle, to move around the civilian floor of the rocket.

"Shall we find the food hall?" I say. I am certain it will be good food, clean food. One of many positives in the journey which lies ahead of us.

"I'm not hungry," Eden replies. She fumbles with the strap of her seat belt.

"You were starving earlier," I say. Her eyes avoid mine. A sprinkle of crumbs decorates the corners of her mouth. "What have you been eating?" I whisper, yet my words of air blow through my lips like rocket-plume.

"Sorry, Mummy." Tears collect in the corners of her eyes again. Have I been mistaken in thinking all the crying would be over now?

"Honey. Eden, sweetheart. What did you do?" I grab her chin and brush away some debris from her cheeks. Her breathing quickens. "Tell me," I insist. I reach for her bag in the cabinet overhead and begin to search. My heart thuds in my throat. Eden remains defiantly silent.

I unzip her back to search for clues. On the top, her clothing is crammed into a messy ball made from a multitude of colours, like the green and red guts which splayed from Father when we found him in the yard a month back. I was left with no choice but to call Pest Control to have him exterminated and chucked on the pyre. I had folded Eden's trousers and tops so neatly in preparation yesterday. It is in this moment, it clicks. Young, careless hands have been in this bag, rummaging. Underneath the clothing, I find food packaging.

"Earlier, when I thought I'd lost you, I opened a packet of biscuits that Grandma gave me last year. This morning, when you told me to check my room before we left, I found them under my bed and packed them in memory of her. I was so scared—so scared and so hungry."

A pulse of vomit rises into my throat. I don't recall ever allowing Mother to ply my child with junk. How dare she go behind my back and give my child plastic-riddled, toxic shit. All these years I've bent over backwards to provide a better life for my daughter. A healthier, safer life. I curse Mother aloud as more tears spill down Eden's cheeks. Through the window behind her, the red ball in the distance grows larger. The timer on the screen at the front of our compartment tells us our new home is under an hour away. I pull my precious daughter, my future, in tight to my chest.

"It's okay. It's okay, love. I'm sorry for being angry with you. How many did you eat?"

"The whole packet," she whispers. Her skin blanches. Is she about to throw up?

It's at this point, I see the neon fly.

It emerges from my daughter's ear. Hovers over it.

And it's red. Not green. Red.

And then, there's another.

And another.

It Started with Placental Encapsulation

Narrow door frames and bulky wheels had pushed her over the edge, to tears again. On her return to Unit 12—baby asleep in one seat of the twin stroller and Mother, glinting blue under the strip lights, slumped in the adjacent—she'd scraped the door jamb while jimmying the pushchair back into her living quarters. Once inside, she pitched the pushchair next to the kitchen table and thought about how she'd inform her husband of the damage she'd done to the steel.

With a bone-aching weariness, she sat down and picked at her sore cuticles. Caring for a new baby who did nothing but gripe and groan was exhausting, and her own mother was no help at all. She's still felt none of the joys of motherhood the others in Unit 12 informed her she would. The bags under her eyes carried bags. *Thank the Gods for the Cafe*, she thought, and rummaged for the items in her pocket.

A year ago, before pregnancy, Mother had warned: "You'll struggle with motherhood, daughter dearest. Most do." But she'd ignored this warning and had applied for gamete release and a pregnancy licence regardless. The baby had been a deal breaker of sorts, between her and her husband.

Relentless night feeds, volcanic nappy eruptions, dawn choruses of ceaseless screaming ensued. *It's so much harder than I thought*, she wailed through her darkest moments and her husband was little use, working late, working early, avoiding responsibility whenever he could. But despite the burden of it all, sat at her table in the privacy of her quarters, through eyes burning with tears and tiredness, she watched on with an innate, irrefutable love as, next to Mother, her little one dozed.

"What would you do, Mother, if you felt old and rotten as I do, a hollowed cocoon?" she asked. She didn't expect a response, but it was important to have such discussions. Speakers at the Cafe emphasized the need for conversation with one's elders, it helped with healing; it made good sense to her.

The silence that followed swallowed her words. She sighed, shook her head at Mother.

"Boil and pour," she commanded. The kettlebot clicked on. She reached into her jumpsuit pocket for the gift another new mum at the Cafe had slid her earlier.

It wasn't the first time she'd been passed something there; visitors went there, after all, in search of healing and empathy. With the intention of providing a discreet place for people to speak safely, the Cafe had remained open downtown despite governmental pushback. Herbal sleeping aids, vitamin-D gels, free UV gym passes to encourage physical well-being were all distributed within. But this, this gift from another mother who'd also been pushing a dual stroller—newborn in one section, great aunt perched in the other—this gift had stirred hope within her. This other mother had looked so fresh.

She'd passed quiet comment while in the queue for cake: *You look so well, glowing, despite your babe only weeks old.* Her own face appeared bloated, owlish from sleep deprivation, too many carbs.

The other mother had blushed, a glimmer of compassion had sparkled in her eyes. *I've something you should try,* she'd whispered, and had beckoned her over to a corner table, a spot out of the Securidrone's scope to explain her secret. After scouring the room for wardens, the radiant new mum slipped her a small packet under a napkin.

"My husband cut off a chunk. Hid it in his skinsuit. Before they took it for combustion," the woman had whispered and smiled. "I feel you need these more than I do. Don't tell a soul!"

The packet contained ten transparent capsules, each filled with a rust-coloured powder. Dried placenta. She tipped them from the bag, played with them on her tabletop, spun each around, and lined them up in a row.

Disgusting, what are you doing, woman? Sort your head out. She knew what her husband would say. But he no longer spoke the same language as her and she knew he'd long since stopped trying to understand her.

She stared at the capsules. They smelt bad. They were made from someone else. Flesh from a stranger. *Foul.* Yet the mother who'd given them to her had looked so radiant ... her husband would never need to know, and she had several hours before his shift at sub-station Mavian-361 was due to finish.

"I'm taking one," she said to her sleeping baby and Mother in the pushchair, "sod the consequences." Mother said nothing. Never did. She leant forward, tucked her baby's blanket in then straightened up the cut-glass decanter in which Mother sat.

The Grief Cafe insisted on displayed ashes, it was a condition of entry. On Mars, there were no funerals, no wakes, no corpse viewings, just immediate cremation. It was a stoic and tight planet under fastidious governmental rule—resources were sparse, the climate, delicate—but its people still grieved. Many residents who'd lost a loved one lugged ash in transparent vessels, tug-along trailers, transparent rucksacks, pushchairs. It was the fashion, no matter how much the government disapproved. Some people yanked carts along holding several containers. It'd become part of the healing process, initiated by an anonymous movement in the face of strict Martian law. To wear one's heart on one's sleeve. To welcome, even initiate discussion around grief, death, the concept of the Gods, wherever one went.

The government had outlawed the historical Earth-origin tradition of ash scattering—the sandstorms were problematic enough without more particulate matter becoming flung up into Mars' delicate atmosphere.

Going up to the surface to scatter ashes, to scatter *anything* into the winds, was something she'd never brave anyway. The surface was where Mother had died.

The knock on the door had come around midnight. She'd been heavily pregnant. Her partner had opened the door to the soldier sent to report her mother's death. The soldier had presented them with the ashes.

Her mother, an engineer, had been fixing the magnetiser for West Division when she'd disturbed a Tenticulus nest. The multipart creature had slaughtered the entire team. Her mother had always said it would be lung disease from a lifetime of inhaling poor air that'd finish her—this was how most surface workers went—but, in the end, it'd been a Tenticulus swarming.

She'd seen documentary footage of the inky beasts that'd taken Mother's life on the holoprojected newscreen at the mall. The Tenticuli moved together like a giant airborne millipede. Composed of many creeping limbs of blue nebulous gas, they poured through orifices, suffocating any life they encountered. The midnight soldier had insisted the solar-dust-borne infestation had since been eradicated, the government had taken back control, but she and her husband were paid to keep quiet. With a baby on the way, they took the money and promised each other they'd never venture to the surface.

She sipped on her tea and rolled the capsules in her palm. *This may be lifeblood, source of pure nutrition, but this is lifeblood of another gene line. It's not mine to take,* she thought. *What would Mother do?* A tear rolled down her cheek.

"Grief is the price we pay for love," a Cafe speaker had said earlier, but she felt she may also be paying with the loss of her husband's love. He despised her grief, sent her to the resting quarters whenever emotion beckoned her.

"Grief is a sign of weakness," he'd say.

It's wrong to take someone else's lifeblood into my own? she thought. *But I'm so tired. Feel so old.*

"Placenta is life source for baby; full of nourishment, full of love," the kind lady at the Cafe had said after passing across the capsules. "Back on Earth, many women consumed afterbirth to replenish energy and spirit."

She took Mother out of the pushchair and hugged the decanter to her chest. "What should I do Mother? Motherhood is overwhelming and I am such a disaster. Help me. Mother. My Mother, my gene line."

She pulled apart the first capsule, tipped its rusty contents into the bin, and lifted the lid from the decanter. The capsules filled with ash and re-assembled into bullet shapes easily. *Spirit bullets,* she thought. She closed her eyes and swallowed the capsules down.

Rest when baby rests, she thought. Exhausted and spent of tears, she lay her head on the table and fell asleep in the chair.

My cheek, I felt it on my cheek! She jumped up from her sleep, not because of her baby wailing, demanding milk, but because a soft hand had brushed against her skin. She could still hear the word Mother had said in her dream: "Liberation."

Her heart battered hard and fast against her skin. But she did not feel scared. She felt refreshed, as if she'd had a full night's sleep, and for the first time, she truly enjoyed spooning rehydrated banana into her little one's hungry chops. She smiled at her baby. Baby smiled back.

An hour later her husband returned from work. He made no offer of thanks for the fine meal she'd prepared. With a mouth full of casserole, he leant and tapped the damaged door frame. "This. This is because of that ridiculous, oversized pushchair. If Unit Patrol spot this, they'll fine us." He pointed at her. "Why can't you just be done with this grief, move on with your life?"

She served up dessert in silence.

After her husband and baby had fallen asleep, she took a framed photograph from the shelf—happier times—wiped the thin layer of dust from it and cried. Cogs of grief cranked up in her stomach, span faster, chipped at the happiness she'd felt since consuming the capsules. She lay the framed photograph down flat and tipped Mother up and out until a grey pile, a handful's worth, sat atop the picture. With a teaspoon, she scooped the powder into her mouth, spoonful after spoonful, and washed each back with glugs of warm tea and tears. She screwed her eyes tight with disgust at her own actions, but continued until the family photo was visible again.

It was then she felt the hug.

"Her arms," she exclaimed, crossing her own arms, rubbing her own palms up and down the outside of her own arms in comfort, thinking nothing of moaning babes or selfish husbands. She floated in an ecstatic place of bliss. "I felt Mother's arms around me."

Days passed.

He was working late again. She wanted to try and make things work between them. She decided she'd surprise him at work with a picnic.

After she'd prepped the sandwiches, she considered pouring herself another dose of ashes. But she noticed Mother looked a little depleted. She'd been tucking into Mother several times a day. *Should I top it up? Scrapings from the oven floor, dust from the shelves? Or should I transfer Mother to an opaque container? Do I want my grief on display, or is my husband right? Grief is best left behind?* She worried.

Staring at the vessel made her miss Mother more. It was as if the ashes called out to her, "Take me into you, or scatter me free."

She couldn't help it. *Tap tap.* Another portion fell into her hand. She licked it up from her palm. Mother's ashes quicksilvered through her veins. Euphoria similar to the initial burst of oxytocin she'd felt on delivering her baby, on seeing it open its eyes for the first time, spread through her core, and replaced any guilt in a trice.

Mother's arms enveloped her. Mother's hand stroked her face. Mother's voice whispered gabbled sentences she couldn't understand. But she could hear Mother's song, the same song Mother used to sing to her as a child: a melody of honeycomb and blossom, a week full of Saturdays. As the rapture eased, she strapped her babe and Mother's remains into the stroller, swung open the front door, jimmied the double stroller out, and set off through the underground channels towards her husband's place of work. She'd a spring in her step, not the usual low-gravity Martian bounce, but the bounce that came with the huge slug of ashes she'd devoured.

She stomped through neon-lit passages, rattled on and off trains, until— there it stood in front of her—the Mavern-361 substation. She hadn't visited him at work since having the baby.

A Securibot directed her to his office and as she approached it, the feeling of ecstasy the ashes gave, the rippling warmth charging through her limbs halted in an instant. Through the glass walls of his cubicle, she saw her husband with his lips and body pressed up against another woman.

No, she cried, *not again.* He'd cheated only once, before the pregnancy. And she'd forgiven him, believed him when he'd said it'd never happen again. Yet there he was, embraced in the arms of another.

She turned on her heels and fled. She pushed her baby and what remained of Mother back towards Unit 12. *How could he.* Her eyes hurt, overwhelmed by the harsh glare of the sunlight-simulator lighting and hot tears of shame. Her chest tightened, she found it hard to breathe. *This is what* '*surface lung*' *must feel like, the curse of particulate asthma,* she thought; one hand steered the pushchair along, the other clasped her chest.

On re-entering Unit 12, she ripped open the medical chest on the apothecary wall and snatched from it the regulatory nebuliser. She loaded up the medication cartridge, pushed the mouthpiece to her lips, and pulled the elastic strap tight around the back of her head. Releasing the vasodilators and inhaling the cloud of gas the nebuliser dispensed did nothing for her breathing. This wasn't asthma. This was a broken heart. She needed Mother. With the nebuliser still strapped to her face, she ran home.

She rammed open her front door and placed baby in its playpen. Riddled with a lowness she'd never touched upon before, she poured the remnants of Mother into the nebuliser in place of the medication cartridge. The release button depressed, navy ash vapour appeared in the nebuliser tube. *This is what I need,* she thought, *I need Mother. Now more than ever,* and then she took the gas into her lungs.

She fell back on the sofa. Warmth flooded her. Her body, a vessel of pure love, her vision as luminescent as the sun, despite her eyes being closed. Swirls of colour. Reds, yellows, neons. She flew over vales and hills, the like of which she'd never seen before. True bliss. And her nose filled with the scent of musk. A million flowers. Mother's perfume.

Mother's voice whispered in broken sentences, echoed fragments of indecipherable love, but she could make no sense of any of it, for she was floating too high, and Mother was speaking too fast.

I feel her arms around me, she thought, *but they're too … tight.* She opened her eyes. "So many arms are around me, and none of them are Mother's!"

A translucent skin of Mother's body and her own body appeared, as one, as if a ghostling shell of Mother had wrapped itself around her slight frame. Mother's limbs moved in line with her own movements. As she screamed, her own voice and Mother's came out together, in unison. She yanked the nebuliser from her neck, threw it to the floor, pulled her distorted body up until she sat perched on the edge of the bed, a blue-tinted spectre of Mother outlining her. She rose onto unsteady feet. An electric storm of energy charged throughout her body and scratched at her skin, a sensation more powerful than love and hate combined.

"We've become one," she screeched. She opened and closed her fists and saw not just her own young hands, but Mother's too, in sync, tracing her very own form.

Words came again, this time as a million blades scraping porcelain; not her own voice, or Mother's: "You destroyed us." And then came the scream Mother had made before blue Tenticuli wisps had forced their way into her mouth and nose and ears. "You burnt human corpse. Destroyed our host, our eggs."

She screamed as her Mother convulsed, and the ghost of Tenticulus screamed. She glanced down at herself and the superimposed shroud of Mother. Their joint limbs bubbled up in white blisters from which, countless cobalt, infantile Tenticulus ghostlets burst free.

Her body slumped.

The Wardens discovered the body when someone complained they heard a baby crying. On his return from work, the husband was greeted by a polybag of ashes and a note: *Collect child from crèche.*

He tipped his wife's ashes into the empty decanter and slid it under his bed. Didn't want to look at it—didn't believe in discussing grief. And he found himself repulsed by the creeping blue glow which ensconced the glass container.

He kept hold of the ashes for his child's sake, although he hoped his child wouldn't be one for flaunting one's emotions.

The Dangers of Ill-Prepared Shellfish

Fresh from her scalloped shell she steps, sand between her toes. Her first day. So beautiful. Her Titian hair, all Botticellian waves, cascades down, passes her shoulders, dusts her breasts in thick fronds, curls around her waist. Her flesh is peach-skin soft.

"You're the image of perfection," the four winds whisper into her delicate ears as she tests out her sleek limbs and glides across the shore. She tilts her head, smiles, uncertain as to what these words mean.

"Perfection?" she asks and inspects the palms and backs of her own hands like an inquisitive child.

"Be careful not to hurt yourself on the glass-sharp mantle edge of the shell," the four winds whisper.

She smiles, thanks them; her smile is the gift of gratitude. Her own skin feels divine under her own fingertips. She closes her eyes. Another smile spreads like sunrise across her porcelain cheeks. She turns back, looks at the sea.

The ocean, it must've been a dream, she thinks. It had been her home up until this moment but she has no memory of what came before, and no idea of what is to come.

Stretching out each graceful limb, she flexes her spine. With her body liberated from the clam, her soft tip-toe gains confidence, develops into a stride, a canter, a skip. Glossy hair whips behind her as she moves with elegance and poise.

In and out of the shallow waters she darts, embracing the cool babble and break of waves over her feet.

From further inland, Man, who calls himself Mars, sees this creature of beauty pacing across the shore; this divine thing who does not yet know she is Woman.

He tells her she is perfection, just like the four winds who had welcomed her into existence had done, and so she trusts him as she had trusted the elements. He steals her from the shore—she, so new, so fresh, so unaware that she has a choice not to go. He makes her his own and she becomes his pride and joy. For a while.

Later that week, he dives for and presents her with fresh sea pearls. "For you. Your beauty outshines even the most polished jewels of the sea," he says. He decorates her in nature's gifts, helps her style her hair the way he likes it, purchases and chooses outfits for her to wear.

She thinks she enjoys the attention. She knows no different, for she was raised in a shell by the cold, knife-grey blanket of the sea, her only guidance a few words whispered in the wind. She knows—because he tells her—that her life with him, in the house, the kitchen, the small fenced-in garden which is not a trap for sun, and the bedroom, is better than anything else she could ever hope for. "I'll provide for you with everything you will ever need," he tells her. And he does. For a while.

He feeds her up on the finest fresh fish and caviar. He kisses and caresses the parts of her body she cannot reach alone. He makes her laugh. Sometimes. At first.

For the first few years, he brings her flowers on her birthday, which he tells her is the day he found her on the shore. He says it is important to mark the event. Although she cannot recall it, she is certain she existed before this moment, has vague memories of the strange, cramped comfort of a scallop womb. But these memories are eaten away at around their edges by the passing of time and his persuasion.

He brings generous cloying bunches of lilac sea aster, golden samphire, to mark her birthday each year, tells her their beauty does not compare one touch to hers, tells her she can't have existed before he discovered her, and each day, she believes a little more in him and a little less in herself.

Each time he brings her flowers, she takes them, thanks him with a bow of her head, a kiss, and places them in a vase, the same vase. Always the same vase. This is the vase he tells her she must use. She does not like the vase, but it is the only vase. *What choice do I have?* she thinks.

As the days that follow pass, she watches them wilt, the flowers, long dead already before she had even placed them in the vase in her kitchen. Over morning coffee, she quietly requests: she would like to see where he picked them from, visit—perhaps—the place where the flowers grow wild. She asks him this just the once—his answer ensures she will never ask the question again, puts to bed her desire to venture away from her home, his house, helps her realise she is lucky he brings her anything at all.

This is, at least, she thinks, *my kitchen, my place of safety, I am blessed to have this humble space,* and she spends time each day watching the flowers decay in a vase she knows like the back of her hand but cares not for.

Other than the journey back from the beach many years ago when he brought her home, she has never been anywhere else. *It is still my kitchen,* she thinks, until he takes that from her, too, as he forces her into a position she never agreed to, pushes himself upon her until no part of the kitchen feels safe to her again.

And as the years pass, her fears and pains ebb and flow. She grows tired of the kitchen. Restless. Each corner is tarnished now with shady memories, shadows, and sometimes he makes her bleed. He continues to bring her flowers on her birthday which is not her true birthday, although she has forgotten who or what she even is. He brings her flowers, too, each time he hurts her. He brings her flowers often. Each time she thanks him, places them in the same vase, watches them wilt, the flowers already long dead.

"You are not what you were, my Venus. Your skin has become dry, and your hair, grey." Mars flares his nostrils, his skin flushes red. He is angered by the smallest of things.

"I'm sorry," she says and pulls up the bed sheet to cover her ageing body.

She feels the back of his hand against her cheek, the heel of his foot kick into her long barren womb. Tears etch rivulets down her cheeks at right angles to the deep lines the passing of time has marked her with. He leaves the bedroom, slams the door on his way out. She rises from the prison cell which is her bed and pulls her smock on, each movement pin-balling pain through her bones. Later in the morning, the stairs play a part in the breaking of her leg, along with Mars' strong arms and overbearing size.

She heals slowly, but never is what she was before, and her recovery is marked by more outbursts, more setbacks, as he tells her with his fists how she is becoming less and less perfect with each day that passes.

Venus needs a stick now, just to move around the house, which has not been a home for a long time. He gives one to her, eventually, in exchange for a further fistful of happiness.

He hides it from her, the stick she needs to walk with, when the food she serves him is substandard. For days she is trapped in a chair in the corner of the kitchen, soiling herself, drowning in a sea of salty tears. *The tears taste better than any kiss he has placed on my lips,* she thinks.

Later, he tosses the stick back, only so she can hobble—her spine is curved forwards, her leg is skewed in an unnatural alignment—into the small garden to bring in the washing from the line.

There in the garden, Venus spots a robin, the same robin she often shares a few crumbs with. The bird tilts its head at Venus, takes the crumbs, then opens its wonderful wings. Venus smiles through tears at her avian chum, mouths the word: "Perfection."

One day the bird does not come anymore, has flown away for a final time. She wonders, as she pegs shirts and socks to the line, if the bird is now happy. Perhaps her robin has found a better garden. She sees a thumb print of swarming birds, a murmuration of starlings, up above in the open blue sky and wonders, yearns to know, how it feels to fly free.

The night before, Mars had brought war to the dining table. The stew, he claimed, had been overcooked, the husk she had baked, too plain. He had put the bread knife through the palm of her hand. She had held her hand to her chest, and the blood had spread, stained the white of her apron red, a robin's breast. She felt no pain, not now, after all this time. As she looked down at the stain which blotted outwards, stretched free from its centre on her clothes, she fell deaf to his shouted words. She merely thought about her robin. Her robin, free to fly whenever it wants.

After pegging out the laundry, she sits back in the kitchen, looks at her bandaged hand, her deformed femur, and with her good hand, she brushes her brittle white hair from her face.

Her husband is sat in another room. *He will not even notice,* she thinks, *until he requires something to be done.* She takes him through a cup of tea, a slice of cake, as cake is what his leather belt had insisted she bake, and then, she quietly slips on her shoes. With the shawl draped over her hunched shoulders, she flaps her wings. Through a hole in the garden fence, she pecks and leaves.

After all these years, she remembers the way. She has played the journey over in her mind many times. Her feet take her back to the beach. The beach is empty, cold. Rain falls gently. She feels it on her skin, tastes it with her tongue, watches the veil of falling water as, in the distance, it returns to the sea. She hopes she will too.

She sees the giant clam shell. After all these years, it is still there. Its open maw beckons her; the four winds encourage each pain-riddled, difficult step.

She sheds her clothes, strips down to nothing, until she is as naked as the day she was born, and then she tosses her stick into the sea. She approaches the clam shell, steadies herself on it with her arthritic hands. Stepping back inside of the place from which she came, she thinks of the wilted flowers rotting in the vase. *The vase is his, always has been,* she thinks, *but this shell is mine, and I, tired bloom, am ready to wilt.*

She curls her old body forward and makes herself as small as she can. Near invisible. Unsurprisingly, she does not find this hard. Venus becomes a beautiful grey pearl, and around her, the clam lips start to close. *It is as if the shell is smiling, happy to have me back,* she thinks.

Inside, for Venus, it grows darker. She feels squashed, but finally, at long last, safe. "Perfection," she whispers and, outside, the four winds echo her final word. The lips do not close completely. Both halves of the crimped mantle pause before Venus becomes too cramped inside. A wavy slice of space is left. Enough for a little light to enter, for long strands of her white hair to poke free and waiver in the gentle sea breeze. She peeks out as and when she pleases. Until the water comes.

The tide pushes forwards, and in time, the shell is submerged and is carried back out, deeper, into the ocean. Water rushes in through the gap. It fills. Brine fills the shell, fills Venus's lungs, eventually bringing her aged body a certain permanent peace. But the spited spirit of Venus, a woman scorned, lives on, haunts the giant clam which now sits at rest, half buried, half exposed, on the sandy blanket of the ocean floor.

A pearl diver clad in neoprene pierces into the water, swims down to the ocean floor in search of marine treasure, eager to pluck nature's gems like fruit. Top predator, he steals from the natural world. The pay is good. He will spend the fistful of notes he will receive for whatever he pillages today at the strip bar downtown, like he does every Friday night. Whisky and breasts. This is what he lives for.

He spots a clam, can't help but swim closer. The sea scallop—the strength of its external shell now appears softly feminine—is coated with pink anemones, some sort of coral. *It looks like a pair of beautiful, plump lips, the lips of a sweet, young woman,* thinks the diver, and he finds himself with urges. He pulls down his swimming trunks, grabs the mighty shellfish tightly either side with gloved hands, and, feeling he is hidden, out of sight or judgment, protected from the eyes of anyone down there on the floor of the vast ocean, he places his hard cock in between the undulating bivalve flaps.

But Venus, the very raw ghost of Venus, is vengeful. And Venus is hungry.

And finally, she snaps.

Juliet, Juliet

First published by Ghost Orchid Press in 2022

I live in a well.

The advert had described our one-bedroom flat as *designer compartment living*, the *perfect starter home for a professional couple*. But without you here, it feels like a smoke-filled well, a place where light is swallowed.

The ket's ready.

I've cooked it up dry on a plate over the pan we used to cook our chilli in. You'd chop the vegetables and with the pestle and mortar we bought somewhere deep in the souks of Tangier, I'd grind the coriander seeds, the cumin, enough to give anyone else a stomach ulcer. The stone set had been ridiculously heavy, but you said you wouldn't leave without it, so I carried it in my rucksack for you for the last part of our travels. Now, there is no more you here, no us, there is no more chilli. Microwave dinners for months. I'm eating trash.

Not that I've a hunger since you left. Not for food anyway.

I've always used something. As a teen, I drank heavily to numb desire, to keep me in a safety net of denial. Then, when I knew for sure I couldn't ever go with a man, I used to numb the rejection when I came out. My family said it was *just a phase*, something I'd grow out of. You said the same about my drug use—until you couldn't handle it anymore.

Corrosive white crystals have replaced you, replaced the hole you ripped in my heart when you left. A void has spread through one side of me to the other and I know no amount of chemical fix, no dubious powders, no street elixir will ever patch it up. Still, I carry on using.

Can't even remember what our final argument was about—me, not taking responsibility for my actions, not behaving like an adult, needing professional addiction therapy? Whatever it was, it hammered the endmost nail in the corpse-coffin of our relationship.

I crush the anhydrous rocks into glassy powder with the melted edge of a store card, a store I can no longer afford now I'm paying all the rent. I'd pay anything to have you back—all the money, all the riches, my soul. What I wouldn't give for another kiss and one more night with you.

Three neat snow-slugs lie on the black plate. When these drugs have worn off, I'll look up from the bottom of the well, at the circle of grey sky forever looming large over me. I'll watch the stars come and go and none of them will be as bright as you. I'll watch the Rorschach test of clouds pass, devastated I'll never feel the softness of your skin or hair again. I'll sit in the throat of the well and watch and wait and wait, knowing the only bait that'll lure me out, make me step into that bucket to be hauled up to the surface, is the promise of seeing you again.

I bend forwards, greet the first line as if it were an old friend, then with a tatty note I'll need for cigarettes later curled up between my thumb and finger, I snort.

Before the inch-worm-lines kick in, and I pass out, dissociate for a couple of hours, I set my phone alarm for five p.m. I've work to do this afternoon.

The ket kicks in. Fragments of beautiful, incandescent truth as convincing and as powerful as the love I feel for you flit in and out of my peripheral vision. These hints at the meaning of life then let go, disperse, become fantasy, geometric pattern, sound and feeling, sensations that have never been made or heard by anyone before. In this lost moment, nothing makes sense and time is a forgotten concept. And this is how I need my life to be right now, through this hideous period of grief.

I'm furious with you because you were the one who chose to end it. You closed our front door behind you with everything you own in your flight case, and said, *'it's over,'* null and void.

A fog stretches around my paralysed body. Under the influence of the strangest drug I've ever taken, the spirit of me edges closer to the circumference of the stone gullet of the well that now exists in my front room. Do I jump in? All the reasons why I should flood my neurones, but the chemicals start to wear off and all I can see now are stacks of duplicate novels we were going to read together and the fractured television screen you kicked in rage when I said you'd never be happy without me.

I'm back on the sofa and my phone alarm is nagging. Time for work.

Sideways sleet penetrates everything but my rain-coat-covered torso on my walk into work. When I arrive and step inside, the rain continues to pelt down against the window. Wet socks, sodden boots, black-with-water jeans.

I ask Margaret on reception if she minds if I take my clothes off, hang them on the radiator whilst I work. She finds me clean scrubs to borrow. I joke with her—even though I feel devoid of humour—and ask her when I can expect my pay rise. Part-time cleaner to surgical vet is quite the promotion.

I greet all the caged animals being kept in overnight, dozy from surgery—there are a few perks to my job—and set to work vacuuming the floor of the veterinary surgery.

I hoover, I dust, I mop. Margaret's shift is finished. She wants to get home to her myriad cats, her inane evening quiz shows. "I still have the bathroom to finish," I say, so she chucks me the spare keys, tells me to drop them off tomorrow morning.

I do what I need to do, take a little longer than I should, take some things I shouldn't, then set the alarm, lock up at eight, and make the lonely walk home.

I rack up my chemical dinner on the plate you used to serve nut loaf on, and waste more time in another place, a place where the smell and softness of your hair is near-tangible. I wish you were here. I pass out for the night on the sofa.

The next day, mid-morning, I slip on my trainers and wait for the rain to stop. In an opportune moment, I head towards the surgery. I need to return the keys I'm not supposed to have. I wish it were still raining. It might help disguise my tear-streaked face.

At the traffic lights, I consider whether to chance it across the red light, then I see you, your hip-length blonde braid. You call it your 'Disney ladder' and it's bouncing behind you. I see your vine tattoo creeping up from the outside of your wrist that matches mine.

It is you. I freeze.

In your hand is the cuff of a familiar gold-studded purple lead. A brindle whippet of sorts, Berry I think, is on the other end of it. The dog is following you, walking to heel. Berry is a regular at the surgery, I saw him there just yesterday.

I want to call out 'Juliet,' make you turn around, see your face, but your name falls silent on my lips. Saying it aloud will hurt too much. You're in Rio anyway, so I know it can't truly be you …

But the dog—I recognise the distinctive circle patch of raised purple-grey on its flank in the shape of a round fruit with two leaves and a stem. It is definitely a dog I know. Definitely Berry. Is it Berry?

"Berry, Berry!" I call the dog's name, quietly and with uncertainty at first, then louder when I'm confident it's him. The handsome mongrel turns and looks at me from across the road, barks and wags his tail in recognition. Then you turn around.

My heart, a caged bird, pulses in my throat.

"Juliet?" I manage, my voice reedy, weak, like the connection between my soul and my physical body when I'm under the influence. The last of my adrenaline quicksilvers through my veins.

"No," you say. Your voice is filled, most oddly, with susurration, but it *is* you—or at least, the very mirror of you. "Not yet."

I don't understand. All I know is that I'm a broken mirror. My life is nothing but bad luck and if the shards of my existence were to jab into my heart, I'm certain I'd bleed out black blood, emptiness, and chemicals.

You look at me. Your face is full of sadness. You're never sad. Even when we split, you were sunshine through the rain. Your eyes catch mine and the exchange feels like a million syncopated firecrackers exploding in my heart. For a nanosecond, I'm stunned and unable to think or move or breathe. Then you continue on your way.

"Please, stop," I manage to call out. A bus with an advert for panto at the Hippodrome Theatre whizzes past—Widow Twankey, Prince Charming, Cinderella—and ten or so miserable commuters come between us, and then you're gone.

I'm clearly distressed when I arrive at the surgery, and I drop the keys on Margaret's desk without a word.

'You alright, chick?' she pipes, her face bright with cheap cosmetics. Some people are eternally cheerful, like Margaret, like you. You were always smiling. Except just then, walking the dog, you weren't smiling then.

"I … I … just saw someone." I want to tell Margaret I've seen you, but I know you're not in the country and why would you be walking Berry? You don't work where I work. You don't really even like animals.

"Who was that then? Look like you need a cuppa."

I decide to keep my tumbling sanity to myself. If I tell Margaret who, what I've seen, she'll declare me positively unhinged. I can't afford to be signed off sick. Besides, work provides too many bonuses.

"Berry. I just saw Berry. He looks well. Mark works miracles, doesn't he?" I ask. How easy we spurt rhetoric, even when we are but a shell.

Margaret's jolly face drops. "Berry, love? Can't have been Berry. Poor thing passed away twenty minutes ago in surgery." She raises her finger and points to the annex, a room to the side of reception where private conversations happen, and bad news is given. From it, the sound of sobbing and tissues being pulled from a box. "Owners are in there."

I must've been mistaken—but it was you and I've never been more certain of anything.

I leave without a word, without offering my condolences, without replying when Margaret reminds me of the meeting Mark, the practice manager, has called for all staff tomorrow morning.

It is evening and I'm at work again, this time to clean. I'm plodding along as slowly as I can get away with. Partly because I'm in physical pain and partly because I have things I need to do that require time at the surgery alone. I've learnt how to be less efficient. My bladder is griping, filtering razor blades from my body fluids, and I can hardly bear the constant burning feeling, this constant urge to pee. They say ket does this to you, when you use for too long, when you're no longer abusing it, but instead, it's abusing you.

"Margaret," I say, "I'm sorry. Don't know what's up with me at the moment. The bathroom is taking me so much longer to do tonight." I fold over slightly, my spine, a dowager's hump, as I grasp and palpate my sides— where my kidneys are—hoping the pressure of fingertips will ease the congestion, the agony I'm feeling there today.

Margaret smiles at me and I prepare myself to lie to her again, say I'm going to need a little longer. Would she mind *ever so much* leaving me the keys again? I can drop them off tomorrow morning, when we're all in for the meeting?

But before I can start, she tells me I have to finish on time tonight.

"Rommy, love"—Rommy, short for Romea. No-one calls me Romea— "Mark's said you need to leave when I do. For health and safety reasons."

I sigh. I'm frustrated. It's never been a problem before. I've been staying late a couple of times a week for a while now.

"Oh," I reply and pause and think and panic slightly. "Best get back to it then. I'll scrub a little faster." I'm mumbling, but Margaret doesn't hear me. She's gone upstairs to carry on with her admin.

It's dark outside now and the animals are being noisier than normal. I put it down to the bad weather and the ones that have been operated on; their anaesthetic starts to wear off about this time. The ones who've been really poorly are waking up, realising they're missing their testes or a limb or the tip of a tail. I hear the surgery door open, even though the practice is closed for business, so I turn around.

The room falls silent.

I drop the disinfectant spray to the floor, clutch my hands to my chest.

Here you are, again.

It's you, but your eyes are dark, your face, sad.

"Juliet!" I say.

You've come back for me! You must've changed your mind. My heart is racing, and I feel ecstatic, but I panic—have I left the frying pan out at home, covered in a thick frosting of ketamine? You'll hit the ceiling if you see it. If you're coming back home. Please, please say you're coming back home. I'm fed up with living down this smoke-filled well alone.

"No," you say. You look at me. A tear rolls down your face, and the tear is red. It's blood red, and your face is so white. I feel my heart miss a beat, my own blood sinking to my toes.

I want to hug you, wipe your tears of blood away, but also, an existential dread like I've never felt before, even in the darkest of my trips, washes over me. The ground is tessellating. Each tile of easy-clean medical laminate flooring is tearing up and dropping down beneath us, into a pit of black.

"No," you say again. "I am not Juliet. I am the light that comes before the dark."

My heart thuds in my throat. You shed another red tear and I freeze. My spine is pressed up against the wall; the wall feels like an iceberg through my T-shirt. I've no choice but to stand rooted and watch you edge towards the bottom row of post-surgical cages. You crouch down, all the while, rivulets of red are trailing down you, behind you, weaving and flowing into each other, into a thick, wide, deep river of blood.

You reach and open the cage in which Mrs. Potter's Siamese cat, Charles, is resting after a tumour was removed from his bowels earlier today.

You pick Charles up in your arms, stroke him. His eyes slowly close and open, his head tilts back in pleasure. You tickle the underneath of his chin and I watch as you almost smile.

My legs are trembling. I press against the wall, it pushes back, thank God. The wall is the only thing keeping me from collapsing with love or fear or both.

"I am the beginning of the end. I am busy. I am needed in one hundred different places with each minute of your living time that ticks by."

I try to speak, but I can't and I'm crying too, but my tears are ordinary, not red like hers.

Am I trapped in a nightmare? Tripping? I haven't had a hit, snorted anything yet today—was trying to wait until after my shift. "Why are you saying you're not Juliet?" at last I wail. Insanity chips at the edge of my thoughts and I promise myself: No. More. Drugs. No more drugs—after I've finished the stash I've accumulated at home.

"At the beginning of your end, you see the one you love the most, the one you trust. When your time ends, you choose who leads you to the other side, you choose who takes you over the bridge. Who will I appear as? Who leads you on your final journey? The one you have loved the most."

My heart can't take this.

You, or this apparition of you, bring the cat up to your lips and kiss him on his head. Your rose-stained lips drain to a shade as blue as a bruise and then you leave in silence, stepping through the spatters of blood, with Charles calmly embraced in your arms.

Your words crash around in my head, ripping at my last threads of sanity.

The door closes and this form of you passes through the wintered-dandelion seed orb-glow of a dim streetlamp, steps past merlons of cityscape moonlight, melds with the darkness of the night. And then, you're gone. I stagger towards the reception desk, vomit with shock and neglected health, and pass out.

"Rommy! Darling girl, darling girl. What's wrong? You're really not well, are you?" Margaret is stroking my hair from my face and I realise I've been out cold for nearly half an hour. I can smell and taste sick. I pull my sack of bones into a seated position and notice for the first time how my ribs and hips jut out now like a broken umbrella.

"I'm sorry. I ... I ... I saw someone, something ..."

Margaret passes me a towel, tells me to wipe the sick from my clothes. I stare on as she clears up the mess I've made on the floor.

"Is it Charles? Did the sight of Charles do this to you? Lovely cat, wasn't he? Mrs. Potter's going to be devastated."

I look at the cage from which Juliet, or Not Juliet, had taken away the old cat, expecting it to be empty, but there he is: milky eyes, dead opals. His body is arranged in a peculiar curled position. His bandages are soaked through, red. The bottom half of his poor body is swimming in a crimson puddle, his paws are covered in the same sticky fluid. Charles's lifeless body is still soft, not yet in a state of full rigor mortis.

"It's a frightful shame when they wake and gnash open their stitches before a solid clot has formed. He bled out. Quite quickly by the looks. He was fine earlier. I checked on him before I went upstairs." Margaret's eyes are dry but soft. Mine are filling up with tears again.

"You need a break, chick. Get the doctor to sign you off for a bit. I can lend you some money for rent, drop you over some lasagne. You don't seem well, Rommy. And you don't look well ... When was the last time you ate a proper home-cooked meal?"

It's all too much. I know she means well, but I need to get out of here. I need to figure out what's going on. I want to be in your arms, Juliet, but I also want to throw myself into the pan, into a sea of white powder. I want to fall down the well.

From somewhere deep within my bones, I summon enough energy to tell Margaret, *"I'm fine, just need some sleep."* I grab my bag and start to launch out of the surgery when she calls after me, says she needs to offer me a word of warning.

"Look, listen love—the meeting tomorrow. You need to be there. Make sure you do get a good nights' sleep. Mark knows it's you, chick." She places a caring hand on my arm. I pull away like I've touched the orange hob. "He knows it's you who's been taking the medications, the class A's from the locked cabinet. He's going to confront you tomorrow in front of everyone. Time to come clean, love. Time to *get* clean. We're all here for you, to help."

I bolt out of the door, run all the way home. There's no way I'll be going back in the morning. I want nothing more to do with the place. Too much blood, and too much you—I can't be surrounded by death anymore. But I am surrounded by death. All I can think of is death. Death, and you.

Why are you torturing my mind, my soul like this, Juliet? Why do I keep seeing you leading dead animals away?

Back at home, in the pit of a well, I put on a final cook. I need this cook. I collapse back on my sofa and wait for the flat to be thick with the pungent caustic, soapy stench of ketamine.

I'm going to take it all: several grams, and the crushed contents of a half-full bottle of pills I found in the locked cupboard. I long to see her again: Juliet, or Not Juliet, the creature of beauty with the Disney braid, the vine tattoo, the red tears; the girl with the same face and voice as you. I will let her take my hand, kiss my lips, carry my frail, exhausted body in her arms from the light which screams out in nothing but grey for me, and on into the noiseless dark.

I crush and swipe and stretch the crystals into lines this last time, taking pride in how it's all laid out. With many white lines, I draw your face. I eke the powder round into curves, semi-circles, ovals, waves, and create an image in your likeness. I curve round the thickest white line to form the tip of your patrician nose. Pressing white grains into almond shapes—I form your beautiful eyes. Weaving white lines around the edge of the plate with the tip of the card, I form the long braid in which you always keep your hair.

You.

I roll my note and push it hard up into a sore, weeping nostril and then inhale every last grain of you, and, once more, fall back into the well of my sofa.

A blanket of bliss rolls over me with a sigh like fog on the moors, peace spreads out from my core to my tips.

But then, my heart rate shoots up and then plummets back down, dropping away to nothing. Consciousness slips into a cloud of smoke all the shade of you, and I step over the edge and allow myself to fall. My eyes, beetle-black, open as I reach the pit of the well. There you are. You are sad again, my Juliet, or my Not Juliet, or this angel-of-death version of you who never raises a smile.

You say nothing but reach out a willowy arm. I see your vine tattoo. We both got one done for your twenty-fifth birthday. Yours starts at your wrist and twists and twirls all the way up your outstretched arm to the top of your smooth shoulder. Mine is similar, a continuation, but extends a little further around my neck to where I like to be kissed the most. I take hold of your hand and you pull me in. Your arm of vines reels me, wraps me up in the softest, most brilliant feeling. Warm yet cool, safe yet unknown. I am next to you again, or this version of you, Juliet Not Juliet.

And then I let you kiss me. Your lips taste of Saturdays and of what I can only imagine heaven is like if heaven were to exist. This is the start of my long goodbye.

I am one thousand candles, all lit up at once, and then I am those same one thousand candles, all blown out in unison. I let you take me from the light, which is becoming greyer by the second. I realise time means nothing anymore, and now, like Berry, like Charles, I have reached my destination and I have become nothingness in the dark. I know now that you, Juliet Not Juliet, are not human. You are, in fact, Death. And now, so am I.

The stench of rotten flesh and ketamine can be smelt from the stairwell. Juliet hammers at the apartment door for ten minutes until the fire-fighters insist their way in is quicker, and they haven't time to waste. Juliet steps back, fearing the worst. She changed her mind, decided she's still in love with Rommy. She raced home as soon as her flight landed. She can't wait to see her girl, her Rommy. Can't wait to forgive her and take her back.

Juliet strokes the tip of her long braid up and down her inner arm, tracing the outline of the vine running up it, whilst she waits for the rescue team to batter down the door.

Juliet will forgive the drug-taking, she'll help Rommy get the professional help she needs. They'll escape the powerful trap of addiction together, the right way this time, with help and support. In time, Juliet knows things can be what they once were. Good again.

But Juliet knows in her heart it's too late.

The door is down. The slam of it hitting the floor is nothing compared to the implosion Juliet feels in the pit of her stomach, or the crush she takes in the chest, two planets colliding. She rushes over and sees her love, her Rommy, flat out on her back on the sofa, a thick ring of dried white residue is around her nose, a powder-encrusted plate, a rolled note just inches from her dead, unfurled fingertips. A mottled patch of dry vomit mats her precious girl's face and hair to the fabric of the sofa. Rommy's cheeks, Rommy's bare stomach, the space between her thighs—are all vomiting with maggots. The busy vortex of flies moving in Brownian motion above Rommy's dishevelled, stiff body is too much. The sight and the smell of her is too much. Too strong.

Juliet's loss is too great.

A crouched fire-fighter with kindness in his eyes speaks to Juliet. She has to focus hard on what he is saying. "Is there anyone we can call?"

But Juliet is struck dumb with grief. She can't be there any longer.

She runs down the stairs of the apartment complex, as fast as a stone dropping down a well; she needs to be out of the building, far away from the memories, the dead body of her lover, the stench of death and ketamine.

Juliet wipes tears from her eyes. They are clear tears, salty tears, tears of the living, not tears of blood. The brightness of the outside world jabs at her pupils like pins.

For a fleeting second, Juliet sees her lover, sees Rommy with an arm extended, with her matching vine tattoo snaking up her arm. She sees Rommy's other hand pointing at her own neck, to the end of her vine, where she likes to be kissed the most. But where the ink of Rommy's tattoo had once been green, now the vines are black, toxic, throbbing; as if close to bursting open through her near-translucent skin.

"Juliet, Juliet," Rommy Not Rommy with the sad, dark eyes calls out. "Let me lead you from the light into the dark."

Juliet swears she's just seen her lover Rommy lifeless, lost forever down the infinite, bleak well of drugs and sickness. But here, outside, Rommy is beckoning her closer, calling to her for an embrace, one more passionate kiss—but Juliet only sees Rommy, and not the speeding truck as she steps out into the road.

And Juliet's light, too, is extinguished.

The Beauty Parlour

First published by Timber Ghost Press in 2022

As Skip pulled the last steel whisker out and through the final cheek-pad hole of her face, Rhea yelped. Sixteen bores had been pierced either side of Rhea's philtrum, through each of which a short length of fishing wire protruded. It had stung a little, but her quest for beauty was never painless. Skip knew how it felt. He'd given himself facial fur using a similar technique when he had transitioned to kangaroo.

Rhea stood and surveyed herself in the salvaged Baroque mirror which hung on the far wall of the beauty parlour. The mirror, seized most likely from one of the museum raids which had taken place long before the Dust had gotten so bad, gave back a clear reflection of pure beauty. Morphed from kitten to lioness in a little under three hours, Rhea's new form was nearly complete. She was a riot of fur and tail and paws, the cat who had got the cream. After thrumming out a purr and stroking her thread-whiskers, she sat back down, placed her hands on the table, and tilted her head at Skip.

"Claws next," she said, her aquamarine cat's-eye contacts almost glowing with feline demand.

Skip nodded. He was tired, but he knew this customer was worth the effort. She not only paid well, she was also the hostess of the Unmasked Ball and she'd promised to reward him with a ticket in exchange for a successful cross-species transformation. Skip was the best beautician in the district and

Rhea was the most influential—and also the most demanding—of the Beauties.

"How long are we going this week, with the nails?" he asked, proffering a display wheel of mounted acrylic and natural keratin talons which ranged from guitar pick to nightmarish in their sharpness and in their length. Rhea took the samples in her hands and ran her finger along each blade-like claw— enough to leave a linear indentation on the skin of her finger pad, but not enough to draw blood.

"Oh, let's stick with two inches. I'm not brave enough to go longer," she replied. "I love the way they would look, but it's impossible to wash my face without injuring myself. You know, I'd slice open a cheek—or worse."

"I understand. I rarely went longer than a half inch myself when I was feline. It wasn't practical. I kept scratching solar units, which made them totally inefficient," said Linux, a second customer, an energy engineer, a friend of Rhea's.

"Yes, I can imagine," said Rhea, despite not having a clue about the ins or outs of photovoltaic energy or biodome construction. She had gotten this far on looks alone.

Linux flashed his finger stumps at his friend. "Now I identify as Phillipine Cobra, I've done away with talons completely. I'm thinking about a semi-permanent finger binding next. Clump them all together with bone staples so I can strap my arms down against my torso and be done with upper limbs altogether—just for the ball, just for one evening." He stood and lifted his T-shirt to reveal a taut stomach, shelled in overlapping black scales. "One hundred percent snake, well, ten percent waterproof adhesive and reptile leather."

"You'll have to go over to Millia's for binding or webbing," said Skip as he filed and prepped Rhea's nail beds. "We don't do anything that requires anaesthetic here."

"Oh, I know. She did my hood, and a fabulous job she did too," said Linux, cupping his hands behind the yellow and black skin wings which stretched from his shoulders to his ears, fanning out either side of his neck.

"I can see the appeal of going reptilian. Julian from dome thirteen has gone iguana and the scale work the tattooist has done down his back is to die for," said Rhea.

Linux flicked out his forked tongue and reached for Skip's portfolio of his influencer sketches and of drawings of his most recent work. Once Skip had finished Rhea's claws, Linux was going to enquire about non-surgical options to enhance his dentition. He had wanted all but his canines cracked and pulled and then all four remaining canines built up with loaded faux-venom chambers, ready to spray on compression, but he knew tooth removal was a permanent modification and might limit future transitions. He knew he'd like to be a large mammal of some sort again in the not-too-distant future—perhaps a polar bear or one of the other Arctic creatures who were some of the first to go—so he wasn't quite ready to give up his bite altogether yet.

Linux looked with admiration and great sadness at the display of images, at all of the hundreds of torn magazine and book pictures and drawings of creatures which decorated Skip's beauty parlour walls. All bar the hardy brown anoles, the cockroaches, the locusts, and a few resilient fish species had been lost since the Great Dust came many years ago. There were thousands of extinct species to choose from, yet so few still alive. All that was left was survival and art, but he knew at twenty-three that he only had a short time left until his lungs succumbed to the force of pollution. Not a soul lived to see the other side of thirty. He already felt the crackle and tightness in his chest on exertion, which they all knew was the beginning of the end.

Most of the human survivors had been forced underground. Partially due to the thick Dust which whipped up into ad hoc towering, erosive tornados, destroying everything organic in their wake. Partially due to the particulate matter too small to see or feel but just the right size to cause almost instant emphysema. And partially due to the power of the new Elite.

When the Dust came, the capitalist society which had reigned eternal toppled like a stack of cards. Overnight, bankers, bitcoin trust-fund kids, and sport stars became worthless, fame and money lost value instantaneously, and the new Elite formed. They consisted of Those That Could: solar panel technicians and bottled gas suppliers, weapon hoarders and hydroponic scientists, engineers, farmers, and the Beautiful. Those That Could rose upward.

As the value of all commodities and all abilities rocked and shuffled over the years that followed the beginning of the Great Dust, so did what the Elite considered to be beautiful. Reptiles, amphibians and mammals all dropped from existence in a matter of months, animal carcasses littered deserted roadsides until scavenged, and scavengers lasted only a little longer, but soon, all who existed under the natural sky became blighted by the perilous toxic dusts. The air held a dryness like no other as the humans kicked Mother Earth into premature menopause. Earth's wildlife, Earth's fruits became desiccated, powdered like trampled sandcastles. The biota of the planet was decimated ten-fold and ten-fold again.

Those That Could built glass-roofed ecosystems with clever ventilation, air purification and toxin extraction methods, and Those That Could survived. And Those That Could, formed allegiances with Those That Had Weapons, and Those That Could and Those That Had Weapons took in Those That Were Beautiful. The Beautiful traded in the Oldest Profession, and together, they formed the Elite.

And the Elite separated from Those That Just Survive.

Beauty had in the past been the slim, symmetrical face of youth and muscle, and those genes still remained. However, a quest to become—or to at least imitate—what had been lost evolved. Beauty parlours cropped up in between the glass domes, and the Elite and the Beautiful travelled bravely from places of safety—where the air was breathable and the water was pure—to the parlours for their modifications, to become animal, to decorate themselves with relics of organisms lost and only now present in posters and books and paintings and myth.

"Excuse me, Skip, I need a comfort break." Rhea stood up and swished her leonine tail behind her. The tail, a gift from a taxidermist in exchange for tickets, had been anchored into her behind, into the ligaments of her sacroiliac joint, under lidocaine injection. "It's such a palaver taking this suit off to use the bathroom."

"Sure. I could use a drink gel anyhow," replied Skip, wiping sweat from his brow. "You know, we sell beta-carotene supplements—take a high enough dose and your skin will yellow all over from within. You could give the skin suit the old heave ho."

She peeled down her lioness cloak until it sat, an emptied sack, on the floor. Made from 'donations' from Those That Just Survive, it was not only buff yellow, but also soft and downy, and unbelievably pelt-like.

Those That Just Survive were a collective of hardy families who were not Beautiful and who were not Those That Could. They'd fled straight underground when the Dust came. They were the underworld, they were redundant. They had nothing to offer bar their own tissues. They bred like rabbits and bartered with the flesh of their own weak in exchange for foodstuffs and pure water. The Survivors, with their average and below average appearances, and their simple fashions, would never be allowed to attend the Unmasked Ball. And they had no gas masks with which to travel through the Dust to reach it anyhow. They were trapped in their caves. But their skin was young and supple and Those That Died were peeled and broken apart like scrap heap cars, and those spare parts were offered up to the Beautiful Elite for their costumes and their modifications and their surgeries. In this process of desperate up-cycling, the Elite and the Beautiful worked hard to bring about the look of the rarest animals and the look of the animals long since lost to the Dust.

The skin, hair, and nails of the Survivors were all good—all good for bargaining with—as they were all young. The Dust, the radiation, the tropical illnesses that spread like wildfire as the planet warmed, and the wildfire and the dust that spread like the tropical illnesses: all of these things kept anyone from reaching death due to age. Time rarely killed the Survivors or the Beautiful or Those That Could. Old age was as much a distant memory as dragonflies, snow leopards, orang-utans and pangolins.

"Good idea. Add some to my list, wouldn't you be a darling?" Rhea shimmied to the bathroom and on her return, her talons were fitted, and she paid Skip in tickets. Skip thanked her profusely and his tapered pseudo-ears, brown and soft, flapped as he did so.

Rhea and Linux donned their protective suits—yet a further layer of costume, this one essential when taking on the Dust and solar glare—and pulled their gas mask helmets on. Skip poked Rhea's whiskers under and in, ensuring not to bend them in the process as the pair got ready to leave.

"The Dust is bad today," said Skip, tucking the tickets into his kangaroo pouch. "Make for home with haste."

"We shall." Rhea's voice was muffled through inches of filter and tubing. "See you at the ball on the morrow."

The Unmasked Ball came and went. Five hundred Elite from the network of biodome cities met and celebrated and compared their transitions and their costumes.

Each month that the Ball took place, Those That Could tried to outdo each other with their extreme modifications. Mini tusks fashioned from elephant ivory taken from a museum long ago were surgically affixed to a young man's upper lip. Brightly coloured toucan bills fashioned from acrylics and resins were welded to the exposed, sanded jawbone of another. Plumes of feathers mounted to sockets drilled into the soft tissues of a lady's back created a bird of paradise. One young reveller, both his legs bound together and smashed to smithereens, like crushed packets of crisps beneath unbroken skin, tarnished himself with grey body paint; an eel he became.

Each month, the competition grew for most modified and most dramatic transition. Slashes to cheek and neck were made and stitched and healed as a Beauty re-identified as an axolotl. Dead Survivors' teeth were mounted on steel hinges and fastened to foreheads: and so, a megalodon attended the Unmasked Ball.

One half-orbit of the planet about the sun later, the Dust had thickened. The Dust became more corrosive than it had ever been and Earth cried tears of acid and grit.

Rhea barged through the safety lock, pushed open the second door and marched into Skip's beauty parlour. Many of her friends were getting prepared for the final ball of the year, the Christmask Ball, the annual pinnacle of the Elite calendar. Those attending would no doubt pull out all stops to come in their most revered, most outrageous and most fanciful attire to bring in the end of the year.

"Skip, darling. You simply must see what I have in my bag. I have a look I want … I *need* you to help me attain. It will be worth five tickets—no—I will give you ten tickets. Bring all of your parlour friends along; Christ—bring Survivors! I care not who you bring if you will only help me achieve this look."

In the parlour room, which stank of epoxy resin and burnt flesh, all the customers turned to look at the Hostess and what she was presenting. "I have found the rarest of images. The most rare of all creatures. You will not believe this when you cast your young marsupial glare upon it, Skip. No-one will beat this. All eyes will be on me, as they should."

She pulled out a folded sheet from her bag, unfolded it, and thrust it forward into the audience.

"There. Isn't it a thing of beauty?"

Skip's brows rose like banners above his brown eyes.

"What is it? What are they meant to be?" he asked. He could tell it was something like a human, for it had a face, and all the parts of the face were where they should be, if somewhat compressed and clouded with sagging skin; it had elements of shar-pei dog, folds of horseshoe bat, and the facial hair of a piglet. Hair sat on the top of its head like that of a sheep—white, yet wispy. Like smoke. "Is it some kind of mammal? Humanoid, but most peculiar." Skip cupped his chin in his hand.

"Can you do it? To me? Do you think you can?" asked Rhea.

"Where did you find this photograph?"

"My guard ransacked the Survivors who live to the east of the Apricot Desert." Pulling up a chair, Rhea reached for the myriad tray of hair weave samples in search of something to match the greyness of the image. "Held them up at gunpoint, demanded they fill his sack with keepsakes; something for us to look through of a dull, dusty evening. I'd instructed him to go out and forage for inspiration, and this is what he came back with."

Linux hissed from the corner, "It's an Old Person, Rhea. A 'Geriatric.' Long before the Dust came and the planet could breathe, in the great Apricot Desert, people lived double, treble what we live now. Rumour has it, some managed until they were one hundred. Can you believe it?"

"That's what I thought," said Rhea. Her cheeks flushed with excitement. "I've never seen one in such detail before. Look how the eyes nearly slide under drooped lids, see how there is the same white, wiry hair as on the top of the head sprouting like clouds of dust from the ears and the nostrils. Isn't it marvellous? Do say you can do this to me, Skip."

Skip took the photo from her hand and brought it close to his face. The small crowd waited, breath-bated, for his answer.

Skip fumbled through his drawers of accessories, piercing tools, glues, then searched his refrigerator for sheets of fresh-primed skin ready for grafting and sterilised needles for stitching. To his pile, he added various tattoo inks for blemishing and marking and pocking and furrowing. "I'll do my best."

He stripped back her yellow make-up, pulled off her lash extensions and unthreaded her steel whiskers. He scrubbed near raw her yellowed hands and dissolved the bonding chemicals anchoring claws to her nail beds. He worked, folding, cutting, charring, and stitching, to try to recreate the look of time and age.

Skip reached completion and a fever of applause erupted from the spectators. Skip swivelled Rhea's chair around for all to see his creation.

She looked ancient.

Skin folded over on skin, some prosthetic, some borrowed, some her own. Her face, corrugated and creased akin to a brain coral. Her hair stood curly and white like the Great Dusts, laced with the sharp ice crystals that came in winter. Her hands, now covered in brown liver spots looked better than anything Skip had ever achieved before when transitioning customers to leopard or Dalmatian or Friesian cow. Rhea looked marvellous: a thing of time and of many winters, an epoch of generations collected.

As she stood to examine herself in the full-length mirror, she gasped. Never before had she looked so rare.

"I wish the ball was tonight, I don't know how I'm going to contain myself for twenty-four further hours," she said, hugging him tightly, placing a ream of golden tickets into the palm of his furry hand.

Skip, swollen with pride, blushed and thanked her for allowing him to work on the canvas she had provided him with. He helped her back into her safety suit and slid carefully her gas mask, all tubes and filters and inches of Perspex and glass, back over her newly old skull.

"Journey safe, home with haste, my most precious piece," he said as he opened the air lock for her, the audience clapping majestically as she left.

Outside, the Dust was spinning, a zoetrope of grit and particulate pollution. The air was custard-thick as she set off on the treacherous journey back to her biodome.

Plodding onward, full of glee and following the route her feet knew by heart even in the blinding desert smog, she could just about make out the wall of hexagonal panels in the distance which she would need to enter.

The guard which stood up on the balcony did not seem to be present. *How odd,* she thought, *that the Dust is so thick, it obscures the guard.* Was the guard lying down up there, snoozing in his safety suit, under the protection of his gas mask helmet … while on duty? She would certainly be having words with security about staff taking absence without leave, napping on paid time.

Out of nowhere through the thick of the evening, a hard clunk to her head. A Survivor with a club of sorts, manufactured from layers of swathes of wound and bound leathered skins, took a strike, knocking Rhea out cold. The Feral tucked his baton into a crudely fashioned belt pocket, knelt over his prey, and tugged and unscrewed and unhooked the connectors on Rhea's gas mask, and ripped the device off from her head before placing it into his sack. Grabbing next her boots and the trouser cuffs of her outer suit, he lifted and tipped the young old girl upside down. The suit peeled away from her lifeless body, and out of it she slid, paste from the tube, onto the white-hot sands of the desert. Rolling up and bagging the costly protective gear, he grinned a smile that only the Dust would see; this one would be his best find yet.

His own appearance, worthless by all current standards, had taken its own battering. When he'd clubbed the guard, his average face had taken the force from the acidic-reflux spit-up of the desert floor. His lungs had pulled sharply at the heat of the Dust he'd inhaled.

The feral Survivor ripped out the purse of coins and tickets from the Beauty's bag and stormed off into the Dust. He returned to his cave, to share news and findings, to launch the next round of attack. That night, the Survivors would snowball the Elite. Three masks would become six, twelve, twenty-four. The Christmask Ball would become theirs.

And the young old girl's hair blew in the wind as the dust whipped up, a writhing vertical snake of sand and grit, a maelstrom of particulate smog. Her hair spread out and into the Dust and melted like licked candyfloss. The layers of skin that were hers and layers of skin that were not hers un-bandaged, melted, dribbled and blew away, and were carried off into the air with the cosmic grime.

The dust and the sand blasted against her cheeks and her nose caved in, a fallen pyramid, releasing her un-mummified ghost to the ether. The vile force of ruined nature, acidic and potent, lifted off the cartilage and sinew and tendons and fat that lay underneath her skin. Up, up, and away it all went, dissolving into the Dust. The weather took years from the girl's face, tens and tens of years, until her skull was all that remained of her head.

Fatty brain corroded, liquefied into sludge, and slid out through her ear canals. Neurone rivulets vanished on contact with the hurricane of pollution that chipped and gnashed and bit at her remnants. On her neck, solar lasers breaking through the Dust burned and teased away young and old and young again skin, layer after layer, until a passing locust swarm moved in to tidy away what the weather had yet to claim.

Her body—all accelerated and modified tissues and trims, all falsely aged arms and legs and torso—followed suit, layer after layer rubbed clean.

Bones and titanium piercings were all that remained of her on the floor of the Apricot Desert as the Dust settled, satisfied, well fed.

Never before had she looked so rare.

Sick Girl

First published in Punk Noir Magazine, 2021

Sick Girl lives in the city and works in the supermarket stacking shelves and sweeping floors.

She is really good at her job and always leaves things tidy and always leaves the little boxes of cereal and the cans of beans facing the right way around and pulled up to the front so it's easier for the customers to find what they're looking for but Sick Girl still only gets minimum wage and occasionally harassed by her landlord even when she is only a day overdue with the rent.

Sick Girl's tale would be a modern-day Cinderella story except she isn't looking for a prince. She went all Sinead O'Connor, all Bad Britney, and shaved her head with a razor blade back at secondary school and no-one asked her why she did it, which was fine by Sick Girl. She's A-okay by herself, thanks.

Sick Girl was raised by Uncle while Ma was on the Horse. Uncle said Horse was Ma's *Bad Medicine*.

Sick Girl never got any medicine. Her uncle did his best until he was on the Horse, too, and then she had to look after herself.

Sick Girl kept her shirt sleeves long and her fingernails short so the germs couldn't get underneath, and unpainted so she could inspect her nails and check for zinc and calcium and vitamin A deficiency and anaemia and heart disease. Didn't need long nails. Always kept her door key to the bedsit she struggled to meet the rent on poking through the knuckle-slits of her clenched fists when she walked home in the dark after stacking shelves and sweeping floors and directing people to the milk. *The milk is always in the same place,* Sick Girl thinks. *It's always in the same fucking place: first aisle as you come in the shop, underneath the massive sign which says, 'Milk.'*

Sick Girl keeps herself to herself, lives alone and has no family now. She is quite content with her set-up; quite content indeed with the way things are. She works hard all week so she can eat organic and drink organic and wash organic and buy the things she wants: minerals and multivitamins and a digital sphygmomanometer, heart rate watch and glucose-urine sticks and a litre a week of hand gel. These are a few of her favourite things; the things she needs to maintain good health.

Sick Girl finds her weekend day trips always make her feel a little better. She packs the same bag each Friday evening: map, pad and fountain pen, phone and charger, neck pillow, and some trail mix in a tub with 'trail mix' written on the top. She decides to leave her gown at home this weekend as it is a little colder now. Winter is in the air. The gown is quite revealing and doesn't always cover up the bits which need covering up all the time. Sick Girl waits until the Saturday morning and blends herself a green smoothie, and makes an avocado and pine nut salad, nice and fresh, and puts it into its tub, the top of which is labelled 'avocado and pine nut salad', then she heads off for the weekend.

Sick Girl walks, she likes to exercise—knows exercise is good for the heart.

She pretends to follow the clear hospital signage while pretending to look at the map she printed out and laminated a long time ago, in preparation, and makes her way through the double doors and down the clinical corridor until she finds the room she seeks. She chooses the chair with the most padding. Sick Girl likes to sit by the window so she can look outside as well as inside and she knows both views will be relaxing as she has been in this room before, but not for a couple of months.

She looks up at the strip lighting—one tube is on the blink—so she searches for a feedback form to complain about the lighting and finds one by the glass window which she presumes is a sub-station Reception as there is a desk and a switched off computer there, but it is currently unstaffed.

Filling in the form to let the caretaking team know the strip light needs repairing—she knows that flashing lights can trigger epilepsy in someone who has never even experienced an epileptic episode before in their entire life. She posts the form into the box by the sub-station desk and takes her seat again and then looks around and counts eight other people, most of whom, except for one, stare constantly at their phones.

Sick Girl smiles at the woman opposite her who isn't looking at a phone and thinks the woman looks like a bit like what her mum would like now if she'd gotten off the Horse before it'd been too late and cost her all her teeth and some of her flesh. The lady opposite smiles back, pulls a crossword from her bag, and stares at that instead. No-one wants to talk here. No-one is asking where the milk is, and she likes that.

She can smell disinfectant and cheap coffee, and no-one asks her to do or clean or stack or lick anything because there is nothing here to stack or lick or do or clean.

Sick Girl sits and looks things up on her phone although the Wi-Fi is slow but faster than at her bedsit where there isn't any Wi-Fi. She starts to write a list of words which excite her which all begin with the letter 'P'— Palliative, Parasitology, Paregoric, Paroxysm, Pericarditis, Polychrest. She writes until her pen runs out of ink. She thinks about asking the lady opposite if she could borrow her pen when she's finished her crossword but before she can pluck up the courage, someone comes into the room where they're sitting and takes the lady away.

Sick Girl continues to add to her list on her phone. She downloads an app which is just like a notepad, only on a phone, and she wishes she'd discovered this sooner, like when she'd been at the beginning of the alphabet fifteen pads of paper ago.

She watches people come and go until she is the only one left in the waiting room and her phone list grows longer and longer until it's no longer quite as light outside and in fact now it's brighter inside than it is outside. She wonders if it's time to reach into her bag for her neck pillow or if her stomach might not be full enough after the salad and the smoothie—maybe she should nip to the onsite shop for something else to eat before having a rest.

No, Sick Girl is content, and decides she can wait until morning for something else to eat. She delves for her travel pillow, although she has no plans to travel anywhere else tonight.

Someone with a clipboard is walking down the corridor so she opts to leave her pillow in her bag for just a little longer. Just a minute or two longer, until the someone has walked on through to wherever the someone is going, but the someone stands in front of her and smiles with just their mouth and asks Sick Girl if she needs any help and *which specialist are you waiting to see?*

Sick Girl was so calm until someone came, but now her heart races up into her throat along with a bit of smoothie. She says she is looking for Pathology and the someone screws their face up like they're stuck on a crossword clue they can't for the life of them work out the answer to and the someone takes a small step back and looks up at the strip light which strobes hard and is quite annoying, and after some thought, the someone directs her down the corridor and tells her she needs to ask at the *Main Reception Desk* where Pathology is as she is sat in *Urology* which is not the right place at all. Then, the someone walks off toward wherever they were going and Sick Girl sighs and gathers up her belongings. Time to move on.

She heads to the Main Reception Desk but walks straight past it and looks at her map for options and chooses Dermatology because it's a little closer and she hasn't been there for a while, and she is a little tired after all the waiting and the listing that she has done on her day off after a long week at work.

She turns left, then left again, then up three flights of stairs, and then through a set of double doors. She enters a smaller waiting room with fewer seats and no people.

She undoes her bag and places her belongings neatly along the windowsill which is just above her head and sits in the chair underneath it. The heating is on full blast.

Sick Girl relaxes again until she sees a man in a wheelchair being wheeled in by a nurse who applies the brakes and leaves him at the other side of the room and she tries not to make eye contact with him because, for a moment, she doesn't feel safe in the room. But he is wheeled away again very soon and once again, she is alone and safe. She notices the strip lights all work in this waiting room. This she finds satisfying, so she places her neck pillow behind her head and closes her eyes.

"Excuse me, madam," are the words which wake her up. Her lids lift straight away. She was only taking a light nap—there is no sleepy dust in the corners of her eyes at all—but now, it's pitch-black outside, and the strip lights feel harsh again even though they aren't the flashing sort.

"Excuse me. Sorry to wake you up, dear." The words come again. Wiping her eyes, she sits up straight and doesn't know what to say.

"Are you okay?" More words. Sick Girl knows she needs to say something back as that's the way conversation operates and she has had training on it and she knows this from the weekdays, when people ask her, 'Where is the milk?'

"Yes. I'm okay." She suspects this someone is a nurse. The nurse stands in the doorway to the waiting room. Or maybe she is a someone who works in admin who gets to dress a bit like a nurse but doesn't have to sit the exams or deal with bodily fluids.

"We're closing the department in a minute. The cleaners will be round shortly. Dermatology closes at 9 p.m. Are you waiting for someone?"

"No. I'm not waiting for someone," Sick Girl replies in truth, her heart thrums faster now and is all up in her mouth. "I think I might be in the wrong department."

"Well, may I see your Confirmation of Appointment letter and I can escort you to the correct department myself," says nursey, who's not even smiling with just her lips.

Sick Girl picks up her travel pillow and her smoothie bottle and her pad and her pen that has run out and her phone and her empty sandwich box and the copy of a health magazine she picked up (on her walk over from Urology, someone had left it on a chair) and the handful of leaflets on Prostate Problems, on Dealing with Dialysis, on Uterine Prolapse, and on Contact Dermatitis, and shoves them all in her bag then swings her rucksack over her shoulder.

"No, I don't have a letter," Sick Girl says. She has never had a letter. No-one has ever cared enough for her to send her a letter. She shrugs and decides to call it a day. She checks her map—even though she knows the place like the supermarket at which she toils through the week, like the back of her hand—and heads towards the exit.

Sick Girl returns to the place an outsider might call home, the room where she stores her clothes and sleeps. She pulls out the box of rusty sharps stashed underneath her bedside table, rolls up her sleeve, and sets to work on the canvas of her skin. A crimson river drips down her arm, decorates her sheets. She collects a little blood in an inkwell. The pain which had accrued, just below the surface of her flesh, the agony no doctor or drug could remedy, momentarily dissipates into the deathly quiet of her bedsit prison. This silence is pierced, split wide open, as she releases a scream. Her voice comes out, at a pitch and volume which would shatter diamond. It exits and spreads and sinks away into the darkness, this sound, until there is no good thing left inside her.

And then she dips her pen into the well of blood and again, starts to write.

The Cool Kids

I was the one who said *yes* when Nick asked if he should go and get The Blanket. His great grandma had made it by hand, or had inherited it from someone further back in the family tree who'd made it by hand—I can't remember the details. I was simply excited to have people over. Friends. It's never too late to try and fit in, is it, to reach out to your peers? Mother says I'm a pushover, that's why I was unpopular at school. Still unpopular in my mid-thirties.

Back in the day, the kids in my class called me an arse-licker. I prefer *people-pleaser*.

Nick forewarned me the blanket would smell bad. Like his grandma had, after the rot and whiff of age set in. But he insisted it was worth tolerating, because it was so incredibly warm. And I'd had no choice but to agree politely when he first unfurled it. Manners are tantamount to social success, surely. And indeed, it was the cosiest blanket I'd ever had the pleasure of touching. But yes, it also reeked of death.

I'd only popped back to Monkton to check up on my folks' house whilst they holidayed by the coast; they'd begged me to come and water the plants, empty the mailbox and so on as their hired help had fallen ill. I hadn't been back for years. My first night in my childhood home felt strange, not because I spent it alone—that, I was used to—but because the house felt so big compared to the shoebox I rented in the city. I felt as lonesome as an orphan on Christmas Day.

I'd not kept in touch with anyone from school in Monkton and hadn't made a single chum in the city, so imagine how excited I'd been when I bumped into Nicholas Granger from school in the village shop. He was working a shift behind the counter.

"Of course I remember you," he'd said. "I've missed your face. We all have."

I hadn't known where to look, the heat in my cheeks burning a tad.

"Gosh, that's awfully kind to hear," I replied.

"I'll swing by later, we can catch up properly," Granger said.

"Sure," I replied.

"So, nine then? I finish up here at half eight."

I glanced over my shoulder to check he wasn't talking to someone else behind me. The shop was otherwise empty.

At school, Nicholas Granger had been one of the cool lads who'd hung out with the hot girls, and I was—and am—definitely neither. "Certainly, Nicholas Granger," I replied. "Nine is perfect. Tickity-boo." Picture my face, alit like a birthday cake, when he insisted, I should call him 'Nick.'

"Is it okay if I bring some others?" he asked. I handed him the correct change for my comestibles. Why Nicholas Granger, the most popular lad in school, had hung around the boondocks of Monkton and was still working in the village shop after all these years, I had no idea. But … *who cares, he wanted to be my friend.*

"Yes. Please do." I laughed. Too loud. Nervous anticipation.

"Sweet. We can have a party. I'll bring some more of these." He winked and tapped the top of the solitary can of beer I was purchasing before placing it into my bag for me.

Shannon and Nell (the latter, my school crush, every upper sixth's school crush), the twins from fifty-two, cross-eyed James who wasn't even cross-eyed, and Tall Mike were going to come to my house. For a party? My carotid artery thrummed in excitement. How odd though, that these kids, the ones who sat at the back of the bus, the ones who (on more than one occasion) had flicked wet peas at me from the corner of the school canteen, were still knocking about, together, over twenty years after we'd all left school.

In my teens, as friendships had formed amongst my peers, I'd felt invisible. I had dragged through puberty ever-present, ever-observant, yet very much on the sidelines—as everyone else whirled boldly around me.

"We've got to stick together now mate, 'Class of '98.' We're the only ones left," Nick said. He tossed a fun size packet of skittles into my carrier bag. "On the house, mate."

I thanked him, nodded, and left the shop.

Sucking on complimentary candy, I scuttled home to think and to prepare.

Mother and Father would not have been happy with visitors inside. Guests had always been strictly forbidden. Not a single soul bar the three of us and the hired help had set foot over the threshold for as long as I could remember. Mother pretended it was because she liked to run a tight ship, but I knew it was because of the abductions.

Kids had disappeared regularly in the nineties. Lots of kids. Missing posters had been pinned up everywhere. Every lamppost in Monkton had been decorated with paper tassels, paper faces. If milk cartons had still printed lost children on their sides, you'd have seen a new set staring at you every morning over your cornflakes.

I spent the afternoon gathering kindling and chopping wood for a fire. We could keep the party low-key. Everything would be fine, tidy. Contained. Outside.

A large part of me expected them not to show at all, but they did indeed all turn up at nine. On the dot.

I led them around the side of the house, to the garden, to where the fire was blazing a treat.

Half an hour after the sun dropped, despite the dancing and the flames, it got a little chilly, and the beers started to run low.

"I'll go and grab the blanket," Nick said. He winked at Shannon and Nell. "And I'll grab more supplies. When I get back, we can drop the acid."

"Acid?" I said. "Okay." I'd never taken anything stronger than paracetamol before, but I was with the cool kids now. Acid was what they do. And acid was what, it appeared, I was going to do too.

"Marcus, dude, I need you to come, too, to help me get up in the attic," Nick said. He downed his beer and lobbed the spent can into the fire pit. They both fist-bumped me before they left. I've seen people do this on TV so I knew the score. As my knuckles smacked into Marcus's, it smarted. I figured this meant I was in.

Part of the crew.

The gang.

Down with the cool kids, age thirty-seven.

Why had Mother tried to keep me from these people? They were awesome. Beer, drugs … and the girls … the ladies … well, they were sexy as hell.

Nell handed me the last beer. "You take it. It's your party," she said. Then she kissed me on the cheek. The tickle of her golden hair as it brushed against my face sent a near orgasmic rush down my spine. Does that count as first base? Closest I've ever come to a woman. A real one, anyhow.

I cracked open the beer. "Thanks. Yeah. Pumping party, isn't it?" I replied, unsure of how this new language sounded in my mouth. She smiled and licked her lips at me then turned to chat with Shannon.

Nick and Marcus returned with a fresh crate of beer and the blanket. My God, it was huge. Must've taken the old lady a lifetime to stitch or weave or knit it, or whatever. Covered with ovals of all shapes and sizes, all different shades, the blanket was hemmed in lacy, red cotton.

"It's so soft." I stroked the nap with the back of my hand. "What is it made from?" I asked.

"No idea," said Nick. "Think she started it as a school project, and it just grew over the years. It's a frigging blanket. Dude, how the heck am I supposed to know what it's made from? Fucking warm though."

We all sat in a huddled crescent as Nick draped the heavy fabric over our legs. I tried to ignore how much it stank.

"S'bad isn't it? The smell," said Nick. "Doesn't matter if it gets beer on it, though, so it's perfect for use outside. Wouldn't want to ruin anything of our gracious host's now, would we?"

And dear Lord, no we wouldn't. My parents would've had a fit if I'd brought their premium eiderdowns out by the fire.

It was at this point that I probably should've excused myself, tied things up, gone to bed. It must've been way past eleven, but I didn't because I was sat by Nell. She had taken hold of my hand under the blanket. Does that count as second base? Her soft fingertips caressing my palm felt way more intimate than the kiss on the cheek.

"I could only find one tab, though, dude," Nick said. "You have it, bro. You deserve it. Great party."

"Tab?" I asked.

"Yeah. Tongue or eyeball, dude?" he asked.

"I'm sorry, what?"

"Tongue or eyeball? Where do you want it? Just stick your fucking tongue out at me, dude."

When Nicholas Granger says *jump, you ask how high*, so I thrust my tongue out in his direction, and he placed a postage-stamp-sized piece of coloured paper onto it.

"Thanks," I mumbled. Sharp. Dry. Nell squeezed my hand tighter under the blanket.

"Pleasure, bud. Wash it down with some beer."

So of course, I followed my new friend's instructions.

The fire started to die down. We were running out of wood.

"Shall I go and search for some more?" I said. I felt uncertain. About whether I should go and collect wood or call it a night and ask them to leave. As I tried to stand, I suddenly felt unsure about many things: where my hands ended and where Nell's begun, whether the zoetrope of racing rainbow horses circling the fire had been there at the start of the night or not, and whether Nell had always had a third eye in the centre of her forehead. Such long lashes.

"I've got an axe," I said. I looked around the dwindling campfire at my friends, for some kind of response. The moon, to my left, was now razzle-dazzle purple-pink and was not sitting still, and the ovals on the blankets had all sprouted tiny faces.

"Nah, mate. You sit and chill," Nick replied. "Let's play a game instead; a sexy game—before we wrap things up."

"Yeah … good idea. A sexy, sexy game," said Nell. She stroked the side of my cheek with the back of her hand. Gorgeous. Except her hand was now a bunch of bananas. Her third eye, sat now on the end of her nose, winked at me.

A game, I thought, *how exciting. Will the striped pygmy marmoset juggling yellow rugby balls by the oak in the corner of my garden join in, too, or is he here purely for the ribbons?*

Nick tugged at my sleeve. "You get under the blanket," he said. "Me and the others are going to choose something that you've on you, on your person, that you don't really need, which you need to take off."

"U-huh," I replied.

He continued to talk at me. "When you've guessed what it is, chuck it out at us."

"So … a guessing game?" Longish pause. "Something I don't need on my person." Long pause. "Take it off. Throw it out." Longer pause. "Got it," I slurred and tried to retain the radiant word fodder he'd scattered like birdseed into the glittercloud which had come to surround me; tried to scoop-stack the torrent of communication bullets he'd fired into some semblance of an order in the pyramid of my mind-zone.

"Spot on, dude. You're one smart cookie."

They all stood up and left me alone. I sat underneath the blanket and studied the little faces. Each one seemed to be smiling at me, grinning and winking in time with the cadent horses and the clapping monkey and the penny farthing wheel which I sensed was spinning somewhere in the distance to the rhythm of the calliope which perhaps only I could hear.

I stared at all the little faces, admired the detail in everyone, and winked back at each with my own open-for-business third eye.

"Okay. We've decided. Start stripping off, you sexy beast," Marcus shouted and then cranked up the portable stereo. Nick responded with a noise like a foghorn.

It was nice and warm under the blanket, with all my newfound oval-faced friends. I did however hope the others, my guests, my full-sized friends, now deprived of the blanket's hospitality, weren't catching a chill. "Are you warm enough, everybody?" I think I asked.

"Yeah, we're fine," Marcus replied. His voice sounded merry enough. "We're all toasty, bro, dancing by the fire."

I lifted the blanket and peeped out at the other humans. "Oh yes, so you are," I said. Yes, and there they all were, freshly horned and fanged, oscillating like flames, and now stood—it appeared—inside of the fire. Or perhaps my three eyes were playing tricks on me.

"Let's start then, bro, pick an item, chuck it out," said Tall Mike.

I threw out my shoes. Then my socks—I didn't need any of them, especially as I was now lying back comfortably, on the floor, under the cavernous blanket I'd got somewhat lost in. Were they bats—the little people, the faces which peered down at me? They seemed to speak at me in echoes; they followed my thoughts with their eyes, offered words of encouragement throughout the blanket game.

"Nope. Not your shoes or your socks," Nell shouted. "I'll keep your things neatly for you in a tidy pile," she said.

I heard feet, hers I presumed, shuffle through the dirt. I liked this woman, a lot. *Is folding somebody's clothes up for them third base? And what exactly are clothes …*

I drew out my tie from my collar and folded it into a Milky Way spiral. It became a hissing adder in my hands, so I threw it out from my cave.

"Nope. Not your tie. Keep trying."

Whatever could it be? I unbuttoned my best shirt, the one I reserve for job interviews, and pulled my arms out of the sleeves. The pressed cotton scrunched up into a ball easily. My most precious shirt became a crying baby which screamed blue murder at me and the oval faces. I lobbed the shirt-babba out towards my new old school friends.

"Nope. Better luck next time. You didn't need your shirt, for sure, but it's not the thing we chose."

And so, the game continued. Belt, trousers, underwear followed. I shed clothing until I became bare-butt naked underneath the ceiling of stitched faces, which all looked on, down at me, laughing, smiling, spitting out their speeches of encouragement double time.

The feeling of my own birth-suit-bare flesh touched close to the rasping blanket fabric. A thousand small mouths licked and puckered at my skin. Naked. The walls of my knitted sanctum drew in, like a second skin. I panicked: I'd nothing left on me to take off, yet Nick had said, quite clearly, I hadn't selected the correct item yet. I still had something on which I didn't need. The words spun in my jumbled mind. I created a small internal space by looping my arms out in front of me. Shadows. Sausages. Snakes in sleeping bags. I could make out loosely the outline of my own fingertips against the blanket wall as the woolly tent I had pitched glowed red with light from the fire. And then it struck me—my fingers. I was born with all ten, but rarely used the little ones. Could this be what I needed to remove, to take off, to throw out to the wolves?

I stared at what I could make out of my hands for an eternity until Nell shouted: "Come on, you can do it. You can figure it out."

I so badly wanted to impress her—after all, she could be *the one*. The oval faces cheered along with Nell's sweet voice in the key of Saturday, the pitch of candy: "Do it."

Do it, the pygmy marmoset whispered into my ear.

So first, I bit off my left-hand pinky—this was the finger I used the least. The first few layers of skin severed with ease, but I had to bite down hard to snap clear through the bone. Off it came, at the second knuckle. I spat the spurting worm out towards my friends. A little blood came. I played with the fluid, spread it all over my pale bare knee: strawberry topping on an ice-cream sundae.

"Delicious," said Nell followed by what could only be described as chewing. *Eating somebody's finger nubbin must surely be considered fourth base.*

"Nope. Try again," said Nick. The other humans cheered. I snapped off a toe. My left little piggy flew out to my audience. My friends cheered louder but informed me it was still not the correct item.

I worked through all ten toes, then through all my fingers, until left with twenty bleeding stumps. Each leaked warm red and left a coppery taste on my lips.

"Great work," said one of the blanket faces. I reached and caressed its tender yarn cheek. A tongue slipped out of its third eye hole which slurped on the juices of my finger stump.

"Smashing job," said another. Then it snapped free and galloped off into the wild.

"You're doing so well," said Nell, her mouth somewhere close to mine, separated only by the thick, pongy blanket. My heart throbbed faster with pride and then I panicked. I needed to impress her but had nothing left to offer. No clothes, no digits. Nothing left on me could easily be removed.

My member sat limp between my thighs, its tip scuffing the dirt floor. Surely not.

"I have nothing left to offer," I shouted from underneath the blanket. The oval faces all nodded in agreement. Above the music and the crackle of the dying fire, I heard the scuffle, swoop, and thump of my human friends as they encircled me.

"Do you give in?" the twins from fifty-two asked in unison.

"Ready to quit?" asked Tall Mike.

Perhaps I didn't have any other choice. I'd run out of sensible ideas and the tiny stripy monkey had, after all, been waiting ever so patiently—he wanted for this all to be over, so he could teach me how to juggle grapefruit aboard the hovercraft he was paddling closer and closer towards me on.

"Yes. Yes. I suppose I have to," I whispered through the fabric. "I give in." I sigh. Another long pause. "What was it then? What have I got on me that I don't need?" Red leaks and leaks from my edges as I unfurl and fray.

"He gives in. He quits," said Mike. The old school new friends all cheered in unison: "The blanket!" And then they ripped it off and tossed it down on the dirt.

They all flapped down on top of me. Fangs and talons tore through my flesh. They made a light snack of my soft parts.

As the fire burnt out and our party became lost to the blackness of the night, every fleshy part of my body was consumed—except for the oval of flesh which made up my face. The pygmy marmoset gnawed my face free from my skull and kicked the ball-bone remnant into the fire. The marmoset passed my face to Nell. She took the meat poppadom of me and thanked the marmoset. Her soft fingertips caressed the edge of the skin of my forehead, my cheeks, temples, chin and neck, as, with a fine strand of her golden hair, Nell wove me into and amongst the sea of oval faces.

Cosmic Spin Class on Deck 112

Waiting to be scanned into the Health & Leisure deck, Varde pulls on her blue unitard sleeves. Beneath it, her skin feels too small, but the instructions state the attire is obligatory.

"Eleventh door on the left," the receptionist says. Varde's eyes are questing in the other direction, searching for another glimpse of the happy family: a couple sandwiching a child, swinging in between them, the young boy with dimples like Benjamin had had, five, maybe six Earth years old. It's no use. She gives up. They're lost to the crowds of holidaymakers and off-duty star-sailors. She now only hears the reverberation of his laughter, feels its tight squeeze on her heart. "Your treatment commences in three minutes."

"Sure," Varde replies, her voice reedy, unsure. "Thanks."

The eleventh door opens automatically on her approach. Hydraulic magnets hiss, the noise dissipates, becoming lost between the whirr and flick of wheels. Inside the padded box room are seven others in blue skinsuits, all taking in the blurred projections on the walls and ceiling, all already in their spots, disinterested in her arrival.

The therapist-come-instructor, green unitard, greets Varde, "Welcome to the well-being trial." He guides her to the last vacant fixed-position bicycle, lowers the seat, helps her ascend. "Comfortable?" he asks. The man smacks of vitality. There is no depression in his eyes. His sparkling, amber-tone pupils are not the shade of ghosts, as people have told her hers have become. *He has not seen death*, she thinks. She nods and forces a tight-lipped, defiant smile. *This therapy will not help me.* The instructor returns to the front, mounts his counter-posed bike.

She starts to pedal. It does not come naturally—it has been so long since her calf muscles, her lungs, have felt the burn of exercise. *This will hurt tomorrow,* she thinks, *but it'll be no match for the abyss spreading in my soul.*

Issued with a formal ultimatum by her line manager—take the experimental therapy or return to Earth—she had almost laughed at the irony. *Return* to Earth? She'd never *been* to Earth. Born aboard the ship, like Benjamin, her son, she knew little about the blue-green ball of pollution, and cared less. Intergalactic Cruiser-3024X was her home. She'd remain on board until Death said otherwise. Her own ashes would be ejected and scattered in space, to become stardust once more. This was the done thing for a star-sailor. Why would someone who has spent their life mid-space want to be buried under six foot of gravity-shackled, alien soil?

Nine corrugated tubes concertina down from the ceiling. At the end of each, a mask. Yanking the one above her station down, she follows the direction of the instructor, places it over her mouth and nose, pulls the strap behind her head tight with one hand and maintains her balance with the other. The instructor flicks a switch on his visual display unit. *Phhhssshhhh.* A funky brown gas discharges, steams down the tubing.

"In ... out," the instructor chants, his demonstration mask retracting back up towards the ceiling, "breathe in time with your footwork."

Top notes of portabello carbonara, fusty mildew, something similar to the archaic ale served to old timers down on the retirement deck. Potent aromatic medicinal vapours penetrate her blood-tissue barrier, adulterate each organ, and mess with her intracellular receptors. Her pineal gland welcomes the novel spores. More scented research pharmaceuticals extracted from wounded Tentilus suppurations gush into the confinement of her plastic mask. Her bronchi are flooded and then her alveoli become drenched.

"Faster," the instructor commands.

Her legs birl in time with his vocal outbursts. *This alien pus vapour is repulsive, thank heck this stage is transient,* she reminds herself, and pedals through the insufflations, knowing the mask should deliver oxygen soon.

She closes her eyes, focuses only on breath-work, the push and the pull of the pedals. She feels the accumulation of lactic acid in her thighs and prays for the elusive endorphins to arrive, the healing to begin.

"One two, one two," the instructor counts, his voice providing the only rhythm.

The last words she hears are 'astral projection' and the instructor's voice is replaced with the *thud thud thud* of her heart, the whoosh of blood through her ears. She opens her eyes: the instructor, gone, the other guinea pigs, gone.

Only one cyclist remains, but he's not one who was there before. The feet of this cyclist dangle far from the pedals. Naked bar his underwear, the young boy's countenance is wan, nondescript, and his feverish, dewy skin is riddled with deathly Jupiter Pox. Each papule blackens, becomes a widening black hole.

"Benjamin?" she wants to say but her mouth is useless.

"Pedal faster, Mother." The apparition speaks. Her heart swells, feels like it may burst and open up its red, but it does not. She keeps pedalling, unsure if she's trying to escape or move closer to this diaphanous silhouette of her dead son. The boy, now more pox, more black void, than skin, is vanishing. Leaving her for a second time. Before she has a chance so much as to whisper his name, he becomes devoured by the expanse of galaxial swirling pustules. Gone.

The periphery of her vision—rolling bucolic videodrome—retreats and becomes replaced by darkness as the drug kicks in and she becomes lost in the depths of a cerebral thalassic journey. No longer clad in Lycra, perched on a bike, she now swims: weightless, afraid, but hopeful.

Liberated, she twirls round. Her body glides like oil in water. As she turns, her eyes narrow, her body arches forward, cups back. She draws in sharp a lungful of void. Is she *outside* of the spaceship now?

In front of her, shining like a celestial candelabra, she witnesses it: All Of The Light. Flickering ruby, garnet, and amethyst jewels dimple the incandescent, golden nebula. Colours blare out their majestic orchestral synaesthesia for her eyes only. And her eyes, still squinting, adjust, and with her hands, she paddles backwards through water which is now not water, but the lacuna of deep space, and she looks again and tries to gain a better perspective. Breathing freely, the fungal stench of the drug trial no more, she now inhales sweet star anise, ozone, asteroid gunmetal, and the reminiscent talcy scent of newborn.

And she knows this is not the Eagle Nebulae with its pillars of creation, this is something else, something better, something long forgotten. It encompasses her field of vision. Unclear, diffuse edges form a gentle shape. Undulating ripples of grey-white-orange love frill out, caress and overwhelm her. The colossal interstellar gas cloud rests in the form of a smiling child, a child reclined on its side. Benjamin.

A crack of curved light spreads where his lips would be, a smile. His skinscape is mottled, not with pox this time in this place, but with gigantic, cosmic pools, each constantly in slow labour, forever birthing new stars, new worlds.

The Child Nebula winks at her, a hundred new galaxies spin free from its eye socket, fling into space like exploding plant pods dispersing seeds in high pressure bursts. Varde hears his laughter—*Benjamin*—and then she's back in the box room. Seven blue cyclists and one green instructor surround her. She stops pedalling, pulls off the mask. Her face feels awkward but accommodates well the broad smile now at home on her lips, her spirit once again in tangible harmony with life and all it has to offer.

It is true, she thinks, *stardust. I have seen death and now I have seen re-birth.*

Labourers Wanted

First published by Brigids Gate Press in 2022

Imagine a factory: smokestacks, billowing towers of grey, steel shipyard cranes like giant skeletal arms lumbering crates away. Lamia Factory is nothing like that. It's like none you've ever seen before or ever will again. It's a one-off.

And so are the goods it produces.

My employment at Lamia commenced five months ago. I signed something, some disclaimer form, and since then, they've paid me weekly in cash. I'm still not sure what it is I do here though.

I see the built men with their sharp suits, their fitted earpieces which dangle down below dark-visored helmets, and their firearms tucked not quite out-of-sight. They take long shifts in turn to staff the Guarded Door.

I see the one-time-only employees who come ad hoc. They arrive with lustrous heads of hair and leave with a crop and a fistful of notes.

And I see the real grafters. They're the boxers—gloved and tubi-gripped to the elbows. The boxers get bussed in every weekday from all over the district, as do I.

We all travel on the bus before dawn, but we never talk. We never even look at each other. For each of us, the commute involves a long stare at our own hands and feet.

Before first light, we spill out on foot where the dirt track ends and the bus can go no further, and we stomp towards the factory doors. A handful of us bring small children. The parents disembark first, with young ones in buggies. We push them along the shamble of a forest path which is marked out by dim lamps and slits of moonlight. The boxers help us lift and carry our prams when wheels hitch against rocky outcrops or gnarly tree roots. But silenced by tiredness, none of us speak much with anything more than our eyes.

Once everyone is safe inside—hair donors, boxers, security staff, me— the low-hanging sun slowly singes winter's mackerel skin cloud away from the inky dawn sky.

It's clear where they all go, what they all do. But me? Not a clue.

I know what the factory makes. That much I do know. Myriad cardboard coffins, each the size of a shoebox, will be found piled up near the entrance, waiting for dispatch at dusk. Each box will have a clear, plastic side-panel through which the sleeping face of a life-size, darling, shut-eyed poppet can be seen. The next day, all this stock will have shifted, and, by dusk again, will have been replenished once more. And so, the cycle continues.

Some of the dolls are boxed bald, some are given a dusting of fuzzy peach-skin-down on their heads. Some are decorated with real human hair: red, brown, blonde and black. All the dolls have the softest skin—a silicon or plastic polymer—and they come in a spread of hues, from incandescent porcelain through to midnight.

Each doll has lips like rosebuds, is dreamy-faced and lies deep in imagined slumber.

Each comes with its name imprinted in curlicue font on its packaging.

The boxers call them 'reborns.'

But who buys these inert replicas? Women who've lost? Women who've never had? Someone with a sense of augmented reality who thinks they still have? No idea, but demand seems to be sky-rocketing.

With sleeping-angel faces, human hair, and cream-touch skin, they're without doubt a close match for the real thing, but as they're dolls and lifeless, I find them oddly unnerving.

I can tell you one thing I *don't* do. I *don't* tell my husband I've taken gainful employment. He'd hit the roof and my glass ceiling is six foot two thick and packed in tightly above me to the point of suffocation. I don't think it can be broken. Not yet, anyway. Patience is a virtue.

Lamia is an architectural mongrel. The outside of the factory is made from rough, dark lengths of timber which meld with the forest around it; more thick brown tree thighs, more stacked chocolate gateaux than boxy grey eyesore. Its wooden skin is scattered with one-way windows. Each window is round and dark red like a flat glacier cherry and allows workers to see out but not a soul to peep in. On interview day, I was told the factory was designed by a female architect, built to be harmonious with nature. And I believe it is. It sits swallowed, near invisible from afar, by a pocket of the forest which skirts my home town.

Inside? The decor exudes warmth, harnesses rich shades of flesh, and is padded and comfortable throughout. The candle-lit room where I start my working day feels as snug as a womb: small, well-filled with draped fabrics, packed with plump floor cushions, and a freshly made bed. Lullaby music is piped through every corridor. The crèche is exceptional.

There is this one room, behind the Guarded Door, where the 'industrial machinery' is kept—I wasn't taken there on my induction tour but was warned not to venture in—it's strictly out of bounds.

Trade secrets? you ask. *Temperamental, high-voltage machinery?* I can't recall the reason but was told my contract would be *terminated with immediate effect* if I even stretched an arm through the wipe-clean, peach-coloured, plastic slit-drape-curtain Guarded Door.

I've no desire to, anyway; no urge to see the magic in action.

I'm happy with my adjacent role, whatever it might involve—the work pays well and, in a few weeks, I'll have a deposit for a new home for myself and my bairns. Freedom.

It is Monday and it is winter.

James just left for his office. On his way out, before slamming the door behind him, he threw the sandwiches he'd asked me to prepare at my feet. I'd made egg and cress—not ham. I've since cleaned up the mess.

Both the twins are screaming, disturbed by the coarseness of his words and the rattle of the door no doubt. I need to feed them. My milk always calms. There is enough time before I need to lay them in the double buggy and head off to the bus stop.

I feed my boy, then insert a clean finger and pop his lip from my nipple. I slip him into his snug space in the buggy and then I feed my second baby, my daughter. I walk as I do, her tucked under my arm like a rugby ball, and gather essential belongings in preparation to leave the warmth of the house.

We make the bus in time. It carries us away from the sleepy, lamp-lit streets, and the rows of cheek-by-jowl houses, every other with a chimney coughing out a scarf-of-smoke. Off we go, into the woods. The day is yet to break. One twin burps. I smile at another mother onboard and she smiles back, but then we each focus on our children, our laps, anything else, until the bus slows down and stops.

Both regular and odd questions were asked of me on interview day: how many hours could I work, when could I begin, was I still exclusively breastfeeding? I was offered the job on the spot without full explanation of what my role would involve, but was informed that my children and I would be provided with the best healthcare in the country and assured that no harm would come to any of us while under the employment of Lamia. The interview had been curt, but when they showed me the crèche and informed me of the rates of pay, I couldn't refuse the position.

Each day on arrival, I drop the twins off in the crèche and make my way on hands and knees through the dark, tapered tunnel all the way in to the milking room.

At my booth, underfloor heating pulses waves of pleasant warmth in sync with my every in- and exhalation.

"Please, take a moment to rest," the automated voice says through the intercom system.

With almost a sentient charm and clarity, it instructs me to hook myself up to the pumping system. I pull the silken curtain around my velour dorm, slip off my shirt and brassiere, and hang them on the hook. Then, I recline on the gurney, which creaks like geriatric joints. I take a moment to bring the laundered linen to my nose. It smells like sweet lavender. Then, I reach for the two dangling silicon cups.

When I first started, any queries I had about which tube, which cup, which bag went where were answered almost before I'd had a chance to give voice to my question. Answers came with a maternal knowing from the robotic female voice. Now it comes as second nature.

Once attached to my breasts, the machine clunks on. The tranquil sound of gentle suction switches on, off, on, off, on, off.

"Allow your eyes to rest," she suggests, and as a tired mother of two nursing twins, who am I to contest?

I drop off shortly after whirr and buzz and suck reach full pace and doze while the machine takes the milk my babies need for their time in the crèche. After my milk's been extracted, I'm sure she whispers further instructions of what I need to do to complete my shift. But time and color blur past, all fever dream, all jumbled thought.

Seven or eight hours pass, then I'm notified: "Your shift is complete," and I hear a mechanical sigh followed by the dulcet tones once more of the piped factory lullaby. One enchanting melody pours through the speakers on loop. It's a tune composed entirely of vocals, in a key that's not yet been invented. I'm certain I'll never grow tired of hearing it.

I'm fully clothed again yet still lying on the reclined gurney. There's a blanket over my knees, a warm cup of tea to my side, a selection of biscuits on a bone china plate, and I've a ravenous appetite. It's time to crawl back, collect my bundles of joy, and catch the bus home.

It's Tuesday. I've been weeping. James screamed at me again in the night. I'd asked for help at three in the morning whilst trying to settle one of the twins. I'd spent most of the ice-cold night trapped in my nursing chair with a feeding baby on my lap. My blanket had been just a little out of reach.

"Get it yourself, bitch. Don't wake me again. I need my sleep," he'd said.

I think I managed to sob myself back to sleep at four.

I make him a coffee at half five before he sets off for the city.

"You can't even make decent coffee. Useless," he says after his first sip. Then he tips the rest onto the rug in the hallway, the artisan weave Mother left me. All the while he sneers at me, with a mean streak in his green eyes. Each time he is cruel, his face becomes more distorted, uglier, more alien.

Black liquid pools on the wool. Sour.

I manage to hold back more tears until he slams the door. Farewell. From outside, he bends down and shouts back in through the letterbox at me.

"Those little parasites probably aren't even mine anyway." Then he beeps open the central locking of his four-by-four, gets in it, and leaves for work.

How on earth could they not be his? They both have his complexion, his green eyes—eyes he once looked at me through with desire and lust. Although I'm not sure now that he has ever looked at me with love.

At least I get to nap at work.

I kiss my twins and we set off for the bus, for the factory.

It's Friday. James came at me with a rolling pin yesterday, threatened to silence me and the 'screaming monsters' forever. I sat up most of last night, rocking my babies in their cribs to try and keep them asleep. Who knows what he'd have done if they'd have woken him? His rage is growing.

It's Monday. There are far fewer workers on board the bus this morning. A mother speaks to me *en route* to the factory today to inform me of a rumour. She takes my hand in hers and tells me a child managed to escape the crèche yesterday, at some point over the weekend shift. A toddler. The child made his way past the guard and into the area he shouldn't have been in. Somehow, he crawled through the Guarded Door.

She looks straight into my eyes and I feel something squeeze my heart as she tells me she is as desperate for money as I appear to be. Can't afford to lose her job, or she would *quit immediately*, like the other mothers who have heard the talk.

"Is he okay, the bairn?" I ask, stomach a-churn. She squeezes my hand a little harder and informs me the babe, the little boy who crept into the Mother Machine, is apparently fine.

Unharmed, she says, *but hasn't made a sound since.* She releases my hand and whispers more: *He's had his laughter stolen. His voice— It's gone.* How can a voice be stolen? Ludicrous. My twins, they're too young to get about anyway. I push my concerns back down.

The bus slows as it reaches the end of the dirt track and off we get. Part of me wants to turn around and make my way back home, but the lion's share of me is more afraid of spending another month with James, so I press onwards and try to block dark thoughts.

It's Friday. My boy rolled over for the first time this morning. I didn't tell James. Can't look him in the eye anymore.

Each day is pure terror. I'm unable to rest at home and home is no longer a home. It's been reduced to a mere house. A house I can't wait to flee. I've enough saved. Nearly. A few more shifts and I'll be on my way.

I unwrap and re-wrap the silver-red wound on my arm. Exposing to the air, it oozes yellow-white fluid and infection. Yesterday, James branded me with the sharp metal tri-tip of the hot iron. I'd failed to press his shirts correctly. What followed that is too difficult to put into words. Let us just say I've had enough. The dawn air today is as iced as my heart. The white of my breath hangs in the air. I swaddle my boy and my girl with three extra layers. We leave the house and head out for work.

We wait alone, at the bus stop. Staff numbers have decimated, but I'm still keen to earn, keen to manifest my own escape. I see the full beam of the bus headlamps creeping up the road but I also see the lights and hulk of my husband's four-by-four travelling in the opposite direction. He must be returning home, must've forgotten something. I'm ripe with panic. He'll notice I'm not there. Will he find the stack of notes I pulled out from the teddy bear in search of change for the bus? Can he see me now, from his car as he spins past?

I crouch. An attempt to hide. I rock the pram back and forth to keep the small ones happy. Then the bus pulls up. I quickly embark. My heart is thumping but I've no choice but to board. I could turn and go home and face him, but then I'd be sure to lose my job and my only shot at an escape.

The bus trundles up to the edge of the path that leads to the factory. No smoke plumes out from the building, and I observe for the first time that no electrical wires, cables, or infrastructure connect it to the rest of civilization. I'm still shaking with panic. The irregular, wooden walls, that encase all that rests within, appear to breathe in and out in time with the fast charge of my own heart. I walk with pace towards the entrance.

Over the crunching of feet and pram wheels on leaves, I swear I hear a call—a deep voice—from the darkness behind me. I turn around and pause, deer in headlights. It's nothing; perhaps a nocturnal animal, a fox or badger, assembling its family before sunrise.

I keep moving. A noise. I turn again, swear I see something move, something tall, some shape ominous. Lightless flesh like wind darts behind a tree. I start to push the buggy faster, with more force, and I find myself running towards the throbbing pink entrance light which hangs above the factory door.

We make it inside. Safe.

I kiss my babes farewell, leave them at the crèche, and head off for the milking suite. This is when I see him through the one-way window. He *did* see me. He *has* followed me. He's running, looks livid. What if he catches me here? What will he do? To me?

I panic and look across at the guard by the Guarded Door, the door with the neon signage above it and on it. The door with signage which proffers implicit instruction that what is behind the door is 'strictly out of bounds.'

I know my husband, I know what he's capable of, so I make a rash decision to scream.

Dropping to my knees, I make a puddle of myself at the entrance to the tunnel which leads to the milking suite. The guard hears me and runs straight over to my aid.

My husband, with his angry eyes—he's on the hunt for me. He barges in through the factory entrance. I make sure he doesn't see me collapsed here on the floor. Drawing my index finger up to my lips, I beg the guard with the drill of my widened, wet eyes to do nothing.

Please remain still, leave my husband be. Just continue to do nothing but shield me with your giant frame. Hide me from my husband.

I mouth, "Please," to the guard and point to the bandages on my arms.

James does not see me or the guard at the entrance to the tunnel, but he does see the Guarded Door with its hanging flaps of plastic and neon warning signs. Sweet lullabies emanate loudly through the pipework, masking the sounds of the concealed machine carrying out its labour. James runs to the door. Of course, he runs to the door—because the door is telling him directly not to.

He elbows through the peach plastic and guttural screams fill the air. But it's not his voice. It's the voice of the machine.

Loud, shrill, sentient. It's almost deafening from where I'm lying. The entire building quivers. The floor lifts up at one side, tips, and creates a slope of the whole hallway. My water bottle slides out of my bag and rolls away. The factory walls bow inwards and squeeze me closer to the guard in black. The entrance of the tunnel exhales, narrows. There's a jolt. The floor re-levels but the screeching continues and the ground beneath us still feels unstable.

We grip each other for safety. His face is printed with terror, but in this moment, as our eyes meet again, the guard remembers his role—to defend the workers or protect the machinery, I'm no longer sure which—and he pushes my hand from his arm.

"I'm sorry. I've got to do my job," he whispers.

I try to stand and try to hold back the guard, but he is two, maybe three of me, and his face is no longer full of panic but determination. I let go of his sleeve.

The guard pulls down his visor of blackened Perspex, reaches for his firearm, and forces his way through the Guarded Door. He is moving towards the heart of the factory. And as he steps into the forbidden zone where the dolls are made, are born, every ounce of the building screams.

It's too late for James. His cries wail over the abrasive noise of the screeching machine and its clashing eternal lullaby. James screams. James's screaming is longer and louder than any woman who's ever given birth, but no new life is being made in this moment though. That I can tell.

He stops screaming, the machine stops screaming, the building stops squeezing and shaking and tilting, and I hear a thud and I know the weight of the bully that is my husband and I know it's his body dropping to the floor like a de-strung marionette.

There's silence for a moment, until: "Eyes! EYES!" A shout. This new voice pierces clarion through the speaker system and it's not the soothing voice of the milking chamber bot.

Shortly after this outburst, the angelic harping music returns to the air. Louder, sweeter, more tuneful and merrier than before.

And then, the new automated voice pipes out again, over the lullaby tune. And I know, this time, it's addressing *me*.

"You're required in the milking suite. You're five minutes late for your shift."

I gather my belongings and shuffle on hands and knees down through the tapering, dark tunnel towards the milking chamber where I'll provide the milk my babies will need for the day ahead, so I can complete my shift. So I can do whatever it is I do.

I arrive, unbutton my blouse, and reach for the suction cups. I'm glad to lie back on the wheeled bed. I'm in need of a little rest.

It is Spring. I've weaned both my darling babies over the last few weeks. My once-wet breasts are now liberated from their role in motherhood. I feel well rested now, born again now I'm dry. Now they're both that bit older, we all sleep through the night too.

Earlier this week, I received a letter and a parcel from the factory. The letter stated that they've terminated my contract with immediate effect. No reason was given other than that I was *'no longer fit for purpose.'* At least the letter came with a leaving gift.

My gift? A boxed doll, of course. A doll with big green eyes—just like the twins have. Like James had.

I've three children now: the twins—one boy, one girl—who will forever be free to sing and twirl and dance with laughter, full of the joys of spring. And my third, this doll. The doll is an absolute darling—he never cries—and his rosebud lips are fixed in one position, suckling, and they're fashioned from the softest, special polymer, a Lamia-patented material. But he never sleeps; appears to be cursed with eternal insomnia. Poor thing—he looks shattered.

And his green eyes seem hexed, full of fear. He looks petrified no matter what I do to try to soothe him.

So, I keep him in his cardboard box, which has his curlicue name, James, printed on the side.

And I keep the box under my bed.

Every now and again, in the darkness of the night, I'll take him out, place my hand over his face—so I don't have to look in his eyes—and I'll hold him against my bare breast. We'll have a little cuddle. He has such creamy-soft skin, and I can't get enough of his newborn baby smell, of mother's milk. Lamia really nailed a likeness.

Today, I saw the guard who followed my children's father into the core of Lamia's machinery wandering in the woods. I recognized his suit and visor, the identification number on his epaulettes.

Most days, I'll walk under the forest canopy with the twins—the woods are the most beautiful kind of haunted. The guard appeared to be still searching for the factory, but I know he'll never find it.

He lifted his visor and nodded as we passed. We shared a reserved greeting with just our eyes, no words. Then, side by side, we stood and stared at the vast swathe of dead earth, at the mounds of soil and leaf litter that have been left behind from where the foundations, the thick thighs of oak, the rooted planks of wood that once anchored the factory in place, had pulled themselves up from the forest floor. At the end of my last shift, the guard and I had watched from the bus stop as the wood of the factory walls split free and shook out into many giant tree stump legs.

The beautiful factory—mother machine and wooden frame—lifted herself up from her spot and scarpered away like a blown cumulus, free.

We both witnessed her colossal retreat from her pocket of forest, watched her become gulped up by thick woodland, saw her take off in search of pastures new.

I understand, and I wish her well. When a woman wants out, she wants out.

But I don't think the guard believed his eyes.

All the Parts of a Mermaid that I Can Recall

First published by Dark Matter Ink, 2023

The longer I stare at it, the more I'm certain it's not the correct way up. I didn't think I was a tattoo person, yet, here I am, trapped in an unfamiliar room, all 'inked up.'

When did I get it done, and by whom? And why can't I remember the reason for getting it etched onto the flesh of my upper arm *upside down*?

My eyesight seems subpar, in spite of the raw brightness of this room. From what I can see of this fresh image scored below my shoulder—from the parts of it I can make out—it appears to resemble a fish-woman.

A tail, I see her tail, is it called a tail? Each rose-coloured, thumbnail-shaped scale glints under these harsh strip lights as I move my arm gently. Gently is as much as I can bear. And what is that? Her red caudal fin? Ah, I see her all now, I think. Her body stretches out, extends around the sagging skin of my upper arm. I can't decide if it's a work of beauty, this mark, or something else entirely. Is it art, or merely an eyesore? It's certainly sore, I'll give you that.

The breasts, they're a little further towards my elbow. Magnificent. Two pert nipples have been covered by the artist with long, red-inked snaking tendrils of crimson hair. Such unbelievable texture. Every lock writhes, giving the appearance that she is alive, this maiden with flowing hair. So vivid. Each strand of hair is a glistening movement of red; the colours are holographic. Almost.

It's her. I'm sure it is. The artist has captured her fair side and chosen to hide the half of her scalp, which, I think, had peeled away, been left undone and exposed. Yes. Shaved free of lustrous locks, one half of her head had been thrumming with what I'd presumed were maggots; pulsating with infested, suppurating growths.

Yes, it is a good likeness of her. Yes, her, I remember her now. My stomach turns at the thought of her open skull, her razor-tooth smile; but despite these horrors, oh, how my heart yearns for her enchanting sound.

While I have your attention, please, hear my story as it returns to me. Listen well, friend; understand why I need out of here. I need to get back to my barn.

We'd been at sea and had decided to set back to the harbor. We yearned for the safety of sand, and the way it would become hard, steady rock beneath our boots. My crew and I had been out for days and had achieved a great haul, but a storm had brewed in our path.

It seems so cruel, deeply unfair, that I, captain and sole survivor, hold alone the burden of recounting this event, and that all of you, who've listened to me this morning, have tried to counter my account of what happened.

A great wave crashed down on my humble vessel, dipped her at the bow. I should've gone down then with the others, as an honourable captain should. But instead, I jumped overboard, into the rowboat which I'd lowered from the side of the trawler.

From there, afloat, I watched my crew tumbleweed down the deck, into the cold, cold arms of the ocean. Screams for help were met with no reply. My fishing boat, my pride and joy—I watched her as she sank.

I must've drifted for days. Blazing sunshine, sharp ocean spray, and dehydration took turns to rouse me from consciousness. And then, when I'd nearly given up hope, on the third day lost at sea, possibly the fourth—my concept of time has become quite distorted—I heard her: Attina. Attina, with the voice of an angel. I heard her sing as I drifted. Her melody brought me back from wherever my mind had sailed away. Through the words in the songs she sang to me, I knew I'd been rescued.

Alana brought me fresh drinking water, mopped my brow, warbled sweet lullabies to me, for minutes, hours, years. Her magical singing voice, backed by the gentle breaking of waves on sand, was a healing, celestial comfort as I recovered on the shore.

From her lips, each honeyed note strung out into the atmosphere as if from a well-plucked harp. Eventually, when I was able to walk—hobble really—she guided me to a sheltered alcove. Each day, or each hour—I'm unsure how often she visited, please forgive my salt-addled mind—she came and tended to me, all the while, singing her songs. What a beautiful creature.

Alas, when my vision returned and my eyes adjusted to the darkness, I managed to focus in on her. Grave disappointment and an unnerving dread followed.

One side of her face was plain. Not offensively so, but nothing to write home about either. But the other side—the thought of it still unsettles me now—a hideous mess of maggots pulsating on the edge of a glitching, bottomless abyss. And when she smiled, *those teeth!* More blades than a butcher's knife block.

I asked her to face away as she sang, contemplated asking her to leave me alone entirely; the quivering, opened half of her disturbed scalp was almost too much to bear. But her voice—her voice was divine, a gift. I closed my eyes instead and let her music wash over me.

Adella sang about her people, the Mers, the people of the sea; how they sought revenge on the trawlers ravaging their oceans, raping and pillaging their fish-stock. They believed the sea belonged to them! Or that was my interpretation.

Her healing songs, bent with violent words, continued to unfurl. She sang to me the tale of how her people, hybrid beasts of fish and human, caused mishap to my boat, how they lured my half-drowned sailors, their lungs topping up with brine, into storms and towards sharp rocks with their voices. Through her harmonious lyrics, I heard how the corpses of my crew had been dragged to the bottom of the ocean, as playthings for her family.

So, as soon as I was better, I struck her over the head with a rock, knocked her out completely, and stole her from the beach.

She screamed out hateful songs when she roused, as I hoisted her slimy body over my shoulder, yet still, despite the rage, there was beauty in her music.

Her tail, which had shone iridescent in the shallow waters of the cave when she'd rested next to me, appeared grey and dull, and felt like iron wool against my skin as it dried. She would not quieten. I had to drop her and gag her with a length of fibrous bladderwrack, which was a shame. I did not want to draw attention, didn't want anyone to rob this gift of her away from me, so she remained gagged for the short struggle home.

She kicked hard—if kick is even the right way to describe the squirm of an angered mermaid: half piscine tail, half breast, flesh, razor-blade-toothed jaw, festering scalp, and hair. The journey back to my countryside cottage was tough, but I'd do it all again.

I locked her in the bathroom while I constructed a better home for my songful muse. It took a week, longer perhaps—in truth I have no idea—but when she saw the three-metre cubic tank of reinforced Perspex I'd constructed in the corner of my otherwise empty barn, I knew she was impressed. Knew she was ecstatic because she said nothing. Silence. She voluntarily stopped singing for the first time. No song fell from her lips.

I tipped her in. She protested to begin with, then relented, realising surely what a gift her new tank was. Perfect fit. Like a horse in a stall, blinkered between two planked-wood walls. In her glass-like box, she was safe. I filled it two-thirds with water and added a hanging ledge of ply for her to perch on so she could get out of the water and sing.

With the lid clamped down, I told her I'd be back with fresh kelp for breakfast, and waved farewell. She sang back, from her tank—beautiful, if a little shaky. She said she'd prefer Slim Jim smoked sausage sticks, but if they were unavailable, kelp would suffice. I said I'd see what I could do.

She did not smile, though, as I backed out of my barn, as I left her to return to my cottage and sleep in the comfort of my own bed. I strolled up the path to my home, wondering where one could buy Slim Jim smoked sausage sticks at midnight in such an isolated place, and I stopped to ponder over this by my back door.

Could I hear her singing? Yes, yes, I could. What a magnificent sound. She'd started to sing again. *Mission accomplished*, I'd thought, and had patted myself on the back. Although, as my ears attuned and picked up on her lyrics once more, I noticed she was singing quite ruefully this time. Different songs to the ones she'd chanted while I'd healed in the cave.

That first night, back in my cottage, I had to sleep with cotton wool in my ears, and all my windows closed, so her voice would not pull me into a depression.

Late the next morning, I took her down a platter of green fruits from the sea and the Slim Jim smoked sausage sticks she'd requested, and again, I heard such saddening, bittersweet tunes coming out from her tank.

She devoured the food, without thanks, but I let this lack of gratitude slip. It can take time to settle in somewhere new, can't it? Which reminds me, listener: where am I now? What is this place? And when may I return to her?

Please. Set me free, she'd begged, I remember that. Over and over, she'd pleaded, her melodious voice wavering like a heavenly theremin. She'd spun in her tank, scowled, flicked water at me as a breaching humpback might do where I'd displaced the lid to feed her.

After such a childish tantrum, she floated there, limp, hiding her ample bosom from me by facing into the corner.

Arista, sing only pleasant songs for me, that is why I brought you here, I said.

She spun back to face me. A strip of light breaking through a crack in the barn roof fell on her, highlighting her ugly side. Her long locks were absent on this side of her head. Odd-shaped bumps distorted the area, and from it, crimson streaks throbbed and ribboned into the water. Hideous. So, I sealed the gap with a nailed plank and left her in darkness.

For days I left her alone to teach her a lesson, but the volume of her songs only grew; so beautiful, but so sad. I couldn't bear it. From every room in my small countryside cottage a stone's throw from the beach, and even from halfway down the road, I heard her sad voice wailing funeral rhymes. It's a blessing my home is so desolate; if I did have neighbours, no doubt through tear-filled eyes, they would've complained about the racket.

Please tell me when, listener, will I be released so I can return to her?

I could take it no more. She needed an ultimatum, though I'm not proud of what I did next. Now, as I lie here, I worry, because I no longer hear her voice—is my Andrina okay?

Dear listener, in your clinical attire, please help me escape the woman in the yellow anorak and the infant with a face I care not for, who together, claim to be my family. They're unstable, desperate for a piece of my precious Aquata perhaps? Aquata must have financial worth. Not that I'd sell her. I wish for her to sing sweetly again, forever, just for me, in my barn.

Let me explain the sequence of events, perhaps then you'll see my situation. I went into my barn, that I clearly remember; yet what followed is less than clear. I think I told her to lower her volume and put a stop to all the heart-wrenching songs. *You must only sing cheerful tunes*, I'd said, *this is why I took you, gave you this opportunity.*

I remember her voice growing louder, from the dark corner of my outhouse. I recall the swoosh of her tail as she batted it against her tank. Her indecipherable chorus caused me physical pain. The words scratched like claws on glass inside my skull.

She, then—the very audacity of it—gave *me* an ultimatum: *swim to the floor of the ocean and retrieve my glowing orb*, she'd sung, *and in exchange, I'll grant you your demand and only sing happy songs.*

Her melodious racket hurt my head so much, I had no choice but to obey. *You've been a bad boy, a very big, very bad boy,* she'd continued, *and I'll only sing sad songs. Loudly. Unless you retrieve my glowing orb.*

Returning to the ocean was not something I enjoyed. After all, my last fishing venture had ended in disaster. Yet I found myself paddling out, until the sand became nothing but a beige line atop a grey line. Then I dove down.

The water—clear, silver, black—pressed cold against my skin. I swam deeper and deeper, descended through the zones: sunlight, twilight, midnight, abyssal. I kicked and scooped until I reached the hadal zone, and there I saw the glowing orb she'd described.

But as I approached it, reached out to claim the prize, excited for my reward, I realised she'd fooled me.

Teeth. Such sharp teeth. Multiple serrated marine fangs. A ring of smoke-yellow teeth, larger than my own circumference. It was no magical orb she'd sent me questing for, but the barb of an angler fish. And it was too late; I'd reached for its bait. The jaws of this other beast, this all-fish apex predator of the underwaters, closed around me. Glass-sharp points pierced through my head and my upper left arm. And that is the last thing I remember.

And now I'm here, strapped to a narrow excuse for a bed. The coastguard must've pulled me from the ocean, I must've near-drowned a second time. I'm lucky; blessed. Or perhaps, my Arial commandeered her sea-people with her angelic voice, and they carried my body ashore? She does care. We're linked, she and I, by something magical.

How tough it is to be in love with someone you adore yet also despise and can't get out of your head. Why can I no longer hear her melody? This silence is deafening. I must get out of here, must get back to my barn. She'll need her Slim Jims soon.

No barn you say? Don't be ludicrous. Although, that is what the woman with the anorak who claims to be my wife said too. She said I live in a terraced townhouse with her and a child. Witchcraft, all of this. I demand to be released. Stay away from me, stay back. Fetch me your supervisor.

You think so? You've an explanation for this? You're questioning *my* truth? I would laugh if it didn't hurt. Tell me then, fill me in, unleash your delusions. You must be in collusion with her, the anoraked woman who was here when I awoke, the one with the child glued to her side, the pair of them with all the tears in their eyes.

No, no, ridiculous. Of course it's a tattoo. A tattoo of a mermaid. Look, here: her tail, the scales. No, don't show me yours. Put your arm away. Stay back!

"Sir, it's not a tattoo, it's an open wound. We removed the multimedia User Interface panel from your arm. See, here's mine, still connected, wired into my nervous system—this is what yours looked like before surgery. We got it all out, from your arm, and the visual discs from your retinas. But ... we need to talk about the situation in your cortex."

What? What the hell is that thing in your arm? Get away from me. I demand to see your superior. This is abuse. What are you trying to do to me with this black magic? Get away. Let me out of here, please, before she returns, the lady with the ghastly anorak, the child.

They're trying to steal me away. I've no idea what their intentions are, but I need to head back towards the coast, to my barn. Why can I no longer hear my mermaid sing? Is she floating in her tank, pelvic fin side up?

"Sir, there is no mermaid. No tank. You've experienced serious problems with your multimedia neuro-implant, largely due to the source and quality of the media you've been uploading. Let me explain again. Where shall we start? The matter of unpaid library fines for one loaned children's brain-book, The Little Mermaid 2: Return to the Sea—"

But ... don't have a child.

"And one further fine for the overdue short-term loan of Attenborough's The Blue Planet. And Sir, with respect, you have an eight-year-old daughter, Matilda, big Disney

and wildlife fan. You also illegally burned several copies of Bjork's Greatest Hits and tried to sell this ripped braincode via black market VR distribution sites. There are a few other issues that have also come to our attention—"

Lies! And why are you speaking to me in this way, rolling your eyes, as if this is not the first time we've had this conversation? Let me out of here, untether me now.

"I'm afraid we can't do that. You're still recovering from your User Interface extraction surgery, and there are still unpaid fines on your account. Your arm should heal—we've managed to extricate the entirety of the UI device, but I'm afraid there may not be anything else we can do."

Recovering from what?

"There's evidence you've uploaded illicit, pirated code into your multimedia brain implant device, including but not confined to: unregulated copies of The Perfect Storm, Jaws, and Titanic (2028). Our investigation systems have also detected a Slim Jim smoked sausage advertising virus, which probably came with the most likely cause of the cortex damage you're experiencing—we discovered a large quantity of DarkNet-sourced misogynistic pornographic material in your brain drive. The illicit content seems to have triggered malicious neuroplasticity which seems to have caused nano-sedimentation in your brain. The damage is too vast, inoperable. We did try—we took out a little of your cortex—and you're currently on a high dose of antibiotic code which we're mainlining in via this temporary USB port which we've installed above your left ear to reduce the chance of further infection. But we can't promise we can eradicate all the corrupt files. The head pain you're experiencing should diminish, but the disorientation ... we're not sure there's anything further we can do."

You. Yes you. Help me down from this bed. That tuneless mess of a woman returned, this time without the infant. Told me she paid my fines, said I was welcome home whenever I was ready, and then she left, but not before slipping me her address on a piece of paper. I, of course, tossed it into the bin.

I'm vexed. I haven't heard my mer-woman's song for months now. I've tried to sleep here, in this strip-lit, medical bed; tried to close my sore eyes, but all I see is her split skull rotting, and her lifeless, starved body, floating in her tank in the dark corner of my barn. Sometimes I see her suspended there, nictitating in and out of sight, even with my eyes open. I can't allow for this to happen. I can't allow her to die. I have to find her and make her sing again.

Thank you. Thank you for finally releasing me from this room. I'm adamant, as I leave this godforsaken place, that if I keep on walking, out of the city, towards the coastline, I'll hear her sing once more. Sad songs, happy songs, any songs—I don't care anymore what it is she sings. But I must keep walking until I find her.

Every Cloud

First published by Bandit Fiction, 2021

Each paper cut I have ever received has brought on an April shower, irrespective of the season. Each grazed knee has brought forward a monsoon.

For a time, in my teens, I would experiment with the sharp end of the compass from my trigonometry set. When I had mastered some control over my power, I used it to my advantage. I'd etch crossed eyes, a wobbly grin with a tongue poking from it onto the back of my hand—Nirvana—and I'd squeeze for the red and wait for the rain to come.

I used my skill to bring on poor weather every Wednesday at three, after enduring double maths. I enjoyed mathematics, but I didn't enjoy the hockey which followed, so I'd sit at the back of the classroom, balance my text book upright on the desk to create an opaque windscreen, then I'd drive the stainless steel needle back and forth through my skin; just enough. Red would flow and rain would start, pitter-patter, and hockey practice would get called off. Another Wednesday afternoon would be spent in the library instead of out on the cold pitch. Huddled up with a book, I'd pretend to read whilst listening to the syncopated drumming of water on the roof, while occasionally dabbing the back of my hand with blue tissue, until home time came.

Eventually, a teacher noticed what I was doing. Referred me for counselling. I didn't bother explaining to the biscuit-proffering serious lady with the half-moon glasses how much I hated sport, or how I despised having to change into my gym kit in front of the other girls—all curves, all hair—as I stood, ashamed, flat and smooth. I certainly didn't bother to mention to her how I controlled the weather with my bodily fluids. I presumed everyone could do this.

I stopped cutting myself in Year Thirteen. The skin on the back of my hand had grown tired of it all anyway, and Ms. Clark took away my trigonometry set.

My father liked a ladder and a power tool. I remember vividly, aged nine, the time he called for me to help him. I had been sitting in the garden. My dolls were drinking 'iced lemon tea' concocted with leaves from Mum's begonias and crud from the compost heap.

The first time my father called out politely, I ignored him, as was standard practice in our house—I had been too engaged in my game for whatever beetle or flower he'd wished to show me.

The second time he yelled out my name, however, it came from somewhere guttural.

On gaining my attention, I ran up the grey path to the large bush and came face to face with the yellow legs of his tallest ladder.

"What is it, Dad? Have you found another nest?"

"Get your mother," he replied. I saw the hedge-trimmer several metres away on the ground, burning back and forth its toothed saw, buzzing hungrily. My father was at the top of the ladder, not holding his power tool.

"Now," he shouted. It was then I saw the blood. This wasn't trigonometry blood, the type which could be caught and spread on blue tissue, folded and pressed into teenage Rorschach ink blot tests (butterfly wings, curled babies, faces of the damned). This was adult-sized blood. Blood that could be collected in demijohns and vases. This blood pumped out, erupted in bursts into the air, and splattered onto leaves and his shirt. It came in flurries keeping time with my own heartbeat and with each squeeze of his. It made a mess of his top. And the buddleia.

"She's in the kitchen," I said. My father vomited into the space between us. I ran to find her as the spray of sick hailed down onto the path behind me; I, Napalm Girl, all flailing limbs, him, hand and throat, explosive. It sounded like the start of a storm. I discovered my mother chopping offal, and brought her out to Dad. She helped my father down from the ladder and steadied him into the car, taking most of his weight despite being half his size. His face became as pallid as the cloud that had drawn over the sun and as ghostly as the bath towel Mother had yanked from the washing line to wrap around his hand and stump. This white towel however, became deep red by the time we arrived at the hospital.

"Carry this, keep it steady. Don't look inside," Mum said. Her hands shook as she passed me something gift-sized and wrapped in a clean tea-towel. I held the tip of his finger in that Tupperware box for three miles and never once looked at it. Every time my father screamed in pain, I was reminded that it was there, dying, cell by cell. He screamed, a lot. But he never shed a tear.

"Your father has lost several pints of blood," said the surgeon who came to speak to us as my father lay heavily medicated in a faraway room. "But he should make a full recovery." I wanted to ask how they knew. How did they know how much blood had drained and spurted out from him—had they weighed him? It? Did they top him back up? I imagined three glass jugs full to the lip with his equivalent loss inside sat on the windowsill of the ward, waiting to be tipped back down his stump before they could reattach the nail nubbin. He'd been very lucky. *People die from lesser injuries,* so the surgeon informed us.

Despite all his blood loss, it hadn't rained at all that day. So that is how I knew I was different to my father.

Mother bled from her gums when she brushed her teeth. Father said a grey cloud followed her wherever she went, but her leaking gums never made it rain. She was not a wet person. In fact, as she grew older, she became drier. I kept a chart for a while, of the times I'd seen her spit red with white when we got ready together in the bathroom, before my breasts came, before I was made to use the downstairs bathroom alone. There seemed to be no significant overlap between her bleeding from her mouth and the weather, so that is how I knew we were different.

But each of the three times she lost an adult tooth, someone our family knew died.

A great uncle died first. Someone we'd spent summer with years ago, but whose appearance I cannot recall. Next, an elderly lady with a face like a brain coral who smelled sulphurous and sickly, like science experiments.

Before she died, she visited every few weeks and coerced my mother to buy toiletries which stank of chemicals from a small catalogue. She would stand on our doorstep and talk at Mother about how her husband, whom none of us ever met, was having problems with his prostrate. I'd heard her sales pitch so many times I'd looked the word up in the library dictionary whilst avoiding hockey on a wet Wednesday. Made no sense to me why a man would spend so long lying face down when there was so much to see in the world. Perhaps he was afraid of his wife's brain coral face. Or the rain.

It was a relief when she passed, the doorstep catalogue lady, although no-one said so out loud. None of us liked the pungent fragrances in the shower gels which had accumulated in the bathroom. We all said that out loud, and even at the age of ten, I could read between the lines.

I bought my first pair of heels when I was thirteen. Of course, they made me bleed. I walked two miles into town in the bastard footwear, without socks on, to try and break them in. Imitation leather won the battle. By the time I'd reached Our Price—to rummage through the cassette bargain bin—my heels were in agony. I wedged tissue down the back of my shoes to sop up some of the blood, but it stung so badly. I took off the shoes, slung them into my bag, and walked through town barefoot. A murder-scene trail of blood played out behind me as I marched to the bus stop.

Of course, the heavens opened as soon as my heel skin broke. As soon as the first red drop trickled down my heel, along the ridge of the shoe and made its way to the front of my foot, the bad weather came on. I got drenched as I waited for the bus. The rain came down sideways. As did my eyeliner.

The first time I bled from my vagina, lightning and thunder joined the party. It started in the night. I remember waking damp and warm in my bed, the smell of copper pennies. I switched on my bedside lamp, looked between my legs, expecting a river of sweat to be flowing out from the space between my thighs, like my dream had suggested. But it was not sweat, it was blood.

Mother had prepared me for this day. She'd shown me a leaflet that came with a pack of pads which resembled small mattresses. She put the pads in my underwear drawer, and I put the pamphlet in the bin. School told us *enough blood to fill an egg cup will come out each month, along with an unused egg.* I saw no egg as I pawed through the mess on my sheets, using tissues to try and clean it up, although—the gloop did have the texture of clotted yolk. Mother heard the thunder too that night and she came into my room.

"Get the pads," she said. "Go and wash yourself. Then put on new sheets." We never spoke about that night again.

It felt most unnatural, wearing a pad, like straddling a hot-dog bun. I couldn't get back to sleep, even with fresh sheets, so instead of trying, I sat on my windowsill in the dark and watched the rain pour down outside.

It rained for five days straight and then ended abruptly, and the eleventh pad in the pack remained white.

As I grew older, my monthlies became heavier, and with them, the weather grew worse.

In my mid-twenties, a camping trip was abandoned as I came on in the night. I'd an idea it was coming—grey clouds gathered in the late afternoon sky and my stomach cramped, dealing itself with internalised thunder. I left the others to toast marshmallows and swig warm beer from plastic cups while I curled up in my sleeping bag. It had been the middle of summer, and I woke in the night. I'd leaked from the 'heavy flow' pad stuck in my knickers. My torch beam revealed clots of congealed red stuck to the lining of my sleeping bag as the tent also started to leak. I screwed the sleeping bag up into a bin bag and wiped myself down with an old T-shirt minutes before my friend awoke too.

Water poured in on us through a slit in the canvas, and the wind picked up outside. Drops of rain the size of golf balls pounded down, making warzone sounds as blood gushed from me. I was leaking from the inside out and also from the outside in. We packed down and abandoned ship. Must have been three in the morning. After an hour bent over, yanking out pegs in horizontal rain, we managed to fold everything up sloppily into the boot of our car and drive all the way home. I spent the rest of the week in bed with a cold. It rained until my period finished.

I found it hard to tell people about my power, and with time, I learnt people didn't really want to know.

A boyfriend ended things with me shortly after I'd explained I couldn't go boating at the weekend—it was my time of the month, and bad things might happen at sea. Or out on the lake.

"When I bleed, it rains," I said to him.

"It's not me, it's you," he replied.

Many years later, in my mid-thirties, I met a man who understood me. I told him my truth over coffee, after we'd decided to move in together. I thought it best he know, before contracts were signed, dates set—he'd find out eventually. Some people can handle the rain, and always carry an umbrella. Others, not so much.

"Sometimes when I bleed, the weather changes. For the worse," I said. He bit into his lemon drizzle cake. His eyes always shone kindness, like the sun. This was one of the reasons why I loved him.

"I understand," he said. "My mother used to get that too." He kissed me and told me when it rained, he'd be there to make a rainbow. Then he offered up a piece of his cake.

We moved in together, and things were perfect for a while; he taught me how to go out in the rain, how to embrace the bad weather. We bought puddle suits and wellington boots and made light of it all and he showed me how to see beauty in the floods that my bleeding body delivered.

One day, things got torrential outside. I was curled up on the sofa—hot water bottle on my belly, mug of hot chocolate in my hand. It was in this moment he asked me to marry him, and I said yes. Then he pressed his forefinger gently to my philtrum and told me there was something he needed to tell *me* first, before I agreed. There was something I needed to know about *him*.

"Go ahead," I said. "Nothing you can say will make me love you any less." He smiled and squeezed my hand.

"When I fall in love, I bleed," he said. His smile fell away and joined a puddle with my fresh tears.

I didn't understand at first, but as time went on, I grew to learn he was a fan of trigonometry too and his body had the scars to prove it. He told me he had been in love before and had bled throughout that relationship. He told me he had known he was in love with me the moment of our first kiss— he had rushed home to let a little of his blood out. He pointed at the scars just below his ankle, then showed me more evidence on the soles of his feet. He said bleeding from his feet meant no-one would ever need know.

Except for me.

I told him his secret was safe. I understood. And so, we carried on: when I bled, it rained, and so he loved me, and when he loved me, his feet wept tears of red.

A year into our relationship, I became pregnant, and the sun put his hat on for six months straight. People spoke of global warming, but I knew there was more to it than this.

My periods ceased and we shopped for small things. My partner got through a lot of socks.

On my drive home from work one day, after six months of pure sunshine, a sensation: a dampness and a warmth in my groin which had been so familiar, so often, and so regular, so many moons ago.

I pulled over into a lay-by, undid my seatbelt and wrapped an arm around my swollen belly. With my hands between the top of my thighs, I felt for something. I pulled my fingers free and held them up in the air in front of me and I knew straight away a storm was brewing. My fingers dripped with blood.

I undid the door, got out of the car, and looked down at the driver's seat. A lagoon had collected there. The clouds drifted in front of the sun, carrying the grey weight of the world's water within them. I reached for my phone and called my partner as the first drop of rain landed on my cheek.

The coldness of it all.

More blood came from my body, down my legs, and with the blood came pain. With the pain, came a crack, and a fork of lightning placed its angry fingers in fields which draped the horizon. A deluge came and stayed.

He found me in the lay-by; took me to the hospital where our baby gave up on us.

A parent who brought rain and another with chopping-board feet—I don't blame the poor soul for checking out. The rain fell more heavily than I'd ever seen it fall that day, and continued to fall heavily for a month. We drove home from the hospital and cried more tears as the sky cried too.

A one-hundred-foot tsunami on the other side of the planet wiped out a quarter of a million people at some point in the time that held our grief. A tidal wave taller than a blue whale, a wall of water higher than a ten-story building, carrying more energy than one and a half thousand H-bombs rose up from the depths of the Indian Ocean and pushed forward onto the land. I felt the pain of every single person it killed as I bled. I brought down a drop of rain for each of those who died.

When my bleeding ended, the sunshine never returned, but my partner stopped dragging blades through his feet. And then he left me.

I Pull My Blanket Up Tight Beneath My Chin

Mumma says *if you stay in your bed all night, no walkies, no tears, I'll take you shopping at the weekend.* Says she'll buy me the doll with the eyes that blink when you rock it back and forth. Not only does the doll blink, but when you lift the tiny trapdoor on its back and pour water in, it fills its nappy. And it cries. You can wipe away its tears. I really want that doll. Really, really, really want it. I don't think I can do it though. The doll will never be mine, because night is when the shadow comes.

At story time, I clamp onto Mumma and she tells me not to be silly when I ask if I can keep the little light on. *Big girls don't sleep with the lights on*, she says, and she swipes on her phone with its shiny bright screen while I super slowly turn the pages of my third picture book.

Mumma keeps her phone by her bed. It glows all night long and tells her the numbers of the time, so she knows when to get me ready for school. I see it when I stand by her in the night.

She reads the words *The End* but Mumma isn't looking at the book because she's swiping on her phone, but I don't mind as long as she's here next to me, in my bed.

One more story? Please Mumma, one more? I beg, but she says *No. You've had your three. Mumma needs some alone time.* Why would anyone want 'alone time'? *You need to sleep now, sweet pea. School in the morning. Won't learn anything if you're tired. Sleep tight.* And that is when I pull the blanket up under my chin and

Mumma pushes the sheets in extra snug and pretends to wrap me up like a birthday present or a burrito. The shadows aren't here yet, on the wall, but I know they'll come.

Mumma slides away from me. The bed feels like a boat and the dark, dark floor which licks against its sides is the ocean and I can't see the bottom of the sea, but I know something swims down there. Freddie is down there. *Night-night, sweet pea* she says, and she pulls the door to as she leaves.

Mumma, I cry, *leave the door open,* and she pushes it open a little wider for me.

Mumma says *you can have it slightly 'ajar,' little pea, but no lights. Light is not conducive to sleep. You need the dark to rest.* I've no idea what she means but the door is open, so I say, *'thank you'* and *'love you.'*

Mumma switches out the big light as she leaves a second time. I am trapped in total darkness with my eyes closed *or* open. *Mumma please, come back and draw the curtains tighter* I say, because that is how the shadows get in. I can still hear her on the landing as she walks away, so I know she can still hear me. She comes back in and pushes my curtains together in the middle where the gap was, the gap that let the shadows in, and then she leaves again.

Love you, she says again, *love you for infinity,* and I don't know what 'infinity' means but she says it all the time because her Mumma says it to her.

The creak of her footsteps at the top of the stairs lets me know she is not lingering like she sometimes does to check I stay in my bed, and she is definitely leaving me and going down the stairs. The door to the living room squeaks open. The low buzz of the switched-on television set hums. If I keep stock-still, I can make out the faint melody of the starting music of her favourite show. It's a comfort—of sorts—but I'm still lying here, in the dark all alone. It's only a matter of time before I see the shadow at the foot of my bed.

The wind outside sends whistles through the vent by my window and—*whoof*—the curtain moves. Dull orange light from the streetlamp outside illuminates a large patch on the far wall of my room. Looks like a tiny, dim, screen. But there are no pictures on my wall. Mumma says we mustn't decorate the room. Something about marking up the paint, keeping it smart for the landlord.

The sight of the orange light makes me fill my lungs up with air, and rock from side to side to pin the sheets that cover me down with the sides of my thighs. My body must stay underneath. Got to keep myself covered up from the *other* blanket, the one that smothers, which is the blackness of the night.

I shift back as quietly as I can. Must get my head propped up slightly against the wall behind me without the blanket slipping off. I scoot back. That is when it happens, and I freeze. The shadow fingers appear on the wall.

Mumma says *it's the tree outside.* The tree the landlord says he'll trim back but never does and Mumma can't reach it herself, too high. But it's not a tree. I know exactly what it is. It's a finger and it creeps along my wall and as the wind blows and shakes outside, the long sharp claw moves ever closer. Something's arm stretches along and around and soon it will reach the corner-bend and travel along the other wall all the way until it reaches me in my bed.

I want to stretch out my own arm and reach for the bedside light and flick the switch but that would mean the dark would touch my skin and if the dark can touch my skin, then the skeleton finger can too. So, I keep the blanket tucked in tight under my legs, my chest, my arms, and the cheeks of my bottom by pressing against it from underneath down the sides of my thighs and around and under my toes. I want to call out, *Mumma, help me,* but if I speak, it will hear, the thing outside my window—

And I know it will reach me first.

Over the bursts of wind outside and the tap of the claw on my window, I hear a thumping in my chest and the muffled television show downstairs where I know Mumma is. I think about the doll with its big smile and flicking eye lids and the little door for water in its back. I want that doll. But right now, I want Mumma more.

The television noise and the promise of Mumma feel further and further away and the end wall of my bedroom with the shadows looms closer, presses inwards.

I rip the covers off and run like the wind, without looking behind me, not even once. I leg it down the landing and pitch down the stairs and push open the door of the living room. Mumma's favourite armchair—I see it, the back of it, in the living room. At the top of the back of the chair, her soft, brown, curly hair which sometimes smells like vanilla ice-cream, and I creep over knowing full well she'll send me straight back to my room. She always does. If I walk slowly, maybe she won't notice me here. I'll curl up next to her chair and stay there, forever, by her side.

I tiptoe towards her. Her cheeks are pink, tight balls, and I see all of her teeth as she throws her head back with laughter. At least she is watching something funny and not another scary movie. A week ago I came down late and watched her watching something full of blood and nightmares and *dink dink dink.* A bad man called Freddie. He might be the one who taps at my window. *Dink dink dink.* Mumma didn't know I was watching her watching it as I'd stood so stiff and quiet behind her comfy chair.

But tonight she laughs. Freddie is not on the screen. But I am not laughing. Not at all.

I hold my breath, edge closer, and then she *really* laughs, like a donkey, and snorts a bit too. The loudness of her laughter scares me more, makes me cry. Why does Mumma laugh while I'm so scared? Why does she find my unhappiness funny? Despite this, she is still my Mumma. She will make me feel safer, so I run up to Mumma so she can see me cry.

Oh sweet pea, she says, *did you have a bad dream? Mumma's here.* Her face changes. She no longer laughs but looks at me with a face that says she wishes I wasn't in the living room but also a face that is her face, my Mumma's face, a face that cares for me. She picks me up onto her lap and wipes my tears and I tell her I haven't had a bad dream; I haven't been to sleep yet because I can't sleep because the monster by my window is back, tapping on the glass and stretching out its claws.

Mumma hugs me tight to her soft chest. Her hair against my cheek feels scratchy, not soft like you think it would from afar, and it smells of spicy dinners. She tells me *everything will be okay,* and *it must have been a dream because there are no such things as monsters,* and she will always protect me because she loves me so much. *I love you so much, sweet pea,* she says, and I ask her *how much?* and she says *so, so much* and I ask her does she love me enough to let me sleep in her bed and she laughs and says she loves me to the moon and back she'll love me for infinity but she needs her rest and I am too fidgety.

I reach out to touch the dark bags under Mumma's eyes that she points to. She does this often to show me she's tired. But she can't be as tired as me.

Please don't make me go back to my bed, I beg, but Mumma is 'staying strong' and she carries me up the stairs and walks with me in her arms along the dark landing.

You must stay in your bed, sweetness, she says, and she draws the curtains back together.

I pull the blanket up and under my chin and squeeze my teeth together until I hear them grate and I think really hard about her not leaving the room. If I think enough about her sliding into bed next to me to make me safe with her arms and her warmth, maybe she will do just that.

Can I sleep in with you? I ask, but I already know the answer.

Darling, no. We both need a good night's sleep. She kisses me on my forehead. Wet. The cold black air makes it feel like an ice kiss. *I've work in the morning, and you have school. Now get some rest. Love you for infinity,* she says, and she goes.

I say, *please,* one more time, *can I at least have the light on* and Mumma's voice changes, deepens, and she says *No.* It is a firm sound and I know not to ask again. *Go. To. Sleep.* She says this in the deep, firm voice, and walks away too quickly because she wants to ignore me, or perhaps she doesn't hear as I ask her to *please push the door open a little bit more so I can still see light from the landing.* Blackness.

I lie there forever and stare at where I know the wall at the end of the bed is until I can sort of make it out. My eyelids grow heavy, and I think I close them for a count of three. But then a gust of wind outside pushes the curtains open again and the orange light and the boney shadows once more cast against the far wall.

I want to scream. I bite down on my bottom lip and my fists become screwed full of bed sheets. Can't hear the mumble of the television downstairs. Hear nothing but the wind and the tap-tap of fingers on the glass of the window. I want to scream. But I don't scream. I can hold it in. Must hold it in …

But if the long claw which seems to grow and stretch around the corner of the room reaches me, I know I'll have to scream. It might be the only thing that saves me, my scream. But then, a scream might draw attention, make it see me, lying here huddled up on my bed with my sheets tucked in tight around me.

So I swallow the scream back down.

If the finger touches me, everything is over. It will take me with it, outside, through the glass of the rattling window and I'll never see Mumma again. Never. Forever. And forever is a long time.

How can Mumma not know what is happening up here? She's a million zillion miles away. Why does she not care? She says she loves me *so much—for infinity* even, and I think that means as much as you can possibly ever love someone. Ever. So why does she make me sleep near this monster? I'm scared like the time we found our cat asleep at the side of the road and it wouldn't get up. I'm angry and also a little bit okay because I know Mumma loves me to *infinity* and she would never leave me in danger—so maybe she's right? There are no such things as monsters.

I need to be a big girl. *Big girls aren't afraid of the dark.* I think about the doll that wets its pants and cries when you rock it. Want that doll. Think. About. The. Doll. If I get it, if I stay here in my bed, I can be its Mumma and rock it when it cries and comfort it and look after it like my Mumma looks after me.

Then I hear the tap again at the window. I hold in my scream, but nearly wet the bed.

Mumma closed the door to the room too much, but I can still see there is no orange glow from the landing light sliding through the slim gap between the door and the wall. Mumma must've turned it off; must've come upstairs; must be in her bed. I can't hear the television. She'll be cross but I can't lie here and face the creature. Its finger stretches further. Closer.

I slip out and swing open the door and charge along the hallway. The hallway is pitch black and never-ending like an underground tunnel and I have to get past the top of the stairs but on the wall at the top of the stairs, there is another patch of orange light with creeping creature fingers shaking up and down in time with the wind and with the snores I think Mumma makes all in time with the thump in my chest. I walk as fast as I can without running because I don't want to trip and go down the stairs and because running is noisy, and I don't want it to hear me.

Somehow, I make it across to the other side of the house to Mumma's room. By her bed, I see the light of her phone. The screen displays the numbers which tell her the time. The white-blue glow tells me Mumma must be in bed because she takes her phone with her everywhere and sleeps with its little light on. Mumma must be there, in the bed. The bumpy outline of her body covered up by and tight underneath her quilt tells me so. As I get closer, creeping now because I don't want to wake her, I know I must slide in next to her so she can guard me while she sleeps. I hear her snores. They are now louder than the thumps in my chest.

I wish she was awake, and it were daytime, and we were down in the kitchen, making pancakes and painting pictures. What if she never wakes up and I am left alone here in the dark forever or until the creature at my bedroom window hears me scream? Because I'm sure I'll scream eventually. Don't think I can hold it back for much longer.

Mumma lets out a loud snore which makes me jump. In the darkness, I move around the bed, closer to the phone light and to the side where Mumma's face is. If I can see her face, know she's really there, everything will be better.

Another snore. I find her face. The bottom of her mouth falls open and then closes. I stand still by the side of her bed in the dark, taking comfort in that face. She sounds like an animal when she breathes and snores, but she is my Mumma, and I love her for *infinity* despite her noises. The numbers change on her glowing phone screen and, lit by the blue-white light, I watch her. It's cold. I want to be under the safety of the covers, her covers. How can I get in next to her without waking her up? Without the monster with the boney claws hearing me? One chance. I get one go at this, because if Mumma wakes, I'll be back in my own bed alone, facing a sort of certain death.

I slide my hand under the duvet in front of Mumma's chest. There is just enough space for me to get in between her and the edge of the bed which is lit by the glow from her phone on her bedside table. The light shines on her face and makes the edges of her cheeks glow too, like a cold angel.

Mumma snores again. I pull my hand back from the bed sheets quick sharp because her eyelids flicker oddly when she sucks in air through her nose and her mouth as the sound of the snore honks out. *Mumma, please don't wake up!*

In the darkness, something runs over my toe. A spider, a hand, a skeleton's finger. Got to be a hand from under Mumma's bed. My scream pops out. I jump onto the edge of Mumma's bed. Mumma's arm flaps up and she makes her loudest snore yet. Mumma's jaw drops down too far. *Crunch.*

Her head flops back off the pillow. Her eyes roll open. By the light of her phone, I see her green eyes aren't green and now point in opposite directions and the middles glow blue-white like an ice angel. A dead ice angel.

Then the phone light dims, and her eyes become scratched buttons. I scream again but she doesn't wake even though her eyes are open, and her head does not look comfortable at all. Another snore comes out of her mouth but this time it is not a snore, it is louder than a snore it is a long, sharp, *screech*, like a fork on a dinner plate. I put my fingers in my ears.

It is not her voice that comes out as she talks in a sharp language I don't understand.

Don't think I want to understand.

Feels like if I understand it then Mumma will be gone for good.

The words are too high and raspy. They ripple up her bent-back throat. Wee runs down my leg. Out from the pit-black darkness of her wide-open mouth extends a bony claw. It pushes out further and snaps off her teeth, one-by-one. *Snap. Crunch.* I scream but can't look away. The claw keeps coming and coming and coming out. Towards me, forever and ever. I can't stop screaming. There's nowhere I can go.

Mumma is awake but not awake and her neck snaps right back. I shift back until I'm on the edge of the end of her bed. The claw taps me on the chest. I screw my eyes closed and squeeze my fists as tight as I can, and realize there are no screams left in me to come out.

I wake up in Mumma's bed. Feel terrible, like the time when I had flu. It is morning. Daylight blazes through her bedroom window but she is not here. The claw is not here either, but I remember everything up until the creature tapped me on the chest. I pull in the sheets around me and tuck them tight under my chin. From another room, Mumma speaks with her normal voice. She's on the phone to someone.

I make out some parts of what she says: *unhinged* and *no sleep* and *I'll take her in late then. You're right, it's best to keep to a routine.* She is talking to Gramma. I know this because Mumma ends the call by saying, *love you for infinity, Ma.*

And then Mumma comes up the stairs and I want to see her, but I also want to be as far away from her as I can ever be.

When she comes into her bedroom and sees me sat pressed up to the headboard with the sheet all tucked in around me like a proper Egyptian mummy, she asks me how I feel.

I say nothing. Mumma looks back to normal, but I know she isn't real now. But she sits by me and strokes my hair and says all the normal things she tells me in the morning: I'm her *favourite sweet pea* and *would you like eggs or hoops before school?* and *we're a little late but we should make it in before first break.*

I say nothing. I want to be with Gramma not Mumma, but Gramma lives miles away, I'd never find my own way there. My teacher at least is kind and understanding—I'll feel safe when I'm at school.

I get dressed, eat hardly anything, then Mumma takes me in. She lets me sit in the front seat of the car and every time we stop at lights, she looks over at me and asks *you okay, sweet pea?* Then she answers her own question, *sure, you're fine. You're a big girl.* Her eyes. They're not ice angel eyes anymore, they're her normal green eyes. And her head is where it should be, how it should be. Normal green eyes and normal curly brown hair and a mouth full of normal teeth and her breath smells bitter and a bit bad which just means she's drunk some coffee.

Love you lots, sweetness. Love you infinity, she says as she kisses me goodbye. I shudder as her lips press wet and cold on my forehead. *You can sleep in bed with me tonight, little pea. No more bad dreams.'* I grab my satchel and back out of the car. A curl in my stomach flips right over at the thought of sharing a bed with her. She blows another kiss and drives away from the school gates.

I make it into the classroom just in time for maths. I can't stop yawning. We huddle around the teacher on the rainbow rug and the teacher asks us all to count in tens together. Everyone stops when we reach one hundred; everyone except for the kid to my left, this brainbox. He keeps on going. The teacher encourages him, says *well done. How far can you go?*

And the kid keeps on going.

He stumbles when he gets to two hundred and ninety and this other kid—who's even smarter—chips in, says she can go all the way to *infinity* and the teacher asks her what *infinity* means and the kid says it means something goes on forever and ever and ever and never ends and I feel myself starting to yawn more because I'm so tired and I don't recognize any of these strangers sat around me and then I feel something tap me on my chest.

I scream.

I scream so loudly all the other kids scream too and then I wet my pants. Mumma comes to pick me up, but when she comes, I refuse to go home with her.

I am seventeen now. Might be eighteen. The old man who tells me he's a priest, the one with the melted face and the glove of blades, visits me each evening to say the same thing: *You've been speaking Enochian, child. The language of dark angels.* He never tells me what I say during one of my seizures. Says if I did know, if he ever did tell me what my tongue had forced out through my lips and teeth, I might lose myself completely.

There are times when I wonder if I ever came down, if I ever went back to sleep. Maybe I never woke up after the night when Mumma's head split open and the fingers of the thing that watches me from the window tapped me on the chest.

Perhaps I never escaped it, and I'm still asleep. If I am, I sleep rarely within this nightmare, only when the medication kicks in. And when I do, I find myself back in my childhood bedroom. There I am with the sheets tucked up tight under my chin. And there I wait for the curtain to slip open in the dark of the night. I dream the same dream, again and again, night after night—always Mumma in her bed, with her cranked neck and her smashed teeth, lit by the light of her phone, and always the claw, which extends forever from her gaping black maw, like an infinite telescope, probing for me, my soul, in the darkness.

And sometimes I know the dream is real, and what's real is dream. And sometimes I know this can't be true.

Each night I lie alone in a bedroom much smaller than my one from childhood, and as the handful of brightly-coloured tablets set me drifting, I hear the gust of wind and the sound of Mumma's snores. It's so peaceful. And if I let my lids fall a little, I see Mumma. Not the Mumma who comes to visit me monthly out of a sense of duty—morose, silent, distant, and grey now that she is—but the Mumma who I used to love. Used to trust.

But if I let my eyelids clunk close, like the doll I'd longed for as a child, I hear the crunch of Mumma's neck as it snaps back, see the infinite kaleidoscope of shadow-bones ratchet out from her toothless mouth. I run. I run in my sleep even though thick leather cuffs tie me here to this bed. Because, if I stop running, it will tap me on the chest, and I will scream.

My neck is cold, my sheets have slipped.

I wish I could pull my blanket up tight beneath my chin.

One Lie for One Soul

First published in Gravely Unusual Magazine, 2021

"Come out, come closer, my lamb," the voice said. It woke us both. My girl with wet eyes kissed me first and then our son, then told me she knew she was the lamb.

She took a deep breath and pulled on her smock. I remained in our bed, rooted by terror, as she followed its call, yet I did not follow her, coward that I am. Beads of sweat dripped from my forehead and collected in my beard despite the frost outside. The linen wick of our olive lamp had long since extinguished and our room was as black inside as it was out. I could almost hear my girl's heart pounding—fast and troubled—from the far side of the room as she tiptoed towards the door. In the weak slit of light the moon offered through the archway, I saw her face, as pale as ash, and her eyes, tired yet wide. She stopped still, both present and lost.

A cackle.

"The fuck was that?" I mouthed. The movement of my lips caught her attention as she stood, bracing herself to exit, but before she had time to reply, the voice creaked through the dark of night again, whispering so quietly that our son did not stir, yet resonating in my ears with the volume of one thousand howling wolves.

"Come to the courtyard. Alone. Get the fuck out here now, bitch— before I hang you to the rafters, slit your throat, drip you out; before I stone you and him and your bastard child to death."

I wrapped my arm around our baby and pulled him closer. Was I protecting him, or he, me? I couldn't muster the courage to take the large rock from under our bed to challenge whatever was waiting.

My girl, shivering, edged out into the yard slowly, like the creep of ice forming on a lake, leaving a puddle of urine which shone in the moonlight on the floor behind her.

"I know what you have done, slut. Liar. Now you'll take your punishment."

Our baby stirred and cried. I wrapped him tightly in swaddling, stood up and held him in the way he liked to be held. I paced the floor, patting and rubbing his back, trying to soothe him, too afraid to venture outside.

Over my child's bawling, I heard my girl speak back, her voice trembling. What was this beastly presence? Why were they luring her outside in the middle of the night with threats of violence?

"What do you want? Who are you?" she asked.

"You know who I am and what I want. You lied to everyone."

My child's screams rose to a shrill peak as a crash of thunder shook our hut. My girl returned moments later, shivering, screaming, and crying louder than the baby. I took her into my arms and tried to calm the pair of them.

Her tears continued until sunrise. At dawn, she fell asleep exhausted, so did our boy, so I left them to rest.

Days passed, and my girl told me nothing. I asked and asked what had happened that night. She shrank within herself when I broached the subject and never answered my questions.

She grew distant.

Her touch, her kiss, it all ran dry. In days, her hair turned white. In weeks, her skin aged years. Months passed. She stopped talking and sleeping. Her face thinned, as did her limbs, her bosom. All of her curves. Her padding appeared to collect in her belly, which grew like it had with our first born.

All day and all night she rocked, sat, or lay on our bed, and would not leave the room. She refused to nurse and comfort our son, all the while losing her mind as dandelion seeds are lost to the wind. Each night she cried red tears and sweated yellow stains into the sheets and furs.

I had to take our baby boy to the temple for the elders to tend to him while I worked. My girl no longer spoke, no longer moved—even the rocking stopped—she just lay on the bed, sipping rarely on broth brought by villagers, which they fed to her from a ladle.

Her belly grew larger.

I sat by her side and watched each evening as her chest rose and fell as if she had run a great race despite her catatonic state. All the while she wept. I wiped away the red tears which ran down her cheeks.

Three seasons passed.

"Fuck, you're bleeding. You're bleeding. Not just from your eyes … your wrists, ears, ankles, my love." Her thick tongue thrust in and out of her mouth as if she was choking on a chunk of grey meat. Red rivulets flowed out of fresh slits all over her body.

"Something is cutting you," I said. I pressed my hands against the openings in her arms to try to stem the blood flow.

She shifted herself up in the bed. Red tides sprayed and dribbled down her robe. A slash of blood spurted over our young son's face and body as he lay there, at her side, still asleep. I grabbed my son. He woke and cried. My heart thrummed in my throat, as if trying to claw its way out.

"What the fuck—Mary, my love, what's going on?" I screamed. She said nothing. Our child let rip.

With her frail arms, she pushed herself out of the bed and dragged herself across the room until she was far from us, then folded over in pain. She grappled at her own stomach. Her breath sounded hurried, and a trail of blood smeared on the ground behind her as she moved. Through the gown she slept in, now claret and sodden, outlines of fists, elbows, horns and claws pressed out and probed through the fabric. The gown rippled, as something within my lover jabbed and pulsated underneath her stretched belly skin.

"Help me, it's coming," she rasped, her long-silenced voice desert dry. She shouted again, this time something indecipherable—all tongues and spittle—and then collapsed on the floor.

"I'm coming," screeched a new, shrill voice. It spoke in a pitch that could shatter rainbows, crack pottery, tear down temples.

My lady writhed in pain and blood and her own fluids as I cowered in the corner, trying to cover my baby's young eyes from witnessing the horror, the mess of woman and blood and flesh on the straw on the floor.

She grabbed onto the edge of our son's crib, her knuckles white and strained as if bones might just burst though. She clawed at it, her fingernails snapping like broken lyre strings. She etched something unreadable into the wood. The pads of her fingers rubbed raw, became stumps, the bone at last exposed.

The birth of our first born was so tranquil, in a stable surrounded by braying mules and sleeping sheep. As she screamed again and again, her eyes rolled into the back of her head. This second child, this thing erupting from my love, was not mine. Of that, I was sure.

A lightning bolt of red jarred down her stomach, from under her shrivelled breasts towards her legs. "Help me," she mumbled.

Her gown ripped open along that red bolt. Claws peeked out—claws like those of a wolverine. A nest of blades and needles erupted from her navel, cutting and whipping and shredding her tissues as they came.

Her head dropped back; her cries stopped. Only my boy's screams could be heard—that, and a noise like that of a hundred cleavers ripping through a herd of goats. I clamped my hands tight over my son's ears.

Red lacy foam spewed from my dying love's mouth as she choked. Then she lay still.

Something dragged itself from her stomach. Led first by its claws, it was pulsing and faceless—yet was fronted by two ram-like horns. A body of organ meat connected with sinew, tendons and cartilage—all smeared in gelatinous clumps of blood. I shouldn't have looked. Didn't want to see the birth that had split apart my love, but alas, I couldn't help but stare.

Whatever it was had two spines entwined, joined together in the shape of a love heart, and more than enough legs for any living thing. As the last of its form pulled out from her, an ocean of fluids spread across the floor, flooding our room with red mucus. A putrid lava.

Absurd appendages tapped and rapped on the stone floor in syncopation. It scuttled off and out of the room and into the depths of the night screaming like a boiling lobster.

My love's empty, dead body was left behind, a shelled cocoon, white and red and limp on the ground of our sleeping quarters. My son screamed and wriggled but I would not allow him to see his mother dead.

The villagers, the temple men, they all had high expectations for our son. To see such a nightmare would give the child a twisted mind; such a sight would create a psychopath, a delusional man who'd surely seek an early escape from life or become a sick fantasist.

I took two coins from my pigskin purse and placed them over the sockets of what was left of my Mary's eyes and moved slowly away, son in my arms. I considered fleeing straight to the temple to speak to the Holy Men, to ask for forgiveness for the great lie we had told. This, surely, must have been the reason for Mary's death. And yet I knew this could not be an option.

Mary had convinced me we should keep our first born. Rather than poison it, or scrape it, or starve it out, rather than simply get rid of it before the bump became too obvious. We should raise it instead as a Saviour. The villagers believed us when we said that an angel had visited and told us that Mary had been chosen as mother to the Son of the Lord. What a fabrication. We'd acted desperately. Mary had been so convincing; I'd just followed her lead. A mother's love for her unborn child is a force to be reckoned with—I didn't want to lose her, and I didn't want to die. To admit we had fornicated outside of wedlock, had formed the beast with two backs before receiving blessings from the temple, would have surely meant we would have been stoned to death.

I knew the wise men of the village would hold me accountable for what had happened to Mary. No-one would believe me. I'd be accused of murder. I also wanted my son and I to get as far away as possible from that wretched mess of placenta embroiled with spine and claws that broke free from my lost, dead Mary. So, Jesus and I fled.

I walked until my sandals split. Barefoot I continued, taking charity and refuge from passing villages. We spoke not a word of our story, only thanked our hosts and hurried away before the cock crowed. On and on we went. I was exhausted, near-delirious. Jesus, distraught and confused.

At the first river we came to, I took Jesus out from his papoose to wash him. And tried too to wash the stains from my soul. That grey evening by the river, we met a young lady, Abigail, who took pity on this lost soul and my young son. Destitute and homeless, she took us both in. In the privacy that dusk provided, she hurried us into her abode, not a soul saw us enter. She fed us well and all three of us curled up together to keep warm. It felt good to touch another human, she seemed to understand the needs and the desires of the flesh as we stroked and tickled each other's bare arms. Jesus lay asleep between us as we whispered sweet nothings about what we hoped for our futures, as she begged me to stay with her for all times.

Hours into the night, we both fell asleep as the lamp on her table burnt out. And I slept for the first time in days, like a heavy stone, without dreams, without horrendous visions. Until I was woken by a voice.

This time, it was a voice I recognised—the babbling sound of my son. He was yet to string sentences together and had only spoken to me with simple words like *fatha*, *don-key* and *water*. Yet that night Jesus spoke no longer with a baby's tongue. He was forming coherent speech.

I lay still, pretending to sleep, listening to my son. I watched him through squinted eyes as he pushed the hair away from Abigail's ear and shuffled his face and body closer to the sleeping maiden. Jesus whispered into his new mother's ear as she slept.

"In the morning, you will awaken and tell the village how a great angel visited you in the night and left you a fair young child—I, Jesus—and the Godly blessing of another on the way. And both children are gifts from the Lord, are children *of* the Lord, and shall be worshipped and praised as such. You, sweet Abigail, have been chosen."

God help us.

My heart raced. My body was rigid with fear. I could not reach Jesus in order to pull him away from her. Images of Mary's death streamed through my mind. The scuttle of bloodied flesh-blades flickered in the dark corners of the room. I was certain, whatever it was that Mary had birthed weeks earlier, the darkness that had split out of my dead lover, still scurried amongst us.

I tried to get up from the bed, to escape from the room, from my own child, but as I flinched, Jesus rose. His body grew large and wide until he became the size of a lion. Jesus grew until he filled the bed, making a mouse of me. My first born lifted his index finger and stared at me, his eyes as beetle-black as the night outside.

"Massacre," he screamed. A coagulated, bulbous mess with two distorted spines rushed out from nowhere. The hell-beast flattened, sharpened in shape, and charged at me, as an arrow flies toward its target.

Black Metal in a White Room

First published by Sunbury Press, 2022

"Mr. Heathfield? Answer the door. The door."

I hadn't wanted to answer the door. At all. I knew full well who it'd be. The Empties, collecting. No-one else had the nerve to bang so hard and so fast for so damn long.

"We're after one pint today. One pint."

They'd been rude and insistent ever since they'd taken over. I detested the way they spoke too, echoing everything, already loud enough without the additional reverb. Their voices hurt. Their words ricocheted in the air like orchestral gunfire, like shards of glass, like black metal. And I am not a black metal fan. I like classic rock. But I didn't dare say anything or ask them to drop their volume—the Empties were not beings to be messed with, and they sure as hell didn't answer requests with pleasantries.

"Yeah, sure. I know. I'm coming," I said. I switched off my screen, grabbed my bag, and shut my front door behind me on my way out.

Everything had changed the day the Empties came to Earth. No-one really knew what they were or where they'd come from, but they weren't looking for friendship, that was for certain. The newsreaders said they'd '*slid down a moonbow*' in the middle of the night. No-one had seen them arrive *per*

se—due to their invisibility—but many claimed to have seen the ominous shadows they cast bounding down from the night sky under lunar light.

We couldn't see them, but we could always hear them. Everyone heard them alright, with their distorted foghorn sounds and their ear-splitting wah-wah voices and their Cradle of Filth tone. The racket they made was no music to your ear. In fact, their voices were enough to make your windows rattle and your molars hum.

He or it or whatever it was that'd disturbed my gaming session by knocking on my door that cloudy morning led me once again to the train station. I tagged along behind it, a knot of apprehension making a pretzel of my innards, all the while trying to avoid placing my foot directly on all I could see of it, its trailing shadow of black static. Distracted by a feral cat darting from behind a bin, my toe fell within the hazy prickles its presence scattered on the pavement. The thing—the 'Empty'—let out a blood-curdling scream. I apologised profusely as fear bubbled beneath my skin, and I stepped with caution for the remainder of the journey. I knew full well I'd be of no use to them with curdled blood.

It was taking me to make a transaction. Each payment journey to the old church hall in the next district was always chaperoned, despite that being totally unnecessary. We all had a damn good idea about what happened to people who *didn't* obey, and it wasn't pretty. Yet still, each week, a knock at the door would pull me away from my VR screen—a satanic shadow hovering over my doormat waiting to lead me away.

At least it felt pleasant to be outside for a while, away from the four ever-pressing walls of my own front room where I'd been cooped up since the Empties arrived. A moment of weak, autumnal sunshine broke through the cloud to give me a little hope. A little vitamin D stirred in my cells.

As far as I could gather, all of the Empties were cruel, but some of them were rogue and took more than just the standard donation. People had been going missing. Society had broken down. Most people had decided to stay in, watching mindless television shows or joining the virtual reality gaming realm, all existing on the just-about-adequate provisions our uninvited guests provided never quite regularly enough. I'd had to make an extra hole in my belt buckle. We had the internet to communicate with though: chat rooms, email, face-time, and so on. But for those of us without close family or friends, existence meant pure isolation.

My VR escape stage—*Classic Rock Concert Pro*—had become the main joy in my life. I definitely wasn't happy, what with the apocalyptic invasion going on the other side of my curtains, but at least I had entertainment to help pass time. An innate urge to survive powered me onwards each day. We were all hopeful things would get better.

I stepped on the train, saw another man across the carriage also sitting under the veil of a doom-shadow. Poor guy was probably heading to the same place I was. Too tired to make conversation—the payment I'd made last week had knocked the stuffing out of me—I simply raised my eyebrows and nodded at him, a gesture which he, looking equally as exhausted, returned. I rubbed my sore arms. I contemplated asking the Empty escorting me if it'd be possible to make my prospective payment from a vessel in my leg instead this time. I had more track marks than a heroin addict, and some of them looked infected. I decided not to ask on the train—I'd wait until I arrived at the payment centre. This decision was partly due to my lethargy and partly because I didn't want to inflict the sound of its horrible, shuddering, thrashing voice on the chap sat opposite me.

An hour later, the shadow wrapped me up with a roar and shoved me through the door of the payment centre. Once inside, I rolled up the length of my trouser and pointed to the back of my knee.

"Any chance we could take it from here today?" I asked, and placed my fingers in my ear drums. The hideous noise from its invisible gob thundered out causing a chill to skitter down my spine.

"Yes. Yes. If we can find a vein. A vein."

I felt a revolting pressure, the equivalent of a fork scraping down a blackboard, a guitar string snapping, as the Empty pushed me back and groped and shuffled its invisible parts all over my body, searching for a suitable blood vessel.

I have no idea which part of its body it used to jam the needle into my groin. The sharp steel spike entered my skin and the vein beneath it, causing me to let out a yelp. Red stuttered out at first in dribs and drabs and then gushed down the plastic tubing. It filled up the bag on the end of the line which appeared to be floating in front of me, suspended somehow by an invisible, rough-handed monster. As my blood collected, the Empty jabbed another needle—this one attached to a syringe-full of black static—into my thigh. "In exchange, exchange," it hollered. I dug my grubby fingernails into the palms of my balled fists, channelling the sharp pain through and out of my limbs. Christ. What the hell was being pumped into my body in exchange for my blood?

Once my blood had filled the pint sack, I was left to pull the canula needles dangling from my groin out myself. It had what it wanted and had immediately lost interest in my de-juiced body.

How long would a pint take to replenish? The internet told me forty-eight hours. Two whole days to top up the volume I'd lost. A further four to eight weeks to manufacture and replace the red blood cells. This was my seventh payment. They'd come every week, like clockwork, to march me to the donation centre, to drain me like the dregs from an upturned bottle of Merlot. No wonder I felt like death warmed up.

On my way out, I glanced back to see the bag of my blood arc through the air—a crimson-sailed boat bobbing along unseen wave crests—until it stopped in the corner. There it was tipped and emptied into what I can only presume was the feeding organ of an Empty. Red dripped down, its shape shifting, glugging, until it became, momentarily, an out-of-focus polygon. The suspended blood throbbed in time with my own heartbeat as if the liquid were still present within me. Then, the air-puddle faded away to nothing and the bag dropped like a stone.

Were the bastards drinking it? A crisp burp—oddly echoless this time, a violent duck-quack—came from the corner above the emptied blood bag which lay discarded on the floor.

Disgusting.

Whatever these invisi-beasts were, they had appalling table manners. The belch was followed by a series of smaller burps and a hideous shriek of a giggle. The sound ripples hit my eardrums. A wave of vomit thrummed against the walls of my oesophagus, eager to escape my fragile body—as eager as I was to get away from the slovenly, blood-drinking toads.

Dizzy with blood loss, I legged it back to the station and caught a train back home.

At least the payment covered me for another week. A pint a week—that seemed to be the going rate. A half-pint for internet, and another half for electricity, food, and water. The essentials. It was rough but manageable. After making a payment, rehydration was key, and maybe eating a couple of biscuits. Then back I went, into my virtual reality game. I was okay with a pint each week.

They'll get bored, I thought, *they'll go home soon. Things'll get better. Life'll return to normal.*

The next day, the familiar, excessive knock at my front door— albeit a little earlier than I'd anticipated. A whole six days earlier. I was mid-performance.

I paused my game, inhaled deeply and admired my faux view before disconnecting. Jack Bruce stood to my left. He repetitively shifted from side to side, his bass guitar hiccupping in and out of virtual existence, his microphone stand flickering on, off, on, off. I glanced behind me—Ginger Baker, head tipped back, a pair of drumsticks hanging blurred in the air in front of him mid-paradiddle. I lifted my foot from the special effects pedal, slung my Gibson Les Paul behind me, and waved goodbye to my incandescent, glitching audience of thousands.

The sound of the unholy transparent beast knocking and screaming at my front door had drowned out the song anyway. I pulled my nose away from the centre of the large wall-mounted screen, and the device *switched-off*—the blank canvas left hanging from the gallows of my white wall.

I yanked my body up from the couch. The puncture wound in my puce groin oozed yellow pus which dripped down my inner thigh. I still ached heavily from the abuse endured the day before. They must've made a mistake knocking for me again so soon.

I fumbled for my bag and coat and caught sight of myself in the reflective screen on my lounge wall. Drawn cheeks, waxen skin pale, and under-eye bags as dark and inky as my black curtains. Must've lost ten kilos since the arrival of the Empties. Loose skin hung from my slouched frame.

I answered the door. Dirty shadows scuttled on the ground by where I imagined its feet might be—or the base of its hexagon or polygon or tesseract or whatever the hell its true form was. But in the visible plain, draped over its rippling nothingness, a cloak! A black, hooded cape was suspended over my doorstep, a menacing shadow beneath it.

"Hurry. Hurry," it said. Its voice shook dust from my windowsill, filled my boots with dread.

"I made a payment yesterday," I quivered.

"Rate increase. Increase. Increase," it replied with extra distortion. I wanted to ask why, why me, why again, why more blood? But I needed its thunderous, searing voice to stop.

I marched behind it to the station, got dejectedly onto the train, waved goodbye to my house through the window. As home shrank into the distance, its black roof became small and insignificant, and then, like the Empties themselves, invisible.

We reached the payment station. This time, instead of being instructed to sit and wait in turn in the loop of seats pressed against the internal perimeter of the old church hall, the shadows were leading people off into side rooms with gusto. Scratchy, irksome black patches flitted back and forth. Tired humans following like sad sheep. The mass of black static chaperoning me pooled on the floor by my feet and screeched, *'follow.'* So, follow I did. Through a side door. Down a corridor. Unseen claws shimmied me into a tiny, make-shift cubicle and instructed me to lie on the narrow bed within.

"Left or right. One, two, three, four, five. Four or five. One, two, three, four, or five?" Christ alive, why did it have to produce such hideous sounds and speak in echoes?

"I'm sorry, I'm not sure what you mean," I replied, my index fingers plugging my ears.

"Left or right finger. Or toe. Finger. Or toe."

Sweet Jesus. I looked down at my hands and realised what it meant.

It wanted more than my blood—that day, it wanted a digit. My flesh and bone.

I stood up and moved to the door. I needed out. This was one step too far. The unit shifted straight through me to the door in front. A wave of acidic hellfire rode through every cell of my body. I gagged as its antimatter gushed through my muscles and bones. It made it to the door before I could, and I watched in despair as the bolt slammed across.

"Fingers or Toes. Left or right. Right," it said again. A leather fedora hat which had been sat atop a small corner table flew up into the air, came to rest mid-air, shoulder height. I watched, frozen to the spot, as the hat floated back across the room. "You must choose. Internet fee gone up. No tissue payment, no internet, no life."

I sat back down on the gurney bed, my heart bashing under my ribs. No life? Did it mean this in the literal sense? Was I to die today if I didn't succumb to its demands? Or was it somehow aware of how much I valued my gaming time, how trivial my existence would become without my virtual stage? Either way, the door was locked, I was trapped. I could feel its revolting nothingness brushing up and down against my thigh, keen for my answer. I had no choice. It wasn't going to let me leave and I needed the internet—I spent over sixteen hours a day doing holographic gigs, touring the world with Cream, performing to massive crowds, all from the comfort of my living room. I had nothing else, no-one else. Without the internet, would I even exist? Betwixt a rock and a hard place was where I was wedged—I just hoped it, the Empty, wasn't going to *use* a rock and a hard place to take this heavy payment.

I shuffled my butt back onto the loose sheet of blue medical paper towel atop the wheeled bed, braced myself, and through gritted teeth, replied: "Left toe."

I clenched my fists and held my breath in preparation. Imprinted on my retina, before I screwed my eyes closed, was the snapshot of a floating, dipped fedora hat and a levitating hacksaw.

I screamed for ages, bled for ages. The Empty tossed a bunch of bandages at me, unbolted the door, and left. Stemming the flow of blood from my foot with my shaking hands, I watched a floating hat escort my toe away in a small dish.

I wrapped my foot. The bandage became red soaked in an instant. I grabbed another roll from the medical trolley and wrapped and re-wrapped the wound until the bleeding eased. I hopped back to the station that day, through sideways sleet, onto the train, a mess of blood and rain and tears, and made my way back home.

I immersed myself in my VR performances for the rest of the week, my pain alleviated slightly by being on stage. How long a toe would buy me. Weeks? Maybe a month?

Ten days after the Empties first mutilated me, another knock came at my door.

That Empty was wearing a necktie with the symbol of an upturned cross on it. I followed its scuffle of a shadow, its hovering black noose, down the road and onwards towards the train station. I psyched myself up to say goodbye to the little toe on my right foot this time. My left foot stump had started to dry and scab over. Four toes per foot wasn't the end of the world. I could deal with that. In a couple of hours, I'd be back at home, in my living room, on stage at Glastonbury Festival thrashing out "Deserted Cities of the Heart" and "Sunshine of My Love" to thousands of virtual, smiling fans.

That time, they kept me in overnight. Paralysed by the medication they'd forced upon me, yet able to witness and feel every scrape and cut the floating scalpel made, I had no option but to watch them hack off my entire foot and imbibe bag after bag of my lifeblood. Each time one of them downed a gulp, I'd see an evil body cloud up, become vermillion fog before my eyes. Some of them started to look a little less empty. Instead of shadows cast beneath spaces of nothingness, through drugged eyes, I swear I sore fleshy, flitting, geometric shapes. Organic. Fluid. Peach, pink, brown and cream. Edges, angles, corners and planes. Dustings of rose. Blockish, translucent organic apparitions sloped from room to room. Was the pain making me delusional? Many of the shapes were wearing black baseball caps, beanies, and studded leather jackets. One had draped over its shifting image a Darkthrone T-shirt held together with safety pins.

Pain pinballed up my left-hand side from where my foot was once attached. Shock punched me in the gut. I yelled a hopeless, 'help me' from the hospital bed but I received no help, just a hard, thick slap around the jaws from a flush-tint, cuboid, Empty appendage.

"Shut up. Shut up. Shut up," it screeched, echoed by ten-fold more of its allies. Fear stapled my mouth closed. "Be quiet or no anaesthetic next time. Next time."

Next time? I yanked out the pouch and needle which had been drilled into a vessel near my groin. It seemed to be replacing my body fluids with something dark, something made of nightmares, something I knew I didn't want or need inside of me. I lobbed the pouch on the floor and then vomited hard into a cardboard kidney dish.

And there was a next time. Against my will and from a pit of unimaginable pain, I bid goodbye to my other foot. That loss bought me a knock-free month. But then they came again. They broke into my home, pulled me out from under my bed where I'd hidden—I was petrified, still feverish, battling an infection from the last amputation. They dragged me to the payment centre where they knocked me out for twelve hours. My last memory before that surgery was of a floating chiffon Victoriana evening gown with matching velour gloves and a disposable medical mask screeching orders at me whilst tethering me down to the wheeled bed. That time, they told me they'd removed a kidney, half of my lung, my right eye, and a large section of my liver.

When I came round, I was on the train. Propped up in a wheelchair, I regained consciousness, sat under the semi-clothed, black-grey cloud of an

Empty; the Darkthrone fan. The train rolled to a stop, and it pushed me along, all the while whistling a shrill, gut-splitting note from its invisible lips. Each toot it made felt like a woodpecker hammering on my eardrums. Disharmonious vibrations emanating from it shook and irritated each throbbing part of my sore, pained body. I was a shell of a man. It wheeled me back home and tipped me out onto my sofa with a bag of medication and comestibles.

"Aftercare package, package," it hollered, and left.

I felt like I was dying. I did nothing but sleep and clamber to the kitchen for water for what felt like eternity, all the while spinning in and out of consciousness until, I managed to muster up the energy to haul my frail body over to the VR screen. I pressed my nose up against the cold black mirror and switched it on. Thank God for VR, an escape from my world of pain. Within a second, I was back on stage, my boys behind me, able one more time to belt out the classic rock hits. Performance euphoria washed over me. The myriad injuries and incisions the 'surgeons' had left all over my body went numb.

Three long blessed months passed before they called again. An Empty knocked, screeched at me in power chords, and wheeled me to the train station. Another Empty with a hint of peach to its nebulous form knocked me out with its knuckles and a syringe of black static. When I came round, one of the bastards told me they'd taken everything that was left to take from within the cavity of my abdomen. I screamed and screamed. It whipped and thrust a horrific, leather-gloved limb out at me which struck me solid. I recoiled in further pain, silenced.

They didn't understand—organs did not replenish as blood did. Yes, the liver had the weak ability to re-generate partially, but not as fast as they had been reaping slices of it from me. My hair had all fallen out. I had just one eye, I could feel no teeth were left. My arms were like drumsticks, bare bones. My hands and feet were long gone. I felt like a tipped-up sack.

An Empty dumped me back home, and through my agony, I realised something new. The Empty—it appeared to have a human shape. A humanoid outline, human legs dressed in human trousers, peachy arms and hands, a torso wearing something woven, soft, possibly angora, in a shade of bruised blue. Under the cap which perched on what I imagined must've been its head, was a writhing mass of tangled, midnight-black hair which whipped like Medusa's snakes, and a pair of soulless eyes. Eyes filled with loathing.

"Cheerio," it said, its voice no longer resonant, no longer overly loud, no reverb—not alien at all, in fact. I didn't have the strength to reply, every breath hurt. I swear as it left, it winked at me and smirked.

I collapsed on the sofa, slept. When I awoke, I scrabbled about, half on, half off my couch, to retrieve the bag of pain relief it'd hurled into my home as it left. Days passed, I felt weak, feverish, certain that death was near. Had I given up? Despite this overwhelming feeling of impending doom, I wanted, needed, to spend my last few moments doing the one thing I loved.

Doped up on pain relief, I hauled myself to my screen. Could I muster the energy to check in on my band? See the boys, hear the crowds cheer with joy just one more time? I pressed my nose up against the black screen and stretched for the 'on' button.

Nothing. Nothing happened. After flicking the button back and forth several times, I realised something serious was wrong.

It couldn't have run out already, the internet. I'd only just made a payment, and that payment had been a rather substantial one. I'd a vague memory of bartering with the Empty surgeon. I'd allowed it to take the last metre of my intestine, the final lobe of my liver, the other one of my kidneys in exchange for infinite internet. That's when I realised. That's when it clicked. I hadn't thought it through. Silly, foolish me. *What an idiot,* I thought—I hadn't made a payment for electricity.

It'd been cut off. And the internet wouldn't work without electricity. I couldn't delve into my VR world. I couldn't stand on stage, complete, with all my virtual organs, limbs, appendages, and drill out Cream classics to baying crowds of fans. Ginger Baker would bang on his drum skins unaccompanied by the thrashing of the battle axe. Jack Bruce's lyrics would sound hollow without my guitar melodies accompanying him. I pressed my nose again and again against the black mirror of my VR entertainment system, hopeful I was mistaken. Again and again, harder and harder. Frustrated, furious, throbbing with pain, fear, anger. I opened what I felt was my one remaining eye and looked into the black mirror of the dead VR set in front of me—

—to be met with no reflection.

No face.

No sallow, concave cheeks, no glazed, tired eye, no strands of haywire, desperate hair stuck out from my scalp. No scalp. No neck, no shoulders. Biting down on the inside of my cheek to hold in screams of anguish, I drew myself up onto my bleeding, oozing sore stumps—and could not see any of them. I couldn't see any of me in the dark reflective screen, none of me at all. I was nothing. I had become nothing. I was gone, empty.

I threw the space where my body should be back onto my sofa and screamed an acidic scream which echoed and bounced around the four ever-pressing walls. I sat my nothingness down in a pile of misery, invisible and alone.

My living room walls were painted white. My ceiling which stretched out above me was as white as a bed sheet, and the floor below, was all whitewashed boards. It was the whitest room in my house yet, in that moment, it felt exponentially dark. It was as if a three-foot-deep, thick padding of virgin snow surrounded me, made a death's row prisoner of me.

With the weight of infinity, my four white walls pushed in.

And trapped within them, I became nothing.

In His Memory

He told her someone had disappeared from the factory floor so he'd been sent home. With a soft smile for the white-haired dreamboat standing in front of her—this other lost man, her husband—she took the sweater he'd been attempting to fold from his hands, folded it for him, and said she'd make his favourite casserole for dinner. She did. Then she went to bed. He said he had to sit up late to watch the multi-news zed in.

"Come to bed, love," she said. "You need to rest."

But I don't feel tired, he thought, *and do people ever go to sleep in dreams?* "Won't be long," he said. "Just need to know a little more. I'd like to try and make sense of what's occurring around me and within me." Much later, he fell asleep in his armchair. His slumped body remained partially submerged in the luminescent screenzone until dawn.

In the morning, he dwelt on the news. Data scientists had been working around the clock, knocking theories about. A hypothesis had been shared, accepted, with little evidence to disprove it: life was a simulation and was running at capacity.

He spoke with his wife. He told her between emotions how he felt this may've been true for some time, how he felt as if he were both here and not here, halfway into a dream, and then again, not. His wife mentioned dementia and returned to fiddling with the sonic head of the warewasher, a hint of wetness to her eyes.

"Love, come here," he said later in the day.

She came to him.

"Good news, dear? Have they found a way to stop this situation?" He watched her necklace blink into a shadow of ones and nils and vanish before she'd finished her sentence. She didn't notice—her mind lost elsewhere this time—and he didn't tell her. Didn't want to scare her. Not yet. Not until he was sure.

"Depends on one's perspective, I suppose. Scientists have spotted a pattern. Watch with me," he said. She loosened his fingers for him which had gripped too tight upon the edges of the chairport in which he was sat. "Thank you," he said without looking at her, his eyes fixed on the screen.

She clapped her hands, and their screen throbbed and doubled in size.

"We've found a correlation …" the scientist said. Generic face, well-pressed collar. The scientist forced a smile but his eyes spoke volumes in a language the opposite of happiness.

"This is interesting," the news anchor replied, "do tell us more."

She's speaking too slowly, he thought, as if the space into which her words fall has become stretched, and he stood up and down and then up and down again.

In the kitchen of their small home, he reached for and squeezed his wife's hand, told her everything would be okay. Told her he would make everything okay. "I will make everything okay," he said, although he did not feel he had the capacity with which to fulfill this weighty promise.

I'm not sure he's okay, she thought. She squeezed her husband's hand back.

"We have found a definite relationship between what we are calling the EXCITEMENT RATIO and what we are calling the LIKELIHOOD OF BINARIASATION AND/OR DELETION," the scientist continued, tugging on his collar as sweat beads collected on his brow. *The white-haired man seemed taken by the sweat beads, the very orbitality of them,* he thought, and peered closer until his nose swam within the screen.

"Are you okay?" his wife asked.

He did not reply.

"And what does this mean for the average person on the street, say?" the newsreader continued.

"The average person, the basic package if you like, those who are least entertaining, well …" The scientist paused, looked left, right, down, and straight ahead, and repeated this rotational sequence in an identical yet opposite form, as if malfunctioning, and then spoke more into his lap than to the anchor or any of the cameras. "Sadly, the lustreless appear most at risk."

As if overloaded, the axonometric screen throbbed and retracted ever so while the scientist seemingly suspended within it unfurled endless threads of peer-reviewed data, evidence, and research techniques.

"I don't think I understand," she said to her husband, despite her face a picture of fearful revelation. "Or I understand the foundations, but not any of this complicated science."

He nodded in agreement but his eyes did not lift from the screenzone. An internal world of panicked thought unraveled within his head—for there was space there, for his thoughts, room for them to discombobulate within his head, at least for now.

He came to the realisation of what he'd perhaps known all along: he, his wife, with their commonplace set-up, were the most basic, entry-level human packages available.

The anchorwoman's eyes glazed over as the scientist continued to delineate, but it was in too much detail for anyone outside of the world of science, and the scientist vanished live on air, leaving the anchorwoman sitting alone.

And, one brief moment after this incident, the HOW ENTERTAINING ARE YOU survey pinged into everybody's z-boxes.

The screen in front of the old man and his wife, swimming with multiple choice questions, stretched from ceiling to floor. "I suppose it is best to start at beginning," she said.

"Is it though?" he asked. "Is it always best to start at the beginning? This quiz is so long, so convoluted, I'm not even sure where it begins."

"Everything has a beginning," she said.

Don't think it does, he thought. "I'm not so sure," he replied, "and I'm not so sure everything has an ending. Zeroes for example. Circles." Aloof, he traced a round shape in the air with his right index finger. "See? No beginning, no end, just one eternal loop—" *Now, what was I doing*, he thought.

"Shall we make a start, love?" she said, and with her papery palm, patted the side of his arm.

He turned from his wife, tapped the screen, zoomed in on a patch of text. "Here seems as good a place as any," he said and shrugged, and as he did so, the mug of milky tea in his left hand nictitated, performed a brief atomic dance, and disappeared.

His wife gasped. He clenched his left fist, grasped at the air where his bland drink had been.

"But ones," he continued, as if he were choosing to ignore what'd just occurred, refusing to accept it had begun, "ones have a clear start, a definite finish. Unless you take the one, singular line that it is"—he drew his finger up and down in the air—"and curve it around, connect its tip with its base … well, then you recreate a circle—"

"The mug!" his wife said.

"We don't have long," he said.

"No, it appears not," she replied. "I'm scared."

He wiped a tear from his wife's cheek and started to read aloud a question from the survey.

The survey took an eternity. At times he felt as if the questioning led in circles, to the end then to the start, an unending circuit, but on its eventual completion, the couple decided to celebrate all the small things while they still could and threw caution to the wind. It was still before noon so they treated themselves to a second bowl of choco-larvae crunch.

She tipped up the box. Bugflakes cascaded down into their bowls.

"Naughty!" she said and a rush of excitement quicksilvered though her neurons.

Ping.

"They're back already, the results," he said and tapped on the floating neon envelope icon above the kitchen table, but as he tapped, the bowls, bugflakes, and kitchen table all flickered, became numerical static, and vanished.

He chewed his cuticles until the nail beds bled as he marched around and around the space where the kitchen table had existed. "What to do," he muttered. "Such low results. I could pace in a circle forever, for eternity, but will it solve this disaster? This needs to stop. An end is needed. Everything needs an end." *But why are these old legs still marching?* Short term memories fluttered away on the wings of spectral butterflies.

She ran into the bedroom, dove under grey-washed sheets and lay there, sobbing into her aged hands. Her husband was not well. And now, she felt, perhaps they were both unwell.

Ping.

A fresh, neon envelope rotated in the centre of the circuit which he'd been marching. He froze.

Should I tap? Do I want to know more? he thought. *Or is what I know already too much? A basic package is not designed to cope with so much information, data, such as what might or might not be pertinent to this simulation called Life, and Life is full to capacity. There is no more room for storage.*

He had a basic grasp on computing, understood the concept of a hard drive, how things, machines and such, people, worked best when half full, or half empty, space being essential for movement and thought, but in that moment, he could not think; could not think of anything except their impeccably low scores. Certainly, they'd be next, to become ones and zeroes and then no things. Nothingness. *Would to become nothing be all that bad?* he thought, and he thought hard about the place he knew nothing of, in which he'd been before he'd been born.

But he had not the memory for it.

But he had made a promise to his wife, that everything would be okay. He had to make this okay. *Surely,* he thought, *from simple concepts of three dimensions or less, from basic packages, miraculous, existentially wonderful situations may arise? If not by deliberation, then by means of chance?* He continued to march and think. *What to do?* And then he decided: he would tap on the envelope.

"Based on the results of your survey—commiserations—we would like to offer you the chance to increase your score. Read on if you wish to raise your statistical likelihood of avoiding the Big Delete. Increase your potential. Raise your entertainment value, NOW!"

He swiped up on the screen and the text rose upwards, revealing more text beneath, as is the way, the way a screen rolls on forever, eternally, until the user decides to take control of the matter, and make it stop. More information followed. More condolences and an invitation.

He had no choice. Does anyone have any choice? Isn't every decision already preordained, isn't free will all but an illusion according to Predeterminism? He thought of his wife, how bland she was. She'd be sure to go before him. He couldn't bear to be without her. He replied: affirmative.

Days seeded with impatience and fear rolled past. He thought about nothing else but attending 'The Trashcan' in preparation, to watch others compete in the show to which he'd been invited to partake, but he decided against this preparation.

The Trashcan. A 200-foot deep, cone-shaped cement pit hollow in the ground, an inner wall lined with rows of vertically stacked seating, a stage at its base lit by myriad yellow-pink neon dronelamps. It appeared overnight where the World's Largest Multi-Storey Car Park used to sit—same date his wife suggested Alzheimer's, same date the scientists made the link between risk of deletion and entertainment value.

While waiting for his chance on the show, his desperate attempt to save them both, he suggested they try everything possible to spice things up, to reduce their risk. No more fastidious cleaning. He threw the vacuum cleaner from the top window, and watched it smash. Chocolate mousse and cocktails for breakfast. Livin' on the edge. They had to.

"Another mass shooting at the mall yesterday," he shouted. "Best stay away from the shops, I feel. And so much looting. Did you see the chap driving blindfolded through the airstream? Nuts."

Nuts, but still alive. *Still solid.*

"Feeling prepared? Ready for tomorrow?" she asked, a slight tremor to her face, a distortion, he thought and pushed a rainbow-coloured cocktail with a paper umbrella and dolphin-shaped ice cubes in it into her hand. Eight thirty in the morning. Lime-green lipstick stained the tip of his straw. He sucked again on his drink and grimaced.

"Isn't it best to not be prepared? It's all written in the stars anyway, isn't it? Will 'knowing' better the experience? Surely 'not knowing' will make it more entertaining, won't it?"

"I don't know," she replied and sighed.

She does not, he thought, and she does not have the bandwidth to process the concept further.

They spent the remains of the day drinking and eating delicacies they'd never before been unruly enough in their lives to accommodate. He'd insisted on it. She loved him, did as he requested.

Sitting in a swinging chair on their patio at sunset, they stared at the cluttered sky. He pointed out the full moon, hidden between myriad low-hanging, white-flickering Wi-Fi satellites, orbital debris, atmospheric junk. He told her again how the sky had once been a blanket of black, pierced only with needle-holes of white. Now, a polar reverse, the original darkness was hard to spot.

She laughed.

"You're deluded, but I love you," she said.

"Only a matter of time," he said and placed his arm around her. "Always only a matter of time before everything got too full ... and time itself is a man-made construct."

Neither of them wanted to state it might be their final night in existence, so they skirted around the topic with existential physics.

"And who wants to live forever?" He laughed. Alcohol lubricated their spirits. "Poor Elon. MindCloned into the operating system of Space X." They both knew, had always known, they'd never have become wealthy enough to have their own consciences uploaded, like all the tech-savvy billionaires had done, because as time had passed, upload costs had sky-rocketed as storage space had depleted.

She squeezed his thigh, kissed him on his cheek. "I will remember you forever," she said, and entwined, they fell asleep outside.

"How does it feel to have made it through to the final round?" The Host zipped, side to side, in their tennis umpire dronechair before landing in the centre of the circular stage. Showers of glitter cascaded down, towards the bottom of the Trashcan pit. The old man could barely hear the Host's incessant questions above the roar of the crowd.

All around him, three-sixty, stacks of people telescoped up the walls, shouting, cheering, celebrating, as if their lives depended on it. From his spot on the stage, on looking up, he could just make out the sky above, a circle of it, a loop of endless yet finite grey at the top of the pit. Despite the hordes, the noise, the blinking neon lights, the buzz and whirr of Brownian motion drones, he felt as if he was sitting solo at the bottom of a dank well.

He focused on the pounding of his heart beat, the wetness of his balled palms, the last few clear memories of his wife and his home he could fathom. It'd been thirty-two hours since he'd last slept.

A filmdrone zoomed towards his face. The corners of his lips tipped upwards, a slight smile. Hoped his wife was watching from the sofa, also hoped she was not. To witness him vanish on screen would fill her last remaining nights with terror.

The Host barked out the same question. His opponent, who'd been sat against the wall, knees hugged to chest, arms looped around knees, stood up. Somehow, his opponent had had another surge of energy. The way his opponent just jumped up, the way the audience's cheers magnified in volume—it was as if his opponent had been shut down and rebooted.

A feeling of sickness in his stomach burdened him, but there was nothing left to bring up. He hurt, but knew he had to give this his best.

"AMAZING," he shouted. Thick spittle dribbled from his parched lips. Purple ropes, veins, pulsated at his temples. "Feel amazing," he said again and steadied himself against the wall, "bring it on."

If he won this round, somehow beat his opponent, he'd elevate to fame. He and his wife would appear on other shows, nice ones, do interviews, become recognised personalities. His one-shot chance to become more entertaining and to save them both was finally happening—but did he have it in him to win? He wasn't sure.

"And didn't they do well in the Slide It Off round, watchers? Didn't they do well?!"

The crowd cheered.

The pit floor was covered in vomit, some his, some not. With shaking fingers, he slicked back his white hair, effluvium fixing it in place. He'd somehow qualified through to the final round. But at what cost? The image of the other six contestants glitching out of existence had burnt a new memory in his retina he feared he'd never blink away.

"And your final challenge is our fabulous, world-renowned Pack Down Challenge," the Host boomed.

And the audience recursed … PackdownPackdownPackdown …

The pair of contestants moved centre stage, shook hands. Two show girls, feathered headwear, multicoloured skin-suits, pranced out from the sides. To him, each girl appeared as one and then as a stream of ones, each identical, but delayed and transmogrified, zoetroping through the air. All too much.

Each girl released a flare up through the vertical core of the Trashcan. Each flare exploded and released a waterfall of neons above. Stage workers rolled out machinery, two airport-luggage-style conveyor belts were extrapolated from the walls. It was at this point he wished he'd prepared, wished he'd known what was coming next.

Packdownpackdownpackdown …

The volume of the crowd hurt his eardrums.

The two girls collected up the concertina paper doll chains of themselves and dipped back into the eaves. Each came back out pulling a large crate; each crate had transparent sides, a hinged lid, and the dimensions of a coffin.

"Thank you, girls. Can we get a round of applause for our girls?" The crowd obeyed. "Girls, I think we're ready for the tools—"

The two girls, pegged grins broader than their fancy headdresses, wheeled in a cabinet each. Each cabinet had hung from it a variety of implements: egg flipper, dusty King James bible, cordless drill, spade, kitchen knife, and many more items he could neither name nor identify. None of the items—glass coffins, conveyor belts, cabinets, tools—were his.

"Dull dull dull dull dull. You two are here because you're mediocre, dull, vapid. You hold no value, have no reason to be kept. Prove us wrong—become saved!

"All the dull items still somehow in existence from your meaningless homes will roll out here, before us, on the belt. All YOU have to do is pack them down, into the crate, using the tools provided."

Packdownpackdownpackdown …

The Host continued over the roar of the crowd. "And on the countdown, the conveyor belts will start … ENTERTAIN US!"

I don't understand, he thought, and he didn't. Although he did understand his life depended on it.

A spinning red number ten z-jected in a void above the stage and the audience chanted each number as the count descended to zero.

"Zero!"

He moved towards his conveyor belt. What is my opponent doing? His opponent punched the red switch on the side of his conveyor. The sound of gears grinding and magnets whirring crunched and curled through the air. *This switch, is this switch the beginning of the end, my end?* Panic showed clarion on his face. I am not ready to go. His opponent took down a mallet from the cabinet. The white-haired man, all fingers and thumbs, copied.

Saucers his wife had brought trundled along his belt and over on his opponent's belt, a small casserole dish. He watched as his opponent grabbed the dish, brought the mallet down on it, picked up the pieces, and smashed them again until what was left was closer to dust than dish. The hum of stale sweat and sick dissipated through the thick air. His opponent dropped the mallet in haste, cupped up the debris and carried and dropped it into his transparent box.

He copied with his wife's tea set.

A folded pair of slacks poked through his opponent's black rubber flaps, the dispensing mouth of the opponent's belt, which the opponent proceeded to grab, roll up, and press into his box.

Item after item swept along the belts. He and his opponent, with speed, grabbed and destroyed each piece, made each piece smaller, compressed each piece into their box. *Is it the first to fill the box? The first to destroy all of the items? How is this contest judged? Who's in charge here?* He had no idea. But he also had some idea. And they were not good thoughts.

The chanting of the audience pulsated in his eardrum. He operated trancelike. His body ached, his mouth became a desert, and his chest longed for it all to stop. But he couldn't. Had to keep packing down, compressing.

Life was at capacity. And life is everything, although life has a beginning and an end, and must be sandwiched between slices of something else.

He glanced at his opponent's box. Half full. Still space. More items rolled out for each of them to destroy and crush and pack away. His winter overcoat, his bathroom mirror, a cuddly toy from his childhood, the blanket his wife had been working on …

The audience fell silent.

On his component's belt, rolled out a panting, black-and-white collie.

"Oh no. Oh shit," his component uttered. "Not Bonnie. No—"

The old man stood and watched, catching his breath, resting his tired arms, curious and fearful over what his opponent would do. Would he do it, to the dog? Could he? The old man had once loved a similar dog as a child.

"I can't," his opponent cried. "Can't." And his opponent dropped his hammer. As the hammer hit the floor, his opponent's hand started to flicker.

The old man watched on, his own conveyor belt running empty, loop-eternal. *Could this be it? Have I won?* His opponent froze, stared at his vanishing hand then at his dog who'd lain down on the conveyor belt, paws over eyes, playing dead.

With his still-flesh hand, the opponent bent down, retrieved the hammer from the floor and, in a fit of rage, burst towards Bonnie. He took the hammer down hard and heavy: an explosion of violence, a guttural wail. The opponent scooped up and placed his limp pet into the box, then fell to the floor and sobbed. But his hand flickered back into focus.

The white-haired man felt sick. He mouthed 'sorry' to his broken opponent, and, in catching his eye, felt a pang of distant recognition: Is that—? Could he be—? *No, no, it's gone,* he thought, and then turned his head towards a sound—his own conveyor belt flaps were parting.

"Packdown packdown packdown," the crowd cheered. Their volume elevated. Tawdry energy filled the Trashcan pit again. The old man turned and gasped and clamped his chest with his hands.

His wife, the woman he loved with all his heart. Strapped to a wooden chair, his wife edged towards him on the belt.

What sweet hell was he in? Blood drained from his head to his toes. He could not do this, pay this price for his own life. The game which was his life was over.

He shook and hung his head first at his wife, then at the Host, then at the crowd. "No more," he said. He moved towards her. If he was going to vanish, it would be in her arms.

He scrambled up onto the conveyor belt, knelt down, and held his wife. She embraced him back, and then she whispered in his ear.

Re-birthed by the words and sweet kiss from his wife, the old man felt as if he had been switched off and then on again, despite his right ear now a cluster of wavering zeros and ones, and his left ear, which his wife had spoken into, becoming a flickering-edged abyss.

Maybe it was not all over. Not yet.

The ladder up the side of the umpire chair had been easy to ascend with its steel rungs. The apolipoprotein-suited Host was lighter than the old man had imagined. The old man grabbed and pulled the host towards him. The cordless drill bit pierced the Host's skull readily, as if it, an inanimate object, were as eager for the Host to die as the white-haired man had been. With each fleck of hippocampus that splattered out, a section of our white-haired man's missing ears phased back into the visual plain. The crowd roared.

Once certain the Host had been slain, with a surge of white-blue might, the old man yanked the dead irritant from the chaircraft, and allowed gravity to drop them both to the pit floor.

The opponent, in his spot against the wall, knees to chest, arms round knees again, sobbed and sobbed until he vanished. *A shame*, the old man thought, can't lift this host-corpse alone.

"Turn away," he said to his wife, and with the best tools for the job, he defragmented and transferred the Host into the transparent crate and closed down the lid.

He turned, jubilant, to address the audience who'd become silent, and at the very top of the pit, where he remembered the watchers had seemed small, as far away as the moon, he saw the rings of furthest seats were now empty. *Have people left or disappeared?* he thought, *Can I truly be sure they were ever there in the first place?*

"They're vanishing," his wife said. They both stared in awe. Ziplights and filmdrones fizzed in reiterating shades of ones and zeroes before disappearing. "Becoming erased."

She placed her hands on his shoulders as he hacked and sawed through the belt which held her onto the chair only to find himself no longer needing to hack and saw as the belt and the chair became nothing in his hands.

Ad hoc clumps of crowd fell away, became minimised and removed, like patches of lawn burnt white by sun, like systems and stars sucked past event horizon. Eventually, all that remained in the Trashcan was the sound of weeping and the matter of the couple.

He took his wife by the hand and led her to the wall of the pit. Together, they studied each of the seats, pointed, compared. All empty. They searched until they were sure they were the only things, other than the clothing they had on and the pit itself, that'd avoided deletion. Their heads tipped back further. They looked up, out, to the circle of now dark sky above.

"The night stars," she said and pointed at the sky, all velveteen and empty bar a scattering of constellations, "the ones amongst the zeroes. I see them now. Vividly."

"Each star is as clear, as preconceived, and as disbanded from one another as the freckles which cover your nose," he said. "Let's get out of here."

Weary limbed, they reached the top. He crouched, lowered his knee on which for her to climb free, and she did so. He followed, hoisting himself up with tired arms.

Above them stretched the endless noir ceiling of sky, cracked open only by stars. Things were not as they'd once been.

"It's as if we're trapped inside a black sphere, and something outside has pierced inwards, multiple times, from a place of great light, with a needle," he said. "Smells sweet, like the hazelnut cakes Mother used to bake."

"It's beautiful," she said.

He agreed.

Behind them, the pit was gone, and in its place, their humble home. Beneath them and the house, where they expected to see grass or concrete or their neighbour's properties, extended only an infinite inky darkness broken just by uncountable, dots of light.

"We're … floating." she said. She stepped forwards, closer to her loved one, his face lit only by stellar lux.

"Shall we go home?" he asked. But their house, the only other object in the starlit void, roiled, became an imploding mass of zeros and ones, and, in a blip, disappeared.

His wife turned to him, her face, restful, still, serene. She cupped his face in her hands and kissed his lips. "It's happening," she said, "I'm going now. I'll never forget you."

A celestial light rippled up her feet, her legs, her waist, until, like a ghost in his arms, she became a ball of white light as bright as a sun, a one. She flickered on and off and then disappeared into oblivion.

He both knew and did not know all this was to happen, yet still, he felt his heart, adrift, become a black hole.

He screamed.

He screamed and the sound waves from his throat spread out in all directions. He screamed until no further sound came. And in all plains, all axes, all he could see was eternal blackness, the occasional neon-clear zip of a line moving towards the perspective of its vanishing point, and on off dots of white light.

He sat down on nothing and waited, until he could remember nothing at all, and his heart filled with a need stronger than any emotion he'd ever felt before, for his own ones and zeroes to begin.

Hag Stone

First published by Gravestone Press, 2021

Reece pushed aside the cobweb strings on the photograph: Aello.

Aello, his grandmother, had worn her black hair long in youth too, but had not cared to dye or mask the keratinous white streak in it, like his mother had with hers.

Both his mother and grandmother, in their midlife, had resembled magpies. Cropped and ashen was how his mother wore her locks now. His grandmother, well she was all ash, too, and scattered in the forest near her home. Reece had not attended the old lady's funeral. He'd never even met Aello—his mother had ensured all her matriarchal connections were severed.

The rye bloomer baking in the oven of his grandmother's home drew him back to the kitchen. From Aello's cupboards, he fumbled together a picnic to accompany the loaf. A few comestibles had not been claimed by mould: a jam of sorts, dried fruit, preserved sausage meat from the larder.

The boat out front, tethered to an oak, was still watertight, and so, after a hard day of boxing trinkets, burning musky, stained robes, and pouring unidentifiable concoctions the old bag had been stewing down the sink, he'd decided he would venture out in it. The liberty of the vessel had beckoned him, and the river had called out to the boat.

There was nothing of entertainment to do inside the cottage anyhow; no Wi-Fi or phone signal and nothing to read bar a few dust-coated novels he'd found the night before by the fireplace. Written in a language he couldn't identify, the books were filled with vintage copperplate-engraving prints of ships, sea monsters heralding tridents, and bird-like creatures with the faces of women, and all were more odorous than his grandmother's deathbed.

"Don't call us, we'll call you," he'd said as he'd tossed the books onto the fire.

When the probate letter had come, stating that everything Aello owned was to be passed to Reece's mother, Reece had suggested he go to manage the property. He met his mother in a motorway cafe midway between their homes. They rarely spoke—she wasn't one for talking, and he wasn't one for listening. She told him she didn't want anything to do with the handling of Aello's estate and Reece, sensing his mother's hesitance to handle the situation, smelled cash.

"I'll go. For fifty per cent of the equity when the sale goes through," he said.

"Okay. You go. Empty the place. Give away or bin or burn her belongings. Don't bring anything back for me, I want no memories saved." He watched his mother's eyes dampen.

"Seventy-five," he said. His mother wiped a tear from her face. "I'll take seventy-five percent of the profit—as I'll be doing all the work."

"Fine. I imagine it'll take you some time to clear it out. Do what you must inside her house." She paused. "But the forest—don't go out into the forest, Reece."

His mother reached out and squeezed his arm gently, in a vain attempt to reinforce her words. She knew her son rarely did as he was asked, and usually did quite the opposite. One could only lead the horse as far as the water.

"If you do though, if you really need to get out of the house for a break, please don't go any further than Phineas Island."

"Phineas what? How can there be an island there, she lives twenty miles inland."

"It's a riverine island—where the river splits and rejoins. Two miles south of the cottage. Tangled mangroves. Nothing good ever happened there."

Reece guffawed and rolled his eyes. "Christ alive, Mum. I'm not a kid. I'm not going to get lost in the woods, or paddle out of my depth, or follow strangers back into houses made of candy canes."

Reece's mother forced a smile, but burnt by his sarcasm, she drew her hand away and looked down at her food. Her lip twisted and with delicate fingertips, she withdrew and flicked away a small, blue-black feather from her half-eaten gateaux.

When Reece woke, he was in a hole; a cave of sorts, dark as a lonely midnight. He pulled his hand up to his head. He had not hit it. There was no blood there, nothing that felt tepid and moist to touch.

His back hurt. Reaching over, feeling between his shoulder blades, he found warmth and dampness. He winced in pain as his fingers probed for a reason. Through his skin-thin T-shirt, his tips fell into deep, fresh lacerations. Something had dug in hard. Blood soaked through his clothing. He could smell the metal of it, warmed copper.

His palms and knees also felt grazed raw, as if he'd dropped from a substantial height down onto them and then crawled through a thicket of needles and scouring pads on all fours.

Placing his picnic sack aboard, setting the boat to water, sitting down on the wooden seat it offered—these are the parts of his venture he recalled. The wind had picked up, enough so to feel the skin on his hands and cheeks ripple. A gale had carried him onwards, forwards, down the river and away from the old hag's house, leaving the oar redundant. After this, he could remember nothing.

Had he blown into this pit? Tripped? Had he been drugged and mugged? He wasn't wet, so he can't have capsized. And where was the boat? His bag?

He stood, rubbed his eyes and brushed leaf litter from his limbs. He looked up, and side to side, and saw the same: nothing. Darkness. His body ached like never before, as if he'd fallen asleep in a tumble drier only to be hurled and spun and rung inside its drum, then burnt with detergent powder; and then yanked out and pegged to the line, with the force of a million winds slapping his face and body as he dried.

He turned to look behind him. The place was as dark as a badger's set and smelled as bad as fox shit. Behind him, he could just make out a warm light resting on a small wooden table.

Reece knelt by the table, the ground beneath him damp, sticky. Had he knelt in some kind of mucilaginous exudate? Blindly, he fumbled for something, anything, to clear off the adhesive residue and settled on a handful of crisp leaves. He used them to wipe his wet knees clean.

On the table was an oil lamp, which yielded him a radius of light no larger than a fistful of bad dreams, at the ends of which, sat blackness again, and the unknown once more. He reached for the handle at the top of the lamp and drew it along the tabletop, towards two other objects, the only two other items on the table, to inspect them more closely.

The first item was a large pebble, which was placed on top of the second item, a note of sorts.

The rock appeared to be placed as a paperweight. It anchored the note to the tabletop, despite the air in the cave being as quiescent and thick and still as a mug of solidified dripping. Reece held the pebble close to the lamp—it was smooth and grey with a white streak like a thin sandwich-filing through its mass.

He held the pebble in his hand. It filled his hand. In such a claustrophobic place of darkness, to hold onto something so solid felt like stumbling upon an old friend, alive, amidst a warzone.

The rock contained a hole with the diameter the size of a fat finger that started on one side and went right through to the other, cleanly so. He slipped the rock onto his forefinger like a Palaeolithic wedding ring, then he pocketed the rock and kept his hand on it, in his pocket, as he moved the final item, the note, towards the dim light. The weight of the pebble gave him comfort, a peculiar reassurance, and his finger fell in love with its hole.

The note was tarnished around the edges—perhaps with time, perhaps with touch—and on it was just one sentence:

DO NOT LOOK THROUGH THE HOLE IN THE STONE, OR YOU WILL GO THROUGH IT.

The words curled out of his lips in silence and again with sound blown into them. He shouted the sentence a third time and kicked the table with force. The table shot across the floor and crashed against a wall which he could barely see. The words bounced back and forth in his mind and oscillated there like a spring dangling between sanity and the alternative. How could he look through the damn hole in the stone even if he wanted to, when he could see no further than an inch in front of his nose?

With time, the cavernous silence became deafening. The words on the note, which had at first shouted at Reece, faded into insignificance as desolation bit back. The soundlessness, as haunting as the darkness, was broken only by his heart which thrummed against the prison cage bars of his chest as his impatient feet snapped twigs on the floor.

Tired, distressed, and confused, he slumped against cold granite. Reece placed the lamp between his legs in an attempt to rest, then promptly stood up again, his silence interrupted by a flicking sound. A snake whipped across the ground towards him. In defence, he raised his foot up and down and stamped and screamed. The reptile's guts splayed across the sticks and leaves and mangled feather litter which made the dank chamber's carpet. His shriek echoed, ricocheting upwards, until it went off with the soul of the snake, up, up, and away.

He reached into his pocket, and once more found the stone with the hole and ran his finger around and through it, around and around and through it again. He found once more a strange comfort in the regularity, the coldness of it, its hardness, and the fact it had an in and an out to it—somewhere his finger could enter and then leave.

He began to circle the dungeon floor; the edge of his foot pressing, dragging against the edge of the pit. He paced the circumference around and around and around again, as the words on the note span and jostled between his ears, bubbling over in his cauldron of madness. He searched for meaning and for a gap in the jagged, rough rock wall through which he could escape. Reece grappled at the wall and ground of the pit with his hands. He brought the dim light of the lamp to each square inch in his quest for help, a way out. He sought for anything other than darkness, twigs, stinking feathers, cold, old rock and patches of slimy mud.

His body ached. His clarity began to crack. The light from the lamp, like his adrenaline-fuelled energy, simmered down and out. In the bottom of the pit, it became as dark as death. Reece fell asleep with one sore, bleeding, muddied arm draped around a broken table leg, and his other hand wrapped around the pebble in his pocket.

He woke. A circle of warm light illuminated something on the twig carpet—the picnic he had brought from his grandmother's. Reece, bitter at finding himself still trapped in such fresh hell, yet ravenous and parched, crawled over to the circle of illumination and reached for his food. He pulled his hand back in disgust. The bread and meat he'd wrapped just yesterday lay riddled, throbbing with dancing maggots, and covered in spores of blue-green mould. His stomach flipped. Dry wretches of vomit erupted onto the pile of rotten spoils.

As he wiped his mouth, he realised: as disgusting as the pile was, in it, he had seen light and colour. Where was this light coming from? He looked up and saw another circle of light above, this one azure blue and laced with white clouds. The circle of light seemed to laugh at his misfortune as it boasted of a better place. With the sliver of light the hole let in, he saw the rope ladder as it unfurled; a ladder which led up and out of the pit.

Reece stood, transfixed for a moment. He looked up and out through the hole in the stone ceiling of the cave. As a prisoner of granite and nightmares, he released a guttural scream. This was followed by his own insane laughter. Freedom.

He had looked up and out through the hole in the stone cave, and yes, yes, yes, and fuck, yes again, he wanted to go through it and go through it he would and he did. Screw the fucking note.

Someone was playing games with him, but he had beaten them. No-one told Reece what to do. He could see the fucking hole. He looked through and out of the hole to way up above at the beckoning blue sky, and then, he climbed out through it.

Reece hauled himself out of the top. In the light of day, his white T-shirt was red and brown with blood and dirt and his legs were covered in bruises. In front of him, he saw his boat, moored, with his bag inside of it. And, as he rummaged through it, he discovered his bag still contained his phone, wallet and keys. Such relief.

He stretched out the crook in his back and felt something hard in his pocket. The stone.

He slipped his hand in and drew it out. It had felt so smooth, a saintly comfort in the night, this salvaged piece of beauty, while he had been immersed in the hellish void of the pit. But under the radiance of the sunshine, surrounded by the beauty and the colour of freedom and the forest, in his hand, all Reece saw was a dull pebble with a hole.

Reece marvelled at the strip of blue above his head where the forest canopy broke. He inhaled the greens of the foliage. He held the lacklustre pebble up so that the hole within it haloed the sun. Inspecting the pebble, he searched it for the beauty he was sure it had held in the black of night in the pit. Did the pebble have anything further to offer? Was it worth pocketing as a keepsake or should he lob it away, into the river or the woods?

He drew the pebble closer to his eye, to inspect it further, for patterns, perhaps for evidence of quartz or fossils.

Zilch.

Nada.

He lifted the central tunnel, the hole in the core of the rock, up close to his face, and pressed the stone against his cheek and brow, making a monocle of it for his right eye. The he opened his right eye, while closing his left, and looked straight through the hole … and saw … straight out of the other side.

Before he had time to sigh, the piece of smoothed rock clamped hard against his face. No longer fresh and cool, it burnt hot like molten lava.

He screamed as he tried to pull the pebble from his face, yet on it clamped, like the suckers of a giant octopus. A pressure built up in his eyeball as the pebble slurped tighter still. Pain pin-balled in his head in response to the satanic fellatio his face was being given.

His white eyeball reddened as the vessels within it burst. Blood spilt into the socket, squirted out with vitreous humour, as his eyeball popped outright like a pus-filled miniature balloon. Gelatinous contents were guzzled in and through and out of the other side of the hole in the pebble, and sprayed all over the forest floor. Nose and cheeks followed, sucked through like light down a black hole. Flesh ripped from bone, claret poured down his neck. The rest of his face threaded through the hole, shredded and pulped like chunks of meat down a waste disposal system. Forehead and ears became ground up into a jammy mess, and then were sprayed out of the other side of the rock.

Reece ran around in circles, all headless chicken, with just a gash for a mouth left to scream through. The rock clamped on firmly to his neck stump. It chomped and sucked and peeled back adipose tissue, and feasted on his cartilage and bone, and mangled his flesh up through its granite mouth.

Like chemical fertiliser from the devil's crop sprayer, a zoetrope of red and pink with shards of grated bone spewed out onto the forest floor, all through the hole.

Torso, arms and legs followed. His testicles popped, overripe kiwi, as they ratcheted up and through the deadly portal. Semen sprayed through and out of the hole, a bukkaki party of one. Macerated, liquefied, dead, in and through and out of the hole, Reece became a puddle—reverse-birthed. Full-sized human returned to a pool of cells and slosh.

And red ran the water that rushed around the riverine island as Reece became no more.

And as the stone with a hole fell to the floor with a thud, all the birds in the trees cawed: "Aello, Aello," and took to the air at once.

The colossal raptor-like creature with the face of a woman cawed the loudest. With her beetle-black demon eyes and a plume of blue-black curled hair streaked with white, the she-beast with feathered wings swooped down from the highest branch, retrieved the stone with the hole from its mossy spot, and dropped it down, back into the pit.

Christingle Service

First published by Madhouse Books, 2022

What use are weighted diving-boots in a land-locked town? Last night, I fell asleep wearing mine. Today, I sit, feet throbbing, at the table opposite Mother. She talks incessantly about Christmas, about the services she is taking part in, as her hands wrap red ribbon around an orange. I drum my fingernails, faster, louder, and wait for her harsh tongue to tell me to stop.

I don't want to be here, doing what we're doing. It's an effort to feign interest in her madness, and my toes and heels are blistered and sore. I want to lie in my room, and float in the lagoon of my ceiling.

The scullery does smell delicious though—cinnamon, cloves, winter equinox cheer—but all the sweet scents in the world won't convince me He exists. None of it makes sense. Each evening, when Mother drags me along, I see her congregation speak in tongues and handle the rattles down at the tabernacle. Mother, once a blind-sided, spiritual groupie, is now leading her own brigade.

I pull out a snapped cocktail stick from the orange Mother has given me, throw it back in the tray, and fold my arms in protest.

Mother's shoulders drop. The smile she wears for her clergy—who are not present, they never come into our house—slips too.

"Why would He want a 'river of blood' wrapped around the planet? And raisins. When have raisins ever symbolised summer? When have raisins ever symbolised anything?" I fondle the dried fruit in the tray of junk she's gathered for her ritual. Shrivelled grapes trickle through my leaf-stained fingers.

"The dried fruit represent all of God's creations; the orange, our planet and all its swamp of sins. They used swedes, between the wars, when oranges were hard to come by," Mother says, attempting to grab my attention.

I roll my eyes.

"Thread on the fruit or go to your room." She drops a fistful of sultanas and four new sharp sticks in front of me, but today I've had enough.

"I'm too old for this." I pause. Should I let out how angry I feel? Well, I can't hold it in. "And I have a direct line with Him upstairs. He thinks wrapping fruit in ribbon and leaving it on the sideboard to rot is a load of cobblers too. That's why there's no mention of abusing citrus fruit in His debut novel."

"Room. Now." My mother's voice is hushed. As if her words are imprisoned in her orange. The whispers are how I know she's livid. But I'm fifteen now, a young woman, and my mother is a fool. This will be my last Christingle-themed facade with her. Six more months of this shit and I turn sixteen, then I'm out of here.

"Gladly," I say and hammer in my final nail, "and don't even get me started on the resurrection—nothing comes back once it's dead. Utter bollocks."

Her eyes narrow, her nostrils flare like a dragon.

In truth, last year I hadn't minded being part of the procession, carrying the mould-green orange up the chequered aisle of the tabernacle. The candle rammed in the centre of my sullied fruit had flickered with each slow footstep. Keeping it alight was the sort of challenge a child enjoys and we'd been promised a taste of the mulled wine after. But I'm older now, wiser. I've found my own religion, of sorts.

Some of Mother's rituals come direct from her faith, others I've no idea where. She doesn't talk about the latter at the tabernacle. On my sixth birthday, after we'd brushed each other's hair—hers thick and black and long, mine mousy, full of lice—she'd shown me, lifted the lid of the half-full glass tank she keeps under her bed in which she poured her monthly menses. Our birds and bees moment. My lips curled in disgust, I pinched my nose to peg out the stench. I could see straight away she regretted sharing it with me. Or, maybe, after she'd given her rambling explanation for why she did it, she realised how crazed it all sounded. She's not mentioned the jar of red since.

Now, her hair is tired and more grey than black and the contents of the red blood jar are scab-dry. But she still keeps it. More than once, I've seen her slouched forward over it in the night, praying, asking Him to breathe life into it, resurrect it.

But it is not my sister.

I tap the orange with the back of my hand, set it in motion. It's happening. Neither of us reach forward to stop it. Her cheeks flush crimson like they do when I move one of her crates of junk. She's getting cross, but I say nothing. I hold my ground and maintain eye contact with this old woman who claims to love me, and the fruit hits the floor with one dull thud.

My chair legs screech over the stone floor and I get up and walk away, leaving her to it—piercing sticks and candles into old fruit.

"*For I am the light of the world. Whoever follows me will never walk in darkness, but will have the light of life.*" She spits out one of her quotes to the spine of me, to my blistered heels, to my middle finger, as I storm to my bedroom.

On my way, I push over the stack of snake skins piled precariously on top of the end vivarium, the infrared tank rammed between old magazines and boxes of broken toasters. The papery skins sigh to the floor and land next to the orange and all the other hoarded rubbish I have to crab past and step over daily.

The man who inseminated her—never referred to as my father (only one Father is in her world—bearded, lives in a cloud)—left her when he learnt I was coming. She blames me. I'm responsible for all her problems: the pain in her back, the leaking roof, when the snakes won't feed before a service. The twin that bled out when I was foetal. Mother says we wouldn't have coped, just the two of us, without my dad. She said we were blessed when the congregation caught us, just after I was born.

In my room, I close the door. As I exhale, my breath plumes out, a white fog in the air. But a red mist heats my core like a furnace. Only my extremities feel cold. I need to breathe deep. I look at my bed. It seems inviting. I sit on its edge and, out of habit, slide my feet into my old diving boots. They are the grim sort: several inches of heavy, heavy sole, cast brass safety toes, ancient, impossible to walk on land in.

Each pair of lead-weighted boots Mother has given me have looked older than the last. She gets them from the vagabond rag-picker in exchange for snake skins and fly agaric. The brass toecaps are cool and almost scold my fingertips as I see-saw the boots on. It's hard to ignore the discomfort from my blisters, but I must. My blurred fingertips and forehead are reflected in the burnished metalwork, dancing on the concave surface as I lift each boot up. My fingers work the waxed-tip laces through each of the reinforced eyelet holes.

The laces are well worn but strong enough to take the tension of my pull as I shape them into double bows. I'm not sure I even need the weight of these boots anymore, but through force of practice, my own little ritual, I put them on when I feel unsafe.

The smell of old leather and lead do their job. My raised pulse subsides.

My lower legs dangle like pendulums over the edge of my bed and the boots press hard on my sore toes and heels, angering the red-raw and white-bubbled skin there, but the pain is worth the reassurance they offer. I reach under my bed for my smokes tin.

Christmas Day, gift swap time. By weight alone, I suspect the large parcel on my lap is something useful before I unwrap it. But it's not the usual shape.

My diving boots pinched hard last night. Straw-coloured fluid dribbled from my toes this morning, and a smell not too unlike the kefir Mother stores in the outhouse followed.

"Money's tight," Mother says. She picks imagined lint from the new scarf I've just given her. She lays each miniscule piece of nothing in a pile on the patched arm of the sofa and avoids looking me in the eye.

"Doesn't feel like new boots," I say and force a white-flag smile.

"You can wear it to service later," she says.

I bite my tongue and pick at melded sticky-tape. I've no intentions of going to a second service today. We've been to one already this morning. I've made plans to see a friend—a dealer—later, whilst Mother handles the rattles and conjures glossolalia.

I break the seal on the tape, tear the cheap paper open, and lift out something dark and waxy. I let the wrapping fall to the floor. Mother tuts. She picks up the discarded sheet, then presses it flat on her lap. She folds it into quarts then 'teenths and forces it into the stuffed top drawer of the side cabinet.

"It's a jacket?" I ask. I know it's a jacket. It's a waxed navy jacket, the sort country folk wear.

"It's new, but I've modified it. Boots were too dear. We'll wait until you stop growing, then get adult boots that'll last. I'm sure you're nearly there, full-sized. You're taller than me now."

"Thanks," I say and shake the coat open. "Is it going to be heavy enough?"

She stands and snatches the jacket.

"Stand," she orders. She cloaks the coat around my shoulders. "Put your arms through. Can you feel the weights I've sewn in?" She points at the lining, a rough fabric riddled with bumps and clumsy, cream stitching, where she's been at it by hand.

I make an effort and feel the lead teardrops she's hidden.

"Lift your arms. Go on, try to flap your wings."

I do as she says.

It is heavy, heavier than the boots. I smile with just my lips and thank her, figuring if I'm gracious enough, I can excuse myself now lunch has been eaten and our gifts have been exchanged. But I feel guilt for leaving her alone on Christmas Day. There are four hours to pass until her evening service.

"They're fishing weights. Sixty-six of them. Lead. Same as the boots," she says.

I sigh. She's expecting me to want to know more. As long as it's heavy, keeps her happy, buys me peace whilst I smoke, I don't care what it's made from.

A drop of water lands on Mother's cheek. She looks up. The ceiling is leaking again. Another drop. Another.

She hobbles to the scullery, retrieves the largest pan and places it under the drip. I take the jacket off and hang it over the back of the couch.

"Will you go up, see if it's a loose tile again? No-one will come out on Christmas Day, and neither should they have to," she says.

I haven't been up in the loft before, and I've not seen Mother go up there for years. It's more than likely close to full. She sent a man up a month back, the last time the drips came, and he patched it up for her in a shake of a lamb's tail, charged more than most earn in a day.

"And what will I do up there? I'm not a roofer!" But I know I have no choice.

I know she'll play one of her cards. This time she settles on the back card.

"My back," she says. "I can't take on that ladder. My back hurts, your fault, big baby. You go."

Of course, her backache is my fault. I head to the scullery, pull an oil lamp and card of matches from the cupboard, and climb up into the attic.

The loose tile is easy to spot. I yank it back into place. As I prepare for my descent, a noise catches me off guard. Something sibilant? It's not the sound of dripping, anyway. Is one of the snakes free again? I'll need to count them. More work for me. Something darts from the corner. It is corpse-grey and moves like wind with flesh and then it is gone. My heart thumps triple speed, but as I move closer to the source of the distraction, I see nothing. It must have been the overactive imagination Mother tells me I'm cursed with. No, there is nothing moving. Nothing of interest up here. All I see are boxes on boxes on boxes—Mother's several lifetimes worth of stored belongings which fill the cold heart of the attic. I arc my lamp one last time to be sure, and the light falls on the collection.

Pushed up against the far wall are fourteen pairs of diving boots, all rust-brown or grey, a cornucopia of sizes. I've no memory of the tiniest ones. I place my lamp down and pick up the smallest pair. Solid and dense yet petite, each tiny boot is like an amulet from a giant's charm bracelet. They're covered in a thick blanket of dust. The smallest pair fit in the palm of my hand. I twiddle the end of the laces. Wire-thin black cords, stiff from time and neglect.

I want to say they evoke emotion, but I feel nothing, so I put the boots back in their place and make my way down the ladder.

Instead of thanking me for putting stop to the leak, Mother cries and demands I count the snakes and go to the service with her. With a small funnel pressed to her cheek, she drains her tears into a glass and tips them into the flood water she's collected in the pan from the leaking roof. Says it'll come in use, perfect for spring seedlings I know she'll never germinate. I try to barter. I put up an argument at first to avoid another service, but she brings up my twin. All the snakes are present, and I go again to tabernacle.

A kid from school is at the service. His mother is in neck-deep too. He gives me some fresh green, enough for a smoke and I give him money from a greetings card from a near-dead relative whom I never see. Mother stays at tabernacle, chasing the aftermath with the other believers, and I head back to the place she calls home.

In the home, the house, out of the cold, I pick up the new jacket, put it on, and go to my room to skin-up.

I roll the papers back and forth between my fingers and reflect on the service and on the nonsense Mother spewed during her moment. Channelling nonsense about birth and death and resurrection, her bulging eyes never leaving my face. "A place. For you. In Heaven." She spoke for minutes with her hands raised in the air. The snakes had been noisy too. Full of Christmas hiss.

Why do believers place creators in the sky, pulling our divinity out from our own viscera? Why do we sieve out the holy from our bones and pour it into an inaccessible domain? Why would anyone wish to extract godly closeness from our presence? The sky is too far away, so unobtainable. I've asked Mother before about Heaven, its precise location. She couldn't tell me with her own words and had to refer to her book.

"The Heavens declare His glory; the skies proclaim the work of His hands," she muttered, her hands slapping through the wafer-thin pages of the old text on her lap, searching, searching. Her answer left me none the wiser.

She insists I'll go there, have my place aside the throne, atop the cloud, under the infinite rainbow.

If.

And there are many 'ifs.'

If I attend service, pray, carry a Christingle once a year, hold the rattles, watch her each week as she channels the Holy Spirit. If I do all these things, she says ascension is within my reach. But there are too many ifs and we both know I won't make the grade.

Yet, from birth, she's tied me down for fear I'll drift up too soon.

I think about my new jacket, all of my outgrown diving boots. I push the pair that now pinch up against my closed bedroom door, underneath the wooden chair I use to stop the handle from levering. The chair I attempt to keep Mother out with. I take my first toke of the day. Hot, creamy smoke rolls into my lungs, tickling them, and I begin to wonder. I wonder if, perhaps, Mother and everyone else are wrong—if perhaps, God and Devil are within me, not above and below. I palpate my stomach with my spare hand—yes—I can feel them both trapped there, writhing between my kidneys and intestines. I lie in silence. They sweat their discourse whilst I finish my joint.

From the age of four, I refused to wear the boots out of the house to school. Mother said she'd pray on it, consult her ministry. She told me He agreed, said the rattles supported His decision. "You can wear patent T-bars for school as long as you put your divers back on when you get home." She also said if I didn't wear the boots at home, she'd use the rope again, pinion me to the truss.

I jump up from my bed and throw the stubbed spliff-nub out of my window.

"You scared me. Don't you know how to knock?" My door swings, and bangs open, Mother barges in. *Ticka-Ticka-Ticka.* Something taps or clunks or thwumps and hisses and scuttles under my bed and both of us turn our heads to follow the commotion. It stops. She looks at me, no doubt my eyes are bloodshot.

"What are you doing, child? What is this smell? Smoke?"

Red-handed. Christmas Day.

She's hit me before. I think she's going to strike me again but instead she speaks to me in a hiss.

"Your sister would never have done this."

She turns and goes in search of her sage brush.

Later that evening, I watch her pour in the snake skins, the tear-water from the leaking roof, her mouldy orange Christingle. She doesn't know I can see her. She pours it all into the jar she keeps beneath her bed and hugs it and speaks to it in tongues. Mumbles about resurrection. What is she conjuring? The sound of her feet pattering along the landing, scuttling back and forth to collect things to add to her jar of madness keeps me awake all night.

Where I live, people leave their unwanted belongings out the front of their house; on walls, tables, in crates. You can help yourself to it. Free. Dust-jacketless books, mismatched crockery, board games with missing dice—many a found thing I've taken home on my walk home from school. Early January, I decide it's time for a clear out.

Mother's words hurt me but I'm never quick-witted enough to fire back. Instead I brew, I ferment. I go up in the roof and gather the generations of diving boots, dust and all, into a burlap sack. I sling them over my shoulder and climb back down the ladder. On our front wall, I line up the boots in attic formation, exactly how I found them. They are now outside on offer to the entire town. I consider what of her stored trash to drag out next.

From the crook of my bedroom window, I check up on my donation to the world. I expect to see all that I leave out, untouched and slowly ruining through exposure. As a land-locked town, what use to anyone are vintage children's diving boots?

I look away and back again for most the afternoon. I read a book, sketch a portrait, and look down on the collection to notice one pair has gone. Size seven. The pair I wore last year.

I pull out my tin, spark up a pipe of leaves and recline on my bed, smug, smoothing my belly with my spare hand. Mother is out with her people again; she'll not be back for a time. And who is she to tell me what to do? I'm nothing but a murderous embryo to her anyway, the unwanted one that has grown too big for its boots.

I lie back and close my eyes—without my jacket or boots on—and allow myself to float freely, higher than high, on the crest of a wave. My fingertips touch the cobwebs up on the ceiling cornices. I wind the frail white spiderfloss up and try and recall if it is true that a spider makes a new web each day. I imagine if my mother were a spider, how would she hoard all her spent webs? I tap grey ash onto my belly. In motes, it dances down, like we all will once done and burnt. Final drag. The burning leaves whistle and glow as smoke curls into my throat. Spliff finished, I sink. My back comes again to lie on top of my duvet, and I stub the herb cherry out on my windowsill and flick it dead into the street below. Outside, I see the sun sitting low in the cold sky of winter.

Hiss. The attic noise has become the bedroom noise. Louder. *Sssss.*

At the end of my bed, there she is.

"Ssssister," she says.

Of course, my twin is prettier than me: her hair is shinier, her skin, clearer, and her feet are a little smaller. A perfect fit in the size seven diving boots.

She reaches and takes my hand and leads me down to the wall at the front of our house. My breath hangs white in the air. The rest of the boots are still there. We collect them and tie them in a chain, lace to eyelet, like you do with sunshine daisies. She drapes the weighty lei of boots around my neck. The thin leather cord digs into my shoulders and leaves lines like strawberry shoelaces.

"Do you want to see if they really work? Hold you down? Stop you floating off?" Her voice is far sweeter than mine. "Let's go to Million Foot Bridge," she says. "I've never seen a sunset. We'll be so close to it there. The sun will be like an orange hanging in the sky, close enough to smell, to touch. It will be beautiful from such a height."

"Right now?" I ask It's been so long, we've so much to catch up on. Sister grins a smile of tombstone teeth and nods.

"And then we can throw off your Christingle. Look, I finished it for you," she says and pulls a rotten orange from her dress pocket. Squeezing it tight in her fragile hand, it bursts like a smashed skull. Vermillion fluid speckled with maggots oozes over her fingers and drips onto the icy path.

"We can throw it from the bridge. Jump after it. See if we can touch the sun on our way," she continues. "Together, maybe we'll reach the place where Mother keeps her Heaven. Let's see if these boots take us up or down." Her outline flickers. She starts to fade as my fists rub haze from my eyes.

And I know this is what we need to do. And we need to do it now, before she slips away again. So, we set off, under the mackerel-skin sky of dusk and head for the highest bridge in the area. She's right. Of course she's right. She was always going to be more intelligent than me.

That's why I kicked her out in the first place.

How to Read a Woman

First published by Black Hart Entertainment, 2022

Freckles: dot-to-dot maps which contained the secrets of the future. To him, each woman was an unread book. Patterns on a lady's skin would always unearth a story; it was his own form of astrology and he'd taught himself to read in this way. Only by connecting the beauty spots and pockmarks on a woman's skin with lines, with the rich red stretches a blade could proffer, could he connect and reveal the prescient constellations and predict his own journey.

But he did not see this coming.

In his bag he carried a variety of tools to help him bisect his next piece: a razor blade, a scalpel, a steak knife, a hacksaw, an axe. But I, Lamia, Spirit Goddess of the Night, saw through the veil of his sack.

Cheek-by-limestone-jowl, he sat amongst the darkness, between the pressing faces of the towering walls of the empty university buildings. He waited under the watchfulness of a strong moon, sure he would find someone suitable—young, marked—with skin that would give him what he needed. No idea yet who she would be, and that she would be I, he sat tight, near the club, with only the deserted cityscape, his rucksack of bundled blades, and the ceiling of yellow light pollution for company. He sat and he waited, and he hoped the darkness of the night would deliver, there, in his nook, hidden from all but the eyes of the ever-knowing. The nightclub would open soon.

Cars started to pass rarely and then frequently. The little hand on his watch crept closer to eleven. Taxis spilt out groups of Friday night revellers, loosely drunk and high on their own youth and everything else the city had to offer, and the night smelt for them of pheromones and hope.

For him, soon he hoped, the night would smell of fear and coppery vermillion; nothing was quite as fragrant as the pages of a freshly-skinned book.

From his crevice, he watched for the right one.

This dive of a student club was a gamble, but he had no better place else to be. A people-carrier pulled up into the taxi rank a few feet from the entrance, a stone's throw from his watchful glare, and, solo, out I stepped.

His green eyes sparkled with the light of Lucifer at the sight of me. I would be his takings, for sure. He could not wait to cut and slice from me the narrative of my very spirit. *What stories would the map of her skin markings reveal,* he pondered.

I wore a black dress. A zipper ran down it from neckline to hemline. Auburn curls tumbled from my high ponytail, the skin on my exposed arms and legs shone as translucent as rice paper, as thin and as marked as pages from an old bible. He stretched his neck to watch me strut into the club, ever careful not to reveal himself too soon—he needed me drunk first, intoxicated, so he could attempt to have his wicked way. His heart revved and pumped fast blood laced with expectation to his keen fingers and toes. I felt all of this and took it in my stride. Because my skin was laced with prophecy. *She'll keep me busy,* he thought. What a read I would be.

Three hours passed. I stumbled out, first through the safety net of bouncers and then, into the mouth of the night, alone. Would I call and wait for a taxi? Should I walk the half mile to the kebab shop, the only remaining source of food in the city at such an ungodly hour? He watched me with bated breath, and I knew that he watched on.

With his bag swung over his shoulder, he scuttled between the shadows behind me. I walked past the empty taxi rank and, staccato-heeled, tip-tapped around the corner. This was his chance to approach. Not a soul other than the pair of us was present. He thought he would surprise me.

"Excuse me, madam," he said.

With my skin of treasure, I turned around to face him.

"Hello," I replied.

"Saw you in the club. Wanted to buy you a drink, but you left before I'd the chance," he lied. He'd never set foot inside of that boom-box building of noise and promiscuity. He was not the partying type, more the studious type, always reading. He preferred to while away his daylight hours alone, at home, amongst his library of hung-flesh fiction. "Hope you don't mind me approaching you like this—"

"No. Not at all," I interrupted. This took him aback. He could not smell fear permeating from my skin and this unnerved him. But I knew he enjoyed a challenge. He would want to make me feel fear. He would enjoy watching the colour drop from my fair cheeks. "I'm Lamia. And you are ..." I said. I moved closer, into his space. He clutched his bag. Even in the moonlight I knew he could see the threads of purple veins which ran under my skin. With his eyes, he traced the ribbons of my blood vessels which snaked around underneath crops of freckles.

"Would you like me to escort you home?" he asked.

"How very gentlemanly—that would be divine," I replied.

I pushed my thin arm through the loop of his and his eyes darted around the translucent, bespeckled skin of my arm which was wrapped in his as I recounted the non-events of my evening. He didn't hear a word I said. In his mind, he was already slicing through my cold body, connecting the largest, protruding moles he might find first with his fingertips—like Braille—with a simple razor blade to provide a sketch of his future, an outline. Then he would hack through this framework with his axe to split the parts of the story my body would reveal. Once separated into chapters, he would wipe away my red ink and join with the steak knife or scalpel the smaller brown and orange marks which decorated every visible part of my skin. This would reveal the beauty in the sentences of each page of my flesh.

"So, this is me." I delved into my purse for my key. "It's been lovely chatting. Divine. Would you care to come in for a ..." My eyes mocked coyness. I playfully bit my lip.

His eyes flitted left and right and behind to check we were alone on the steps of my apartment.

"Yes. Yes, I would. That'd be ... divine," he said, too distracted by my beauty to select new words of his own.

As he followed me up the steps to my front door, his eyes traced the star-charts of the heavens that scattered in freckle-form over the backs of my legs. I felt this. I saw it play out, as if I had eyes in the back of my head.

"Red or white?" I called from the kitchen. He sat perched on the edge of the sofa. I expect he was considering where he would place the pages of derma once he'd ripped apart my flesh, the story of Lamia, the story of what I was.

I came back in with an opened bottle of Malbec and two glasses.

While I'd been out in the kitchen, he'd sequestered his tools—the axe lay hidden beneath the sofa cushion, the steak knife was tucked in the cuff of his boot. I knew.

"You've beautiful eyes," I said. I did not lie. I perched next to him, on the sofa. I let my bare leg skin brush against his knee.

"Thank you," he replied. "And you have beautiful skin."

"You've seen nothing yet." Between my fingertips, I took the zip which lay above my décolletage. "Would you like to see more?"

"Very much so." His night about to peak, his future about to be revealed, between the cushions, his fingers felt for his weapon. His other hand, he placed on my knee and traced upon it a small crucifix patterning of freckles. Further up my leg, his index finger slid over a stretch of pigmentation, age spots, which curved round like a scythe. Old Father Time. He pressed on the curve of my hip. I was an hourglass. He couldn't wait to carve and connect the grains of sand which lay speckled on my skin.

I drew down my zipper. He drew up his weapon.

I continued to peel open my skin-tight dress. A scream ripped from his throat. His face, stamped with the mark of terror, could not believe what I had revealed. Before his own eyes were tens of others, a hundred more. Blues, greens, browns, and all shades of hell in between.

From breast to pelvis, myriad eyes burst out from my skin; clusters and patches of eyeballs, small and large, some lashed and some not. Many ogled side-by-side a matching partner, some bulged alone, others blinked centrepiece, encircled by more. Where my nipples should've been, poked out the largest two—irises of red, pupils like black holes. The eyes blinked and twitched like faulty Christmas tree lights. Pupils dilated and flitted around the room before all settling forwards on him.

He froze.

"Your eyes," I said. I draped my slim arms around his thick neck and pulled my face closer to his. My crimson lips spoke two inches from his face. "I need your eyes." I pressed my lips against his and stared directly at him with the two eyes on my face. My hands now gripped and forced open his eyelids so he could not close away from the terror of me.

My eyes held the suction power of an oceanic drain hole. They yanked out from his sockets the lashes and the lenses first and then the white sclera, which split apart like a cracked egg. I let my full lips slurp the vitreous juice up and then let it trickle down, inside my throat. The fluids within his orbital sockets sprayed out onto my face, each drop absorbed through my translucent skin. Like water down the plug hole, his face and body became sucked up and through my infinite pupils, portals to the underworld, doors to the outskirts of the universe.

In the blink of an eye, he was gone, and I sat alone on my sofa.

I felt the familiar tickle, this time on my inner thigh. Where before, two dark moles of the warty variety had been, now, two new green eyes were rolling through. The visionary opals throbbed and blinked against the top sheet of my paper-thin skin until, like miniature volcanoes, they erupted up and through and out from my flesh. Crowning the surface of the skin on my thigh, his green eyes opened, full of emerald lava and fear, and started to weep. Tears of regret or confusion or perhaps insanity trickled down my thigh and fell in between my legs and onto the sofa.

I zipped back up my dress and rubbed my two new sore spots through the fabric. His eyes had seen enough for now. Satisfied with all my accomplishments of the night, I finished off my wine.

Acknowledgements

I'd like to thank Heather and Steve at Brigids Gate Press for taking a chance on my debut horror collection, Mark Peters for his invaluable feedback and enthusiasm over many of my stories, Daniella Batsheva for her beautiful cover art, and Robert Shearman for all his sage advice and for consistently making me laugh. Finally, a big thank you to all the presses and magazines who've published my work and to everyone who reads my stories – you rock my world.

About the Author

SJ Townend, an author of dark fiction, has stories published with *Vastarien*, Ghost Orchid Press, *Gravely Unusual Magazine*, *Dark Matter Magazine*, and Timber Ghost Press. Her second horror collection, *Your Final Sunset*, is coming in 2025 through Sley House Press. Twitter:@SJTownend

www.sjtownend.com

About the Illustrator

Daniella Batsheva is a self-proclaimed "Illustrator with a design habit" whose aesthetic straddles the line between underground and mainstream. Her art boasts the beautiful intricate linework of traditional Victorian illustration mixed with imagery inspired by horror films, 90s toy packaging, and macabre history.

Batsheva's art has been published internationally. Her work can be seen everywhere from "Whole Foods" to London's biggest punk venues. She has worked with brands such as Kerrang!, Pizza Girl, and multiple musicians from Paris Jackson and Ben Christo (Sisters of Mercy). Her work has recently been featured at ArtExpo, New York, and The Crypt Gallery, London.

While her work can comfortably fit in multiple contexts, Batsheva's work is always recognizable. Her main motivation is fostering local alternative communities and contributing to the future of illustration in Goth/Metal scenes. Batsheva is also passionate about researching obscure folklore from across different cultures in an effort to preserve legends that are at risk of being lost.

More From Brigids Gate Press

CLAY BOY

Craig E. Sawyer

Caleb Jenkins is a bullied middle schooler that everyone calls Clay Boy, due to the way he uses clay therapy to cope with the tragic murder of his mother at the hands of a serial killer. While at school, he discovers a playful video on how to create an imaginary best friend called a tulpa, but the more he interacts with his mental creation the more real and self-thinking it becomes, eventually convincing Caleb to sculpt a body for it to inhabit in order to unleash the hate that both share upon his bullies and the entire community of Wheeler's Cove, Tennessee.

CITY OF SNARES

April Yates

Hazel crosses an ocean, moving to the City of Dreams, not for stardom or the limelight that comes from rubbing elbows with celebrities, but for the chance to be her true self. So she's stunned when fading star of the silver screen, Diana Blake, wanders into the diner where she works and declares her intention of turning Hazel into the next, hot ingénue.

While the idea of following in Diana's footsteps is not the path Hazel would've chosen, the prospect of being close to Diana, of realising the impossible dream of winning the affection of her lifelong obsession, is too seductive to pass up.

Hazel agrees to let Diana mould her into her protege and is thrown headlong into the Hollywood star machine. Glimmers of sexual interest from Diana keep Hazel on the hook as she offers herself up, piece by piece to showbusiness. But Diana's behaviour grows increasingly controlling, suspicious accidents on set begin to pile up, and Hazel will have to fight to maintain any shred of herself, lest Hollywood eat her alive.

Love the Sinner

Mo Moshaty

According to Dante, a sin is the misdirection of love - the human will, or essentially, the direction of our beings. *Love the Sinner* is an examination of just how those sins can kaleidoscope into horrific consequences creating a distorted and deadly landscape. These stories stand stark before you in full glaring misstep and macabre to show the human psyche in all its twisted reality.

From grief and its rage to medical meddling to ensure a new world order to bloody revenge within a quantum leap, these stories seek to solidify one absolute truth: man is the scariest monster.

They Hide

Francesca Maria

Who are we if not for the monsters that we keep?

They Hide: Short Stories to Tell in the Dark collects thirteen chilling tales that weave through the shadows, exploring the nature of fear, powerlessness, and control.

- A series of murders in a New England colony
- An untamed beast in pre-revolutionary France
- A mysterious stranger who invades 18th-century Ireland
- A traveling circus that takes more than the price of admission
- A gathering of the Dark, telling tales on the longest night of the year, and more.

Come play with vampires, werewolves, ghosts, zombies, ghouls and the devil himself. Make sure you check under the bed and don't turn out the light

Visit our website at: www.brigidsgatepress.com

9 781957 537979